PRAISE FOR COUN

CW00494217

"I absolutely love this story. I love these characters, and I love the dynamic between Bear and Jackson...This series could go on for a really long time with the two of them."

— CHARLY COX, AUTHOR OF *THE DEVIL'S PLAYGROUND* AND *ALONE IN THE WOODS*

"*Country Roads* is an unputdownable, adrenaline-charged read that cements Jackson Clay's place next to other iconic avenger-type heroes. With terrific storytelling and characters that are topnotch, B.C. Lienesch delivers a page-turner that breathes new life into the action/thriller genre, giving us all a new favorite hero to root for."

— SHAWN BURGESS, AUTHOR OF *THE TEAR COLLECTOR* AND *GHOSTS OF GRIEF HOLLOW*

"If you liked B.C. Lienesch's debut action/thriller, *The Woodsman*, you'll love the sequel *Country Roads* which features again heroic protagonist Jackson Clay and his wisecracking companion, Bear. Once again, Lienesch delivers an action-packed story with new characters that are as fully developed and engaging as his returning cast. It's been a while since I've both loved and hated fictional characters this much."

— DAVID A. VOYLES, CREATOR OF THE *DARK CORNERS* PODCAST

COUNTRY ROADS

B. C. LIENESCH

CARPE
CREATIVE
LLC

ISBN: 978-1-7373752-2-7 (Paperback)

ISBN: 978-1-7373752-3-4 (Hardcover)

Library of Congress Control Number: 2022905990

The subject matter is not appropriate for minors. Please note this novel contains profanity, depictions of violence, drug use, and sexual situations including sexual assault.

Book edited by Austin Shirey

Book designed by Carpe Creative, LLC

First Digital Edition: June 2022

CARPE CREATIVE, LLC

3422 RUSTIC WAY LANE

FALLS CHURCH, VIRGINIA 22044

www.bclnovels.com

For Angie
Reading from Heaven

Montani semper liberi
"Mountaineers are Always Free"

—WEST VIRGINIA STATE MOTTO

The woods are lovely dark and deep
But I have promises to keep
And miles to go before I sleep
And miles to go before I sleep

—ROBERT FROST, *STOPPING BY WOODS ON A SNOWY EVENING*

PART I

MANHUNT

1

_____

The last hour of Emma Miller and Mason Westfall's lives began with an empty tank of gas. Emma watched the orange fuel-light flicker on as Mason said something to her from the passenger seat.

"So, what do you think?" he asked.

"About what?" she said.

"Blake's offer to move in with him. You want to see the place again?"

"No, I saw it. It's great."

"So?"

Emma stretched her arms and sighed as she sat back in the driver's seat of the old Chevy S-10 her father had recently given her for her eighteenth birthday.

"You're serious about doing this, aren't you?" she asked. "Moving to California. To L.A."

"Of course I am," Mason said. "I was born here. I grew up here. I'm tired of here. I'm ready for something different."

"And you think we can make it? On our own? Out there?"

Mason turned toward her and brushed her chestnut-brown hair away from her warm, amber eyes, giving her his signature everything-will-be-all-right smile. She smiled reflexively back at him.

"It won't be easy to start," he said, "but we can make it work. We'll get jobs waiting tables or something while you work on your music. Maybe even bartend a few joints looking for performers. Get your name out there."

The thought tickled Emma. When he talked about leaving Rion, West Virginia and moving across the country to a city they'd never been to before, it didn't sound reckless or crazy. It sounded like it was meant for them to do it. It's what Emma loved about him. Where every other girl had adored him for his looks – that flowing, sandy-brown hair atop a tall, trim frame bronzed from hours working in the fields – she'd been drawn in by his heart.

"And when are you going to let your friend out there know about all this?" she asked.

Mason turned and looked up at Bobbie Casto's house, its weathered baby-blue facade tinted an ugly brown by the orange barn light over the front door.

"Soon," Mason said, the excitement in his voice gone. "I just have to figure out when. He's not going to be happy."

"You can bet on that," Emma said.

Mason looked out the window a moment longer before turning back toward her. "The *real* question is, when are we going to tell our friend out *there* about our new friend in *there*."

Emma instinctively placed a hand on her abdomen. It wouldn't be that flat for much longer. She smiled shyly. "I don't know. Maybe we wait and tell him when we're in California? It might make it easier on him. Two of us leaving him instead of three."

"Em, he's our best friend. We've got to tell him. And sooner. Not later. Definitely not after we've already left."

"Okay," she said. "Tonight then, maybe."

A big smile stretched across Mason's face, which brought an even bigger one to hers.

"You sure?" he asked.

Emma nodded as a happy tear rolled down her cheek. Mason caught it with his finger as he cupped her face and brought her in for a kiss.

"I love you," he whispered.

"I love you, too," she whispered back.

They held each other a moment longer before slinking back into their seats. Emma arched forward to look out Mason's window.

"That is," she said, "If tonight ever happens. Where on earth is he? Did you tell him we were out front?"

"I texted him," Mason said. "I'll text him again."

He pulled out his phone and punched in a message.

YO, DIPSHIT. WE'RE WAITING.

A minute later, Bobbie replied with a laugh emoji. Mason frowned.

"I'm guessing he'll be a minute," Mason said, sliding his phone back into his pocket.

"No, here he comes," Emma said.

The front door of the house swung open and Bobbie Casto jumped over the front railing and ran down the hill as if he were a dog that had gotten loose. In one clumsy motion, he opened the back door of the S-10, threw himself and his bag in, and shut the door behind him.

"Took you long enough," Mason said.

"Hey, I had to wait until my stepdad was passed out to grab his Natty Light," Bobbie said.

He pulled the hood of his sweatshirt back, revealing curly, dark-brown hair trimmed into a mohawk fade and dyed caramel on top. The freckles on his golden skin—a perfect union of his mother's rosy hue and his late father's swarthy complexion—scrunched together as he smirked and held up the case of beer.

"Natty Light is piss," Mason said.

"Oh, I'm sorry," Bobby said. "And what beer did you grab for us?"

"None, but I got us this." Mason reached over and flashed the pocket-sized pouch of weed and pipe he carried.

Bobbie snatched it out of his hands before he could put it back. "Nice, dude."

"Are we ready?" Emma asked, an edge of impatience in her voice.

"Yeah, I just gotta stop at Wawa real quick," Bobbie said.

"Fine, we'll stop. Put all that crap away, though."

Emma put the truck into gear before reaching across and squeezing

Mason's hand. Mason looked back at her, his head bobbing to the music as he turned up the truck's radio.

The two of them would be dead in 43 minutes.

2
_____

R onnie Franko watched the silver Chevy S-10 pull into the Wawa
   station from across the parking lot. He took a long drag from
his Winston Red, blowing the smoke out the open window where it
formed a cloud with the truck's exhaust in the crisp night air. Two
young men got out of the far side of the Chevy. A woman stayed
behind in the driver seat.

"They might work," Franko said. "Silver pickup. They look young.
And dumb."

His partner, Arsen Bragg, nodded as he looked up from his flask.

"Looks like juvees," Franko added.

They watched as the two went into the store and split off in opposite directions. One, in a red hoodie, ordered something at the hot food
counter while the other, sporting a denim jacket, filled two cups with
Coke at the soda fountain.

"Think they're holding?" Bragg asked.

Franko took another drag of his cigarette, his stubble-laden face
frowning as he pondered the question.

And nothing we can't fix."

"Do you know the black one?" Bragg asked. "Ain't many of them
in the county."

"Don't think so," Franko said. "We ought to introduce ourselves. To protect and serve and all that."

Bragg chuckled.

Both six feet and change, the two Hopewell County sheriff's deputies were an intimidating sight draped in their bullet resistant vests. Bragg was clean-shaven with a military buzz-cut while Franko's face was framed by greasy, blonde hair that ran down to his shoulders. His skin was weathered and aged, like it'd seen too many dive bars and not enough dermatologists.

Bragg shifted his weight in his seat as he watched the boy in the red hoodie grab a bag of food.

"They're gettin' a bite to eat," he said, "No booze or nothin', though. Twenty says they've already got some in the truck."

The two boys rendezvoused at the checkout counter to pay before heading back to the truck with the girl. The one in the red hoodie came over to her side and said something that earned him in a punch in the arm.

"You think she's fucking that one?" Bragg asked.

"Shit, she's probably fucking both of them," Franko said.

"Probably is," Bragg muttered. "Goddamn slut."

The guy in the red hoodie jumped into the bed of the truck. The woman behind the wheel yelled at him for it, pointing to the back seat before giving in and firing up the engine. The reverse lights lit up their dark corner of the parking lot as the truck backed out and turned for the small highway the Wawa was nestled on.

"That's a minor in the bed of a moving truck," Bragg said, grinning. "Dumb kid just gave us probable cause."

Franko shifted their truck into drive, the transmission clanking with a brief but audible objection.

"Sometimes it's almost too easy," he said.

The black truck's headlights flicked on as it rolled forward, stalking the smaller pickup with the three teens in it as they headed away from the convenience store.

Two of them would be dead in 29 minutes.

3

Emma drove the three of them to the top of Cooper's Hill, where the highway ran through the trees and alongside an empty lot perched on the edge of a steep hillside. When she parked, the trio climbed out onto the hood of the truck together, overlooking the valley below. Downtown Rion was a smattering of fireflies clustered together in the autumn night. To the north, at the edge of it, brilliant light towers illuminated the high school football field, calling everyone around to come and worship at the only religion that mattered until Sunday morning. The trio could hear the *rat-tat-tat* of the snare drums as the marching band played in the stands.

"You think Hopewell's winning?" Mason asked.

"Shit," Bobbie said, snorting with a laugh, "they ever win when we were there?"

"Hey, you never know. Things change."

Emma leaned forward and shot Mason a look. He chuckled and leaned back, reaching for the case of beer behind Bobbie. He pulled out a can and opened it.

"I thought that was piss," Bobbie said.

Mason chuckled as he cocked his head back and poured lukewarm beer into his mouth. Swallowing, he rested his elbows against the

windshield and looked up at the night sky. He scanned the stars until
he found the only constellation he knew. Orion's Belt. The three stars –
Alnitak, Alnilam, and Mintaka – all similarly spaced in a straight line.

"Orion," Mason mumbled. "Oh, Rion..."

"Jesus, you take a few hits off your pipe before I got in the car?"
Bobbie asked.

Mason laughed. "Nah, man. Orion, *Oh, Rion*. It's just funny."

Bobbie packed a bowl into the aforementioned Rick and Morty
pipe and took a hit. Coughing, he offered the still-smoking piece to
Emma; she politely shook her head. Mason sat up and took it from
Bobbie, but didn't light it. He clasped it between his hands and
looked out over the valley. Emma unwrapped one of the burgers
they'd grabbed from Wawa and bit into it. The three of them sat in
quiet.

"I'm almost nineteen and I haven't been farther than I can see from
here," Mason said after a while.

"There's more out there. You just can't see it," Bobbie said.

Mason smiled, seeing the segue he needed to bring up California.
But just as Mason opened his mouth, an engine roared behind them.
Together, the trio turned and look back to see a black truck pull sharply
into the lot and skid to a stop just short of their own. As the two doors
on the black pickup opened, a pair of red and blue lights began
flashing from the windshield.

"Oh, fuck," Bobbie said.

A man came around the driver's door of the pickup and clicked on
a flashlight, shining it in Bobbie's face.

"What's wrong, boy?" The man asked. "You got a reason you don't
want to see the police?"

Bobbie shook his head.

"No, sir," he replied, "I just—"

"You just what?" asked a second man, coming around the pickup
from the passenger side. "Go on, out with it."

Bobbie didn't say anything more. The two men stepped in front of
their truck's headlights. The three teens could see now the two men
were wearing bullet resistant vests with badges draped around their
necks. They both had pistols holstered on their hips.

"I'm sorry," Emma said, trying her best not to sound confrontational, "you said you were the police?"

"I don't know. What does this badge here tell you?" The man who'd been driving the truck asked.

"I see it, sir. I was just asking who you are," Emma said.

The two men stepped closer now. Emma couldn't make out their faces with the bright lights behind them, but the driver seemed to have long hair while the other had something like a buzz-cut. The one with long hair moved within an arm's reach of Emma and stopped.

"You ask a lot of questions for some princess trespassing after hours," he said. He grabbed her shoulder and spun her around to face her own car. "Hopewell County Sheriff's Office, if you must know. Hands on the top of the car."

"You boys, too," the buzz-cut officer said from the other side of the S-10.

Mason and Bobbie looked at each other before looking at Emma. Her expression told them to do as they were told. Reluctantly, they raised their hands and put them on the car. The officer with the buzz cut stepped behind Bobbie and began patting him down.

"You guys have anything on you beside that pipe and weed there?" the long-haired officer asked.

"Yeah, don't think we didn't see that shit," the other officer said.

"Sir, I'm sorry about the weed. It's mine and I'll take full responsibility for it," Mason said.

"Well, that was easy," the buzz-cut man said. He stopped searching Bobbie and moved over to Mason. "Makes me wonder what else you got."

Mason's body jerked back and forth as the man jostled him. Emma could see the look on Mason's face—he was getting frustrated.

She worried he might do something to make the situation worse.

"Well, would ya look at that?" the long-haired man said.

The officer had taken a step back from Emma and was now shining his flashlight on the grass in front of the teens' truck. A crumpled plastic bag full of small white rocks lay on the ground. Emma felt a sharp pain in her chest as a wave of panic washed over her.

"That's not ours," she said.

The long-haired officer laughed. "Yeah, sure. It never is, huh?"

"Seriously, man, that's not ours. We don't do that shit," Bobbie said.

"Well, maybe you don't," the man said. "Maybe you just sell it. Looks like you got some good clothes on you, boy. Did you check him, Bragg?"

"Not all the way, no," Bragg said.

"The fuck you didn't," Bobbie said. "You checked me, bro."

Bragg stepped away from Mason and came up behind Bobbie again, shoving him against the truck.

"You're done being checked when I say you're done being checked," the officer said, "You understand me, boy?"

Bobbie seethed at the man calling him "boy". He scowled as the officer rifled through his pockets. The other officer with the longer hair caught Bobbie's expression and grinned.

"Oh, we got ourselves a big, bad guy here, Bragg," the man said. "Well, Mr. Bad Guy, I'll ask again: who had the crank?"

"I don't know what you're talking about," Bobbie said.

Bragg yanked Bobbie's arms behind him and shoved him hard against the car once more.

"Stop being a smart ass," he barked.

"The meth. Whose is it?" the long-haired officer asked.

The three teens looked at each other, suspicion showing in their eyes.

The long-haired officer chuckled. "Uh oh, they're starting to turn on each other, Bragg."

"Here we go," Bragg said, pulling his hand up from behind Bobbie to show everyone another plastic bag filled with white rocks. "Guess this is our boy."

"What the -- I don't do that shit," Bobbie protested. "I – I don't touch that shit, man."

"That's funny, considering it was on you."

"Fuck you, man! I don't have shit on me. You – Someone gave you that."

"Yeah, who? The meth fairy? C'mon." Bragg reached for his pair of handcuffs as he pressed Bobbie's wrists together. Bobbie jerked away, but Bragg put his forearm to Bobbie's head and forced it down against the car.

"Hey! Let him go!" Emma screamed.

The long-haired officer moved behind her, pulling her arms tight and placing a hand on the back of her neck.

"You got a mouth on you," he said, "Bet you use it, too, huh?"

Slowly, the man ran his hands down Emma's figure, but nothing about it was procedural. It was personal. Invasive. He was enjoying what he was doing. Emma shook, angry and terrified.

"Nope, never can be too careful," the long-haired officer said. "Never know who's got what these days. Never know where they're keeping it, either."

His hands crossed over her denim shorts and found her bare thighs, then turned inwards. When Emma felt his hand grab her buttocks from inside her shorts, she kicked her legs free and spun around.

"Don't touch me!" she screamed.

"Hey, leave her alone!" Mason shouted.

"He – He just fucking grabbed me! Underneath my shorts!"

"What the hell—"

Mason stomped around the front of the car toward Emma as the long-haired officer laughed. Bobbie screamed for him to stop, but Bragg pinned Bobbie to the car with one hand and drew his pistol with the other.

"Stop moving!" Bragg ordered. "I will fucking shoot you!"

The long-haired officer used his elbow to shove Emma aside. He smiled as Mason closed in.

"Uh oh," he said, "here comes Romeo to save the day."

"You don't touch her!" Mason shouted.

"I'll do whatever the fuck I want!" the officer shouted back. "Starting with arresting your ass."

Bragg stepped away from Bobbie, both hands now wrapped around his gun as he aimed it at Mason.

"Hands up!," he shouted, "Do it now!"

It was 8:53 pm. The gas light in Emma's S-10 had come on exactly 59 minutes earlier.

4

Emma moved to place herself between Mason and Bragg.

Bragg pivoted and pointed the gun at her. "You don't fucking move, either."

Mason tried to step in front of her, but Emma kept him back with her arm. The long-haired officer unholstered his gun and held it down by his side.

"Relax, Bragg," he said. "Book the black one over there."

"Stop it, he didn't do anything," Mason said.

"Yeah? That meth says otherwise," the long-haired officer said.

"I told you that shit ain't mine!" Bobbie shouted.

Bragg turned back to Bobbie and moved in. Bobbie tried to evade the man, but Bragg brought his arm down to corral him. Bobbie swung his arms wildly, hitting the hand Bragg held his gun with. A round shot off with a boom. Bobbie looked at Bragg and then across the pickup.

Emma's face was expressionless as her body slowly slumped to the ground behind the body of the truck. For a moment Bobbie thought he was only imagining the bullet-shaped hole just below her right eye.

"Fuck," Bragg said. "Jesus Christ."

"God dammit, Bragg! Get that boy in cuffs now!" the other officer shouted.

Bragg looked at Bobbie for a moment, still shell-shocked. It was all the opening Bobbie needed. He elbowed Bragg's chest and reached for the gun with both hands. They fell to the ground fighting for Bragg's pistol.

The long-haired officer raised his gun and aimed it at Mason's head.

"Do not fucking move!" he ordered.

Bobbie tried to pull Bragg's pistol toward him as he and Bragg rolled together on the pavement. Bragg kept one hand on the gun and reached down across himself with the other. Bobbie watched the man's free hand and noticed the knife Bragg was reaching for, strapped to his belt on the opposite side of his body. Before Bragg could reach it, Bobbie surged forward, grabbing the knife and jamming the blade into Bragg's leg. The man screamed and dropped his gun.

"Bragg!" The long-haired officer called out.

Bobbie rolled off Bragg and left the officer clutching his leg. Something in Bobbie told him he had crossed a line he couldn't come back from, but he was fighting for his life— doing nothing wasn't an option.

The long-haired officer stepped toward the truck to check on his partner just as Bobbie was reaching for Bragg's pistol. The officer swung his gun toward Bobbie and fired.

The bullet crashed into the pavement next to Bobbie's ear. Bobbie grabbed Bragg's pistol and fired back at the long-haired officer but missed him. He got to his feet and scrambled for cover behind Emma's truck.

"He's got my gun, Franko," Bragg said through clenched teeth.

"Yeah, no fucking shit," Franko snapped.

Bobbie posted up against the front left tire of the truck. Some guys named Bragg and Franko—they'd just killed one of his best friends. He rose, slowly peeking through the driver-side window. A shadow moved around the truck. When the long-haired officer, Franko, came around, Bobbie squeezed the trigger a second time. Again, he missed, but Franko lurched backwards and retreated.

"Look, boy, you haven't killed anyone yet," Franko said from somewhere on the other side of the truck. "You put the gun down now, we can help you."

Bobbie didn't know what to say, but he knew giving up the gun to these two men wasn't an option.

"Come on, you don't want to make things worse on yourself," Franko said.

Bobbie could see the man's feet below the pickup. He watched them, waiting for them to move when another pair of shoes came up quickly on Franko. There was a dull thud, then Franko was on the ground, Mason on top of him, beating Franko with his fists.

"The gun! Get his gun!" Bobbie shouted.

But Mason didn't reach for it.

Something was off. Bobbie didn't recognize this Mason. Bobbie had seen him get in fights before, but not like this. This Mason unleashed on Franko with a fervent rage. Bobbie felt helpless, paralyzed by fear as he watched.

Whup. Whup. Whup. Whup.

KA-BOOM.

Mason's body kicked backwards in a spray of blood. He landed on his back with a hole the size of an orange in the center of his chest. Bobbie rose to run to Mason, but Franko rolled over and pointed his gun at him. He dove behind the front of the truck.

Franko fired and one of the headlights exploded in a cloud of shattered glass. Bobbie hit the pavement and kept crawling until he got to the passenger side of the truck. He heard Franko get to his feet. Despite the ringing in his ears from the gunfire, he could hear the thumps of the man's boots getting closer.

"Bragg, get the fuck up," Franko said.

Bragg was working on his wounded leg near the back of the truck. Bobbie heard the distinct click of a metal magazine sliding out of a gun and hitting the pavement.

Bobbie jumped to his feet, spinning around to face Franko as the officer reached for another magazine. Bobbie raised Bragg's pistol and squeezed the trigger as fast as he could. Franko threw himself to the ground. Bobbie fired until the gun was empty. He'd lost sight of the officers. Bobbie knew he needed to make a break for it, but the road was narrow and bordered by woods. The two men could run him over just as easily as they could shoot him.

Someone groaned from the other side of the truck. Bobbie was running out of time and ideas. He looked at Mason, his friend's lifeless face staring sightlessly up at the night sky. Bobbie turned, noting the steep hillside and the town beyond. Someone must've heard the gunshots, he thought. But gunshots weren't uncommon around here—and they didn't necessarily mean something bad was happening.

Bobbie did the only thing that came to him: he ran for the hillside.

Franko got back to his feet and slid the loose magazine into his gun as he came around the truck. Bobbie was nearly to the edge of the hilltop when he heard the gunshot behind him and felt a searing pain in his calf. He took one more step before his leg gave out and he collapsed in the grass.

Franko grinned at the sight of his target going down and slowly made his way toward the wounded teenager. Bobbie could feel warm blood running down his leg, but he was nearly to the hillside. One good push and he could let gravity do the rest. He didn't know if he'd survive, but he knew there was no surviving up here. His friends were proof of that.

Bobbie grabbed a nearby tree root and heaved himself down the hill. He heard Franko fire twice as he tumbled over the side. Bobbie had gone a good ten feet before he got his hand around a tree branch and caught himself. He swung down behind the trunk of a tree, and concealed himself in the darkness beneath its foliage.

Franko came to the crest of the hilltop and fired three times into the darkness below. When none of the bullets found their mark, Bobbie realized Franko had lost him. He tried to slow his breathing as he heard Bragg join his partner at the edge of the hill.

"We gotta go down after him," Bragg said.

"He's wounded," Franko said. "And when we put it out over the radio, he'll be an attempted cop killer. We've got to make this right."

"What are you talking about?"

"The shooting, dumbass. We're the ones with the guns. You want to explain how two unarmed kids ended up dead?"

"But the kid down there, he saw the whole thing. He'll know the truth."

"We make this look right, Bragg, and it'll be the word of two sheriff's detectives against a meth dealer. Besides, he's shot. Maybe he'll do us a favor and just fucking die."

"So what do you want to do?" Bragg asked.

"Get a burner out of the truck. Put it in the dead boy's hands and put some rounds in our windshield," Franko said.

"What about the girl?"

"Collateral damage. Shouldn't have happened, but she was there with her two drug dealer boyfriends shooting at us."

"You sure this will work?"

"It'll work if we take care of it right."

Bobbie hung there, clinging to the tree, hearing everything: The sound of two more gunshots as Bragg followed Franko's orders; the sound of his best friend getting set up for something he didn't do; the sound of his truth disappearing. Tears formed in Bobbie's eyes. What just happened? He was some sort of cop killer now? He wasn't. But he was.

"30 Victor, 10-71, officer involved shooting," Bobbie heard Franko say. "Multiple 10-53's. Start me backup and the Vice supervisor."

Moments later, wailing sirens made their way up the hillside. Bobbie looked down below his feet. There was nothing but darkness. He didn't know how far he had left to go or what was at the bottom of the hill, but running was the only thing that had worked for him so far.

So Bobbie let go of the branch.

And when his feet finally found the ground, he ran.

5

Bear Beauchamp backed his old red Chevy Suburban into his designated parking spot until he hit the metal 'Private Parking' sign with his bumper. What had started out years ago as a simple misjudgment had now become a part of his morning routine.

He slid out of the driver's seat and approached the front door of Piedmont Ammo & Supply balancing two coffees from 7 Eleven in one hand. With the other, he unlocked the door with his keys, pushed his ample frame inside, and locked it behind him. He breathlessly placed the cups of joe on the front counter.

"Ray," Bear yelled toward the back of the store. "Ray, you here?"

No response. Bear slid his keys back into his pocket, grabbed a coffee with each hand and headed down an aisle of camping equipment, making sure not to knock over the cardboard cutout of NASCAR Driver Denny Hamlin, as he was prone to do.

Bear was a large man, thick in the waist and nearly six and a half feet tall, with tree trunks for arms and legs. A bushy, brown beard wrapped around the lower half of his face and a baseball cap sat atop his shaved head. Today it was a black and red Miller High Life hat.

"Ray, you in yet?" Bear shouted again.

Again, no answer. As he approached the back office, he could see the door was open and the light was off – telltale signs Ray wasn't in. Bear snorted and set the coffees down on an archery target. He was surprised he'd beat his business partner into the store. In fact, he couldn't recall the last time it had happened. Ray lived in South Boston, Virginia, about an hour from where their store sat just outside Martinsville. Bear pulled out his cell phone and punched in Ray's number. It went straight to voicemail.

"Hey, buddy, I'm in," Bear said after the beep. "Don't get coffee on the way if you get this—I already grabbed you one."

Bear ended the call, returned the phone to his pocket, and took the coffees up to the front of the store. He had a small television stashed there to kill time when days were slow at the store. After locating the remote and turning the TV on, he flipped to the local news to see if a bad wreck was maybe holding Ray up in traffic. A mousy-looking woman with long blonde hair was giving the weekly weather forecast. As Bear watched her explain what the green blobs on the Doppler radar meant, his phone buzzed in his pocket. Must be Ray, he thought.

But it wasn't. Instead, it was an automated text letting him know his breakfast – the second of the day – was out for delivery from Door-dash. He closed the message and tried Ray again. Again, right to voicemail.

Bear stared at his phone, unsure of what to do. The news program had moved on to coverage of some shootout in West Virginia—a couple of kids had been killed and an officer was injured. The police were looking for a third suspect.

It wasn't like Ray to be incommunicado, but Bear wasn't one to worry. Besides, there was still another hour before the store officially opened. He sat back in his computer chair, kicked his feet up on the front counter, and drank his coffee as he continued watching the news.

6

Franko burned his way through his third Winston that hour as a paramedic tended to Bragg's leg. In the hours since the call went out, the area around the roadside overlook had become a beehive of first responder activity. Vehicles of all sizes idled with emergency lights flashing as people went about their various jobs. White sheets covered Emma Miller and Mason Westfall's bodies.

"Ow, Jesus," Bragg said as the paramedic applied something to his wound.

"Shut up," Franko said. "You'll live."

"He'll live, but this is probably going to need stitches," the paramedic said. He looked over at the two white sheets on the ground and then back at Bragg. "You can probably ride along with us. I guess we don't have any other customers today."

Franko snorted. He took one last drag on his cigarette and looked out at the chaos of the crime scene. He noticed a husky man struggling to make his way through the sea of emergency workers.

"Here comes the boss man, Franko," Bragg said, watching the large man come their way.

"Let me handle it," Franko said.

Little about Lieutenant Red Starcher was physically intimidating –

average height, beer gut, dwindling hairline – but it was well known amongst the Hopewell County Sheriff's Office Vice Squad that being on his shit-list was the last place you wanted to be.

"Before you say anything, it was a good shoot, LT," Franko said.

"It sure as shit better have been," Starcher said. "I've got every agency from here to Charleston crawling up my ass asking what the fuck you two did."

"Our jobs, boss," Bragg muttered.

Franko slapped Bragg's shoulder. Starcher snorted. The mustache part of his goatee twitched with vexation.

"The next time you want to do 'your jobs', leave the bodies upright and breathing, if you please," Starcher growled.

Franko smacked his pack of Winstons before pulling out another one out and lighting it.

"So, this third suspect," Starcher said, "the one that stabbed you, Bragg. He shot at you both? Where are we with him?"

"We've got an APB out statewide," Franko said. "Deputies swept Rion twice. ID'd his car. It's still at his house – or his parent's house, I guess – so he's probably still on foot."

"He better be. If he gets out of state, that means the feds get involved, and that's the last fucking thing we need." Starcher said before tapping the paramedic on the shoulder. "I need a minute with these two, please."

When the paramedic was out of earshot, Starcher stepped closer. "Are we clean on this? And I don't just mean the shooting. I mean *everything*. I assume y'all were up here trying to squeeze them. I don't need some kid telling different tales than the official record here."

"Bragg tried pinning some meth on him. Easy job for the business. That's about when it turned to shit. The weed and the beer are theirs. You take that, then it's some delinquent's word against two police officers," Franko said.

"Why didn't you just fucking shoot the twerp after shooting the first two?" Starcher asked.

"I tried. I told you: it all turned to shit."

"And why didn't you go after him?"

"The situation wasn't right up here. We had to make it right."

Starcher sighed and stepped back. He turned and saw a deputy across the crime scene pull back police tape to allow an unmarked police car through. A tall gentleman with an athlete's build climbed out and stood, taking his surroundings in.

"Oh, for fucks sake," Starcher said. "Of course they sent the fucking boy scout."

"What?" Bragg asked.

"First Lieutenant Colton Sayre. The State Police golden boy. That's him over there."

The three men watched as Sayre methodically walked through the crime scene, scanning the array of emergency vehicles. He was tan, so tan his skin nearly blended seamlessly with his short, styled, dirty blonde hair. Turning toward Starcher, Franko, and Bragg, Sayre ran his hands over his large, pronounced Adam's apple and straightened his tie before coming over to them.

Starcher turned to face Franko and Bragg.

"This guy is not your fucking friend, you understand me?" he said. "Your story better be tighter than a virgin's pussy on this. This guy isn't fucking stupid and he's not going to look the other way on some good ole boy shit. Watch what you say around him."

Then Starcher was greeting Sayre with an outstretched hand, laying on his best professional politeness. Sayre returned his pleasantries before approaching Franko and Bragg.

"Good morning," Sayre said. "Colton Sayre, State Police."

"You're the dick they sent over, huh?" Franko asked.

Sayre smiled at the intended insult. "I am indeed. You guys are a pair of dicks yourself, no?"

Franko spat a large brown wad of saliva as close to Sayre's Oxfords as possible as he looked the man up and down. Franko was only a hair shorter than him, but Sayre's square shoulders and toned physique made him appear even bigger.

"Looks like you guys had a rough night last night. I mean, not as rough as the two teenagers you left dead." Sayre said.

"It was a good shoot," Franko said.

"Of course, but go ahead and walk me through it."

"We came upon a suspicious vehicle out here after dark. Three people with the car. Drugs and alcohol in plain view."

"And you knew by the look of them they were underage?"

"*Drugs* and alcohol."

"Go on."

"Right, so we're checking one of the boys and the girl for anything more when the third draws a gun. We draw ours, he fires at Bragg on the passenger side twice. We both step back to cover, he fires another shot. We return fire. He takes one in the chest and goes down."

"And the girl?"

"Shot in the crossfire. Shouldn't have run over to her boyfriend, what can I say?"

"Hell of a shot for collateral damage. And there's no video? Body cam? Dash cam?"

"We're Vice—we don't do body cams. Our cars are made to look completely unmarked. That means nothing except for a pair of hidden emergency lights. No dash cams. Even the radio is concealed under the dash."

"And how did the third suspect manage to get away in all this?" Sayre asked.

"Made a run for it in the shooting. By the looks of the blood going over the side of the hill, I'd say we clipped him," Franko said.

"Why didn't you pursue him?"

"We lost visual during the shootout. By then, it was better to put it out over the radio and set up a perimeter."

Sayre flipped through some papers, making notes along the way. "It says you searched this third suspect, Bragg. Why didn't you guys put out an ID with the call? He not have one on him?"

Bragg looked over at Franko. Franko ignored him.

"I didn't get his ID before shit went sideways," Bragg said. "I found meth on him. They said we planted it. Then—"

"Did you?"

"Did I what?"

"Did you plant the meth on him?"

"Go fuck yourself. Whose side are you on, anyway? The other kid got all mad. A minute later the shooting popped off. I was never able to get the guy's ID. Kiss my ass."

"Well apparently it took a good hour to figure out who he was as a result. Probably why he's still in the wind now," Sayre said.

Franko stomped out his cigarette, clearly annoyed. "The kid's shot and on foot. We're going to find him before lunch and then it'll be up to the little black punk if he wants to come in alive or dead."

"Oh, you haven't heard," Sayre said. "Mason Westfall's car isn't at his house. Bit strange since Mason is dead, right over there."

"Bullshit," Franko said.

"No bullshit. The kid probably has four or five hours on us in whatever direction he's headed."

"He'll turn up. Are we done here?"

Sayre nodded and jotted down a couple more notes. Franko and Bragg climbed up into the ambulance and signaled the paramedics they were ready to go. Sayre finished what he was writing down as the ambulance departed.

A man in a black windbreaker walked over to him. "You the state investigator?"

"I am indeed," Sayre said.

"I'm with the county coroner," the man said. "Boss wants to know if we can take the bodies. Crowd is forming, Sheriff's Office would rather not have photos of dead kids circulating online."

Sayre noticed a group of onlookers being held back near where the ambulance had pulled out, The group was young, mostly teenagers.

"Sure, go on and take them," Sayre said.

The man stepped away.

"Hey," Sayre called after him, "what's with the kids? Did they close the school for the day?"

"Student holiday," the man called back.

Sayre looked at him, puzzled.

The man shrugged.

"First day of hunting season," he said.

7

By half past ten, Bear was starting to worry about Ray. He'd tried Ray's cell phone a half dozen times; each time it went straight to voicemail. He'd called Ray's neighbor – whom he'd met one time while housesitting for Ray – but the man hadn't seen him today. Not that that was unusual, the neighbor assured Bear.

Business was slow, which only gave Bear more time to fixate on the situation. He sat in his office chair, looking at the TV but not watching it. It was the same story that had been on all morning, anyway: Police in West Virginia were looking for a teenage boy, Bobbie Casto, wanted in connection with a shooting that had occurred last night.

When Bear heard a car door shut, he leapt from his chair and rushed to the front window—but it wasn't Ray. It was only Jake West, the pale, scrawny college freshman Bear had hired for part-time help at the store. Bear stood watching the kid as he pushed the front door open.

"Uh, hey, Bear. Everything okay?" Jake asked.

"Yeah. Well, no. Yes," Bear mumbled. "You haven't heard from Ray, have you?"

"Not since yesterday, no."

Bear went quiet. He couldn't recall a time when Ray had been out of contact this long. "I tell ya what—I'm going to run over to his house in South Boston and just double check everything's okay. Been slow here anyway. You mind holdin' down the fort for a couple hours?"

"No, sir," Jake said.

"Great," Bear said as he grabbed his keys and shifted his gut around the counter. "What did I say about that 'sir' business, though?"

"My bad...Bear."

"That's better. Be back in a bit. Get yourself pizza or somethin' for lunch."

THE DRIVE to Raymond Byrd's house took just over an hour. At a quarter to noon, Bear pulled into the U-shaped driveway that bowed in front of a modest red brick ranch house stretched out lengthwise on a large lot of freshly-mowed grass.

Bear parked at the edge of the driveway and climbed out. Ray's bronze Lincoln Navigator was parked just by the front door as it always was. Nothing seemed out of place.

But as Bear began walking up the driveway a line of matted grass through the otherwise pristine lawn caught his eye. Then another line, both the width of a tire's tread. Side-by-side, like a car had driven through. Bear stepped into the grass to follow the tire marks.

The two lines split off in a Y-shape from the driveway before turning parallel with the side of the house. Bear walked out wide to get a better look. The tracks continued on, fading into the grass somewhere around back. A little strange, but probably easily explained once he found Ray. He turned back and headed for the front door.

Bear was just a couple steps away when Ray opened the door and stepped out, hurriedly shutting the door behind him. He smiled at Bear, but something about the smile felt forced.

"Hey, man. What's going on? What are you doing out here?" Ray said, a little out of breath.

"Hey, yourself," Bear said. "Came out to check on ya."

Ray chuckled, the edges of his eyes curling. Bear thought he looked like one of those masks you'd find on comedy or theater advertisements, and with his big eyes and large mouth, there was no denying Ray's face held such features well. His peppered white hair had yielded control of the top of his head to a shiny scalp highlighting his ochre skin, and despite his paunch, he looked downright skinny next to Bear.

"Oh me? Pfft, come on, Bear. I'm fine," Ray said.

"You haven't been answering your phone. Not to mention, you're here and not at work," Bear said.

"Ah, c'mon man. You're going to bust my chops for being late to work *one* day?"

"Hey, I'm good with it, brother. Assuming everything's okay."

"Everything's fine, man."

Bear grunted in acknowledgment, staring openly at Ray, trying to read his friend's face. When Ray didn't give anything away, he decided to try a different tactic. "Say, did you have company over or something? I noticed the grass matted down like someone drove on it."

"Ah, no, just a delivery driver," Ray said. "You know how it is. Had to turn around and all."

"But it goes all the way back around your house," Bear said.

Ray paused, then forced out a chuckle. "I don't know about *all* the way back, but you're right, he certainly took his liberties on my lawn."

Bear grunted again. He wasn't buying it. "What about your phone? I musta called you nine or ten times."

"Shit, you know what, it must be dead. Sometimes I hit it in my sleep and it stops charging, damn thing. I'll check on it."

Bear sighed. "Alrighty then. You goin' to be in sometime today?"

"Yeah, no problem," Ray said, reaching for his door. Bear thought he looked eager to be rid of him.

"Say you know what," Bear said, "I gotta piss like a racehorse. You mind if I hit the head real quick?"

Bear made for the door before Ray could answer. Ray jumped to his left, blocking Bear's path. His smile was gone.

"What's going on, brother?" Bear asked, cooling his usual jovial tone.

Ray looked down, silent.

"Come on," Bear said. "It's me, man."

Ray let out a heavy breath and stepped away from the door, motioning Bear forward. Bear slowly twisted the knob and pushed. As the door swayed open, he saw a hooded figure slumped on the couch. A teenager. The teen looked up at him. It took Bear a moment to place his face, but when he did, he suddenly felt queasy—as if someone had punched him in the stomach.

It was the boy from the news.

It was Bobbie Casto.

8

B ear reached past Ray and pulled the door shut, then led him off the front stoop, hoping that was far enough out of the kid's earshot.

"Good god, Ray, that's the kid from the news," Bear said.

"I know, Bear," Ray said. "Just hol—"

"What the hell is he doing here?"

Ray took in a deep breath in and sighed. "He's my nephew."

"What?" Bear said.

"My brother John—Bobbie in there is his kid."

"So what's he doin' here?"

"He showed up in the middle of the night scared out of his mind. Said some cops shot two of his friends and he was in trouble. He's family, Bear. What was I going to do, turn him away?"

Bear looked at the house, scratching his beard as he thought.

"I get that, brother," he said, "but there's like a shit ton of people lookin' for him."

"I know. And, truth be told, I don't know what I'm gonna do. But I'm not gonna let him fend for himself," Ray said.

Bear was quiet, still thinking.

"Look, I didn't mean to get you out here and involved in all this,"

Ray said. "You shouldn't have to get dragged into it. Lord knows it's not your problem. You go on back to the store. Just forget you ever came out here and saw him."

"And let you deal with all this by yourself? Bull-fuckin'-shit," Bear said.

"Bear, really, it's okay."

"I'm serious. We're goin' to figure this out."

"Bear, I—"

Ray exhaled as if a weight had been taken off his shoulders. He looked down at the driveway and kicked at it, trying not to let his emotions overwhelm him.

"Thank you," he muttered.

Bear patted him on the back. "You got it, bud. We just gotta figure this thing out. C'mon, let me say hello."

Ray led Bear inside, locking the door and drawing the curtains behind him. Bobbie Casto looked like he was being eaten alive by the corner of the sectional sofa he'd wedged himself into. He sat there with his feet up and his hoodie pulled over his legs, eyeing Bear from just over his knees.

"Bobbie," Ray said, "this is Bear. He's a good friend of mine. He owns the hunting store with me. He's going to help us figure this all out."

Bear extended a hand toward Bobbie.

"Good to meet ya," he said.

Bobbie didn't move or say anything.

Bear shirked his hand back and turned to Ray.

"Tough crowd," he said.

He could tell Ray was about to admonish Bobbie for his lack of manners, so he spoke first.

"That's alright. I'm not much to look at, I know," Bear said. "Your uncle's a good guy, it was smart comin' to him for help."

Bobbie mumbled something Bear couldn't make out.

"Speak up, son," Ray said.

"I *said*," Bobbie emphasized, "I didn't have much of a choice. Not a lot of places to go."

"You din' have anywhere closer to go? No other family or anythin'?" Bear asked.

Bobbie shrugged. "I figured they'd be looking for me at my mom's. Ray's the only other family I know."

Bear remembered Ray talking about his brother John and how he'd been killed in a car accident some 15 years back. By the looks of Bobbie, he must've been only a kid when it happened.

"It's good you're here now," he said. "Lemme talk to your uncle for a minute."

Bobbie didn't say anything as Bear gently grabbed Ray's arm to usher him aside.

"I hate to tell ya, brother," Bear said quietly, "but if it's like he says it is, it's not going to take the cops long to come down here askin' questions and snoopin' around."

"That thought crossed my mind, too. I'm all ears if you've got an idea," Ray said.

Bear rubbed at his chin, thinking. Bobbie couldn't be more than 18-, 19-years old. He had his whole life ahead of him and this—whatever *this* was—threatened to end all that, and quick. Bear had once helped a man who helped young people in trouble—the sort of trouble that Bobbie now found himself in. Bear had helped the man give a young woman her life back. Together they might be able to do the same for Bobbie.

"As a matter of fact, I think I do," Bear said.

He pulled out his phone and called Jackson Clay.

9

Lane Wolfe sat quietly poking at his lobster risotto as the men around him talked. The lobster itself was overcooked and rubbery, the rice mushy and bland. An undiscerning tongue might find it at least somewhat palatable, but to him it bordered on inedible.

He'd had European lobster fished fresh off the Greek isles; the best sashimi Tokyo had to offer; Paella in Valencia; and the couple times he'd allow himself the guilty pleasure of pizza, he didn't settle for a delivery joint down the street—he had it flown in from Naples.

So he couldn't understand why his colleagues – all various industry leaders throughout West Virginia – lapped up this overpriced chain restaurant slop, though he suspected the watered-down whiskey played a role. But Wolfe was tactful. And cunning. He didn't ruffle a feather he hadn't intended to and never did a favor that wasn't cashed-in down the road. It's how he'd built VigilOne, the largest private security services contractor in the mid-Atlantic.

Wolfe was thinking about this, still toying with the dead crustacean on his plate, when his phone buzzed inside the breast pocket of his Brioni suit. He slid the phone halfway out and glanced at the name: Red Starcher.

Wolfe excused himself from the table, walked over to the bar—empty on this Thursday lunch hour—and answered. "This is Lane."

"Mr. Wolfe, it's Red Starcher. Lieutenant for Hopewell County Vice."

"Yes, Mr. Starcher," Wolfe said, "what can I do for you?"

"I thought you might need to be apprised of a situation we may have. With business," Starcher said.

"All right, go on."

"Did you hear about the shooting last night?"

"Something on the way in to work. Two sheriff's deputies in a shootout, what have you."

"Right, but they weren't deputies. They were Vice detectives. On the payroll."

"And?"

"They were working a few kids when it went sideways. Two ended up dead. A third is in the wind, wounded. And he's got one of the detective's guns."

Wolfe turned sharply so even the bartender couldn't hear him, a cut of his raven black hair flipping over one of his steely gray eyes.

"And this kid knows things?" Wolfe asked. "Things he can talk about?"

"He knows what he did and didn't have on him. But it's his word against our detectives. And that's assuming he even comes in alive," Starcher said.

Wolfe closed his eyes and slowed his breathing, allowing his heart rate to fall back to the overly efficient resting rate of 55 beats per minute he'd worked so hard to attain.

"Is this kid going to be a problem for us?" he asked.

"The truth? Hard to say, sir. He's scared. Scared people do stupid things. We're counting on that. I've got the whole Vice Squad kicking down doors looking for him, but there's basically a statewide manhunt for him. The FBI is already looking over our shoulder, ready to jump in."

"That does *not* happen, understand me?" Wolfe said.

"I'll do my best, sir," Starcher said. "But it's largely out of my hands. That's why I wanted to bring you up to speed. Perhaps there are levers you could pull from out there."

"Levers I can pull? Let me ask you, who made this mess? Because if you're saying this all happened last night, I was in bed with a Czech girl who spoke about as much English as the bumfuck hillbillies you police. So it sure as fuck wasn't me. And you're asking me to clean up the mess? For you?"

"I was just saying, sir. You have reach I don't."

Wolfe exhaled, his breath fogging up the floor-to-ceiling window in front of him. This was a pissant's problem, but it could fuck him just as easily. Which made it his problem.

"If there's a move to be made, I'll make it," Wolfe said. "In the meantime, you find that fucking kid. And if shit went sideways again and he ended up dead like his friends it would fix a lot of problems. Understand me?"

"I got you," Starcher said.

Wolfe ended the call and slid his phone back into his suit pocket. He turned and looked at his lunch company, carrying on just as well without him. They may all be uber-successful businessmen, but he bet they'd never had a phone call like that.

Everything about him was special. Even his problems.

Wolfe sighed and headed for his seat.

"Back to the twerps," he muttered.

10

It was nearly five o'clock by the time Jackson arrived at Ray's house. Bear couldn't help but grin as he watched the black Dodge D100—a truck he'd loaned to the man and later sold to him after Jackson took a liking to it—rolled up the driveway and parked behind Bear's Suburban.

"Calvary's here," Bear said.

He opened the front door and stepped out, approaching Jackson with two outstretched arms, looking like his grizzly namesake.

Bobbie came to the door to get a glimpse of the man they had called for help. He was tall and tan, but older than Bobbie expected. In his 40's, if he had to guess, though he couldn't see the man's face very well under his ball cap and wraparound sunglasses—just a graying beard and tufts of brown hair ending short of the long-sleeved shirt that hung squarely on the man's toned torso.

Bear wrapped his arms around Jackson. "Thanks for comin' out."

"No problem," Jackson said.

"That's Bobbie over there," Bear said. "Why don't you go over and introduce yourself. I'll grab your bags."

"Don't you think we should get moving?" Jackson asked.

"What do you mean?" Bear said.

"You said the boy ended up here because he didn't have much in the way of places to go to. You were right to be worried about police showing up here."

"So, you want to move?"

"Seems like the smart thing to do."

"Okay, where?"

"Somewhere else, anywhere else for now. You don't want to be here aiding and abetting a fugitive when the authorities show up."

"I suppose there's my place. Or the store."

"Those places won't be much farther down their checklist after here," Jackson said.

Although, the fact that it had been some 20 hours and they hadn't tracked Ray down yet was a good sign.

"On second thought, let's make it your place," Jackson said.

"You just said they'd figure that out," Bear said.

"They will, but it'll buy us some time. Right now, distance is everything. If we can't figure out anything better, we'll need a cash motel or a campground. We'd need equipment for a campground, though."

Bear looked back at Bobbie. Ray had joined his nephew at the door.

"Your place for now, Bear," Jackson repeated. "We'll figure out our next step there. But we should go. That Lincoln is the uncle's car, I assume?"

"Yeah," Bear said.

"You take your Suburban, have him take the kid in the Lincoln. We'll all meet at your house," Jackson said.

"What about the other car?" Bear asked.

"What other car?"

"When Bobbie ran, he took his friend's car. One of the kids that was killed when it all went down."

Jackson removed his ball cap and scratched his head. The friend's car was a problem. If they left it here, and the police found it – which they undoubtedly would – his uncle would immediately be tied to everything the kid was into. But moving the car was far too risky. By now, there were probably BOLO alerts for the car in every surrounding state. Getting stopped in a dead kid's car wasn't something any of them would be able to explain—better to leave it here and let the police think what they may if they found it. The boy couldn't run forever, anyway.

"Leave it," Jackson said. "It's too risky on the road. And we should hide Bobbie in the Lincoln in case his uncle gets stopped."

"Good call," Bear said.

Jackson watched as Bear walked over to Bobbie and Ray and explained the plan. Soon enough, Ray disappeared inside with Bear – likely grabbing a few things to pack – but the kid stayed, watching Jackson. Jackson raised a hand and waved. Bobbie took one hand out of his hoodie pocket and gave a tepid wave back before Ray reappeared and ushered him into his Lincoln.

11

The sun was just beginning to dip below the horizon when the convoy of Jackson's pickup and Ray and Bear's SUVs pulled up to Bear's house, a quaint two-bedroom Craftsman on a generous piece of unkempt land. Jackson followed the other two cars into the driveway, slowing as he turned, checking the road in either direction for someone following. It was clear.

He pulled up behind Bear's Suburban, where Bear was already out and helping Ray unearth Bobbie from the mountain of junk they'd buried him under. Even with the sunlight fading, the world was bright enough that Bobbie winced as he climbed out.

"You guys go inside," Jackson said. "Bear and I will get everything out of the trucks. You two need to stay out of sight."

"You go on in with them, start figurin' out what the plan is. I'll start grabbin' stuff," Bear said.

Jackson looked over at the large shed he knew Bear used to house his hodge-podge collection of vehicles and machinery, and nodded at it. "Do you have room in there for his Lincoln?"

"I can move some stuff around," Bear said.

"Do it," Jackson said. "Then lock it up. And cover up any windows."

Bear nodded, and Jackson followed Ray and Bobbie inside. The interior of Bear's home was not furnished with company in mind: a lone recliner and end table sat in front of an absurdly large television in one living area, while a couple of pleather sofas were placed around a ramshackle coffee table littered with empty beer cans in the other.

"Bobbie, why don't you have a seat on the sofa there. I'll, uh, find a trash bag to clean some of this up," Ray said.

Jackson stood in the entryway, watching Bobbie do as he was told. He heard a medley of bangs and knocks as Ray searched the kitchen.

"Bear said we aren't staying here long," Ray said, speaking loudly so both Bobbie and Jackson could hear him in the other room. "Where are we headed?"

"Not sure. We need to know exactly what we're dealing with," Jackson said.

He stepped into the living room and leaned against the wall.

"Tell us everything that happened last night Bobbie," Jackson said, "From the beginning."

Bobbie wiped at his nose and cleared his throat.

"We were just going to hang out," he said, "Do whatever, you know. We got some food from Wawa and went to go chill at this over-look off the highway. I took some beer from my house. Mason had some weed. We were just gonna, you know, chill."

"Then what happened?" Jackson asked.

"All of the sudden this black truck rolls up on us," Bobbie continued. "At first I didn't know who it was, but then blue and red lights started flashing on the truck so I figured it was the cops."

"These police officers were in a pickup truck? Unmarked?"

"Yeah, except for the lights or whatever. They got out and split us up. Mason and I were on one side of the car and Emma was on the other. We didn't try to hide that we had booze or weed on us. That's when they started searching us, and things got crazy."

"What do you mean?" Jackson asked.

"The dude who was searching me up and pulls out a big bag of something," Bobbie said. "Says it's meth and it's mine. I swear to God I've never touched that stuff in my life. I don't know who had it, but that wasn't mine, I'm telling you."

"Could your friends have had it?"

"No way, man. We might smoke some weed sometimes but we never touch that toxic shit. I told the cop it wasn't mine, but he didn't believe me. I looked at Emma, could see in her eyes she didn't know if she believed me or not. You know how much that fuckin' hurt? To have someone you love like a sister think that of you?"

"So, it made you mad."

"Yeah, I got agitated, you know? Then as the other cop searched Emma, she screamed. She said the cop felt her up. Mason got pissed – I mean I was pissed, too – but Mason went around the car to Emma's side. That's when the cop behind me shoved me against the car and pulled out his gun and pointed it at Mason."

"So," Jackson said, "your friend Emma says the other cop touched her inappropriately, and the only thing the one behind you did is draw his gun on your other friend?"

Bobbie nodded. "He didn't skip a beat, either. He pointed his gun at Mason, and the other cop didn't pull his out, but he said something, talking shit to Mason."

Ray brought a trash bag into the living and started picking up empty beer cans. Bear shoved the front door open with his foot and carried two large bags in. He dropped them in the entryway as Ray tied off a bag's worth of Bear's trash.

"Oh, yeah," Bear said, a little winded. "Sorry about the mess."

"No problem," Ray said.

Jackson nodded at Bobbie. "Go on. The cop behind you drew his gun. Then what?"

Bobbie lowered his head as tears began to form in the corners of his eyes. He sniffled and wiped at his nose.

"It's all my fault," he said. "It... it should never have happened."

"What's all your fault? I thought you said you didn't have the meth." Jackson said.

"Not that," Bobbie said. "The gun. He drew it on Mason. But, but he was shoving me, you know? I wanted him off of me. So, I shoved back. That's when it happened."

"When what happened."

"The gun. It went off. I—he—it shot Emma. He wasn't aiming at her but I hit his arm with the gun. I swear to God, I'm so sorry."

Ray, holding a broom and listening intently from the kitchen, shook his head.

Jackson took a deep breath and sighed. "Christ."

Bobbie sobbed.

"Everything just got so out of control," he said. "It all happened so fast. The cop with Mason told the one with me to cuff me. I thought they were going to kill me. I fought to get free. I started fighting with the cop. I got a hold of his knife and stabbed him in the leg. I swear I thought I was fighting for my life. I didn't want to hurt anyone. I didn't want any of that to happen. I took the gun from the one cop, the one I stabbed. But the other cop saw me with it and shot at me. He missed, but he was shooting at me. Trying to kill me. So I shot back. I didn't know what else to do."

"You shot at the other officer?"

"I'm telling you," Bobbie said. "I had no choice. They were going to fucking kill me, man. I was trying to get somewhere safe. That's when I saw Mason attack the other cop. The one that shot at me. He was beating on the cop when I heard a gunshot. The cop fucking killed Mason."

"You saw him actually shoot Mason?" Jackson asked.

"Yes. He'd shot at me and then he shot and killed Mason. He was going to kill me, too, I just know it. I didn't know what else to do, so I made a run for it. I ran for the hillside. That's when I got shot in the leg, but I kept going. I got over the side and fell a ways and hid. Then I heard them talking about making the scene look right or something, and I heard a few more gun shots. After that, I didn't stick around long. I ran."

"These officers. You saw what they looked like, right? You could ID them? I mean, they said they were police, right? Did they say from where?"

"They said Hopewell County Sheriff's Office. I might know their names. Or maybe nicknames. They called each other Franko and Bragg. Bragg was the one who was shoving me, saying I had meth on me. Franko was the one that groped Emma and shot Mason."

Bear came back in with the last bags and dropped them carelessly on the floor. Huffing for air, he wiped his brow and sat down on the couch opposite Bobbie.

"Franko and Bragg. That's good, Bobbie," Jackson said. "So you ran. Ran where?"

"At first, nowhere really," Bobbie said. "Then, when I saw Church Street in the distance, I knew I must be near Mason's house. I was going there thinking maybe I could tell his parents and maybe they could help me or something. Then I saw his car in the driveway. I remembered how he would leave his keys in the visor when he parked at home in case either his mom or dad had to move it. I thought maybe his parents wouldn't believe me. Maybe they'd turn me over to those guys that tried killing me. So I took Mason's car instead of going to his parents."

"To your uncle's house?" Jackson asked.

Bobbie shook his head. "Not right away. At first I didn't know where to go. I thought I should get out of the county. Then I thought the state would probably be even better. When I got into Virginia, my uncle's the only person I know from here. I thought he was far enough away it might be safe."

Jackson took a deep breath and exhaled slowly, digesting the information.

"Which brings us to now," Ray said, walking back into the room.

"Well, I'm glad you're alright, Bobbie. Who wrapped your wound?" Jackson said.

"I did," Ray said.

"You mind if I take a look? Redress it, maybe?"

"By all means."

"Bear, I've got a kit in my rucksack, would you grab it for me?"

Bear did as he was asked and Jackson slowly unwrapped Bobbie's bandage. The wound was a clean through-and-through, hitting mostly muscle. He was lucky. Had it hit his tibia or fibula, he wouldn't have been able to drive with the leg, much less run on it. Had it hit either of the nearby arteries, he'd most likely have died along with his friends.

Jackson cleaned and redressed the wound with fresh gauze, then wrapped the ends with tape. "That should be good for now. Are you hungry?"

"Kind of, actually," Bobbie said.

"Good deal," Jackson said. "Let me talk it over with Bear and your uncle and see what we can do."

Bobbie smiled his thanks. Jackson got up and motioned for the other two to follow him into the next room. There, next to Bear's recliner, the three huddled.

"So, what do you think?" Bear asked.

"Well, he's not wrong. He's in some real trouble. But all of this doesn't add up. Planting the meth, escalating the situation, it doesn't make sense," Jackson said.

"Wouldn't be the first time the police framed a black boy," Ray said.

Bear pointed a finger gun and nodded at Ray, agreeing with his point.

"Even so," Jackson said, "why? Bobbie and them were off on their own, not bothering anyone. Even if these guys planted the stuff, there had to be a reason they wanted to jam the kids up."

"They're racist assholes. Been good enough a reason for 400 years," Ray said.

"I still think there's more to it. But we need help. *He* needs help."

"I thought that was where you came in."

"He needs more than me. For starters, he needs a lawyer. And a damn good one. Either of you know one?"

Bear shrugged.

"We have a guy that helps us out with business stuff from time to time," he said, "but he doesn't do this sort of stuff."

"I'll make some calls," Jackson said. "See if I can get Bobbie some legal representation. But we need something more."

"What do you mean?" Bear asked.

"Right now we have no leverage. Bobbie is an attempted cop-killer on the run. We need to change that narrative, and get some leverage of our own. If we can figure out what really started everything last night, that might be the first step."

Ray and Bear nodded.

"In the meantime," Jackson said, "we should get him some food. It wouldn't hurt for us to eat, either. Could be a long night."

"Antonio's delivers. The pizza ain't bad," Bear said.

Jackson shook his head.

"No deliveries," he said. "I'll run out and get something."

"I can do that, if you want. Or Ray can."

"No, I'll go. Ray and Bobbie stay out of sight until further notice. And you have to be here in case anyone comes around. But Ray and Bobbie are *not* here. You got it?"

"Got it, brother."

"Good. I'll make those phone calls on the way. Then we'll know what to do next."

Jackson fished his keys out of his pocket and headed out.

12

Antonio's Pizza was only a quick fifteen-minute drive away. Jackson pulled out his phone and called one of his contacts with the Virginia State Police—someone who'd helped him on the same case where he'd first met Bear. Now, this Special Agent was Jackson's go-to when he needed information or a favor from someone with a badge. Or, occasionally, an introduction.

"Jen Bailey," she answered.

"It's me," Jackson said.

"How's it going?" she asked. "Haven't heard of a recent missing persons in the news, but I'm guessing this still isn't a social call."

"No abduction. You hear about this thing with the three teens in West Virginia?"

"Yeah, two are dead, one is in the wind or something. You looking for the missing one?"

"Found him," Jackson said. "But I could use some help."

There was a chorus of rattles and clanks on Bailey's end of the line. Jackson assumed she was moving somewhere more private.

"I don't think I need to tell you this, but if you've got him, you're aiding and abetting a fugitive right now," Bailey said.

"I'm working on that, but it's complicated. His story isn't the story on the news," Jackson said.

"His story? What did he tell you?"

"There's something off with these two Hopewell County Sheriff's deputies. I was wondering if you could do a deep dive on them for me."

"I can look them up, but I'm not going to step on anyone's toes over some kid's story."

"Understood. The officers are Franko and Bragg. Not sure on the spelling. It's possible they're some special unit or detectives based on what the kid said."

"I got it. But you really ought to bring this kid in. From what I've read, he doesn't need you – he needs a lawyer. And probably a damn good one."

"That's the other thing. You wouldn't happen to know one, would you?"

"I know plenty. Occupational hazard."

"Well if you've got a name, I'm all ears. One in West Virginia, obviously. And like you said, he needs a good one. Someone that'd be a headache for you. And cheaper would be better. I don't know how much money the kid's family can throw together."

"Okay, give me a little while, I'll see what I can do."

"Thank you, Bailey."

"Sure, Jackson. I'll get back to you."

Jackson killed the call and pulled into the lot in front of Antonio's. The pizza joint was a small brick-and-mortar storefront in an otherwise abandoned four-store strip mall; a physical symptom of the local economy deserting this particular part of town.

Inside, a milky pale teenager losing a battle to his facial acne looked up at Jackson with a hundred-yard stare. Jackson ordered two pies — one pepperoni and one veggie — and paid cash, leaving a tip neither too big or too small that the workers would have reason to remember his purchase. Seventeen minutes later, he was leaving the store with the pizzas in-hand when he felt his phone buzz in his pocket.

That was fast, Jackson thought.

But it wasn't Bailey calling him back. It was Bear.

"I've got the pizza," Jackson said. "What's up?"

Jackson nearly dropped the group's dinner as Bear answered him.

"Cops are here."

13

Jackson got into his truck, fired it up, and began speeding back toward Bear's house before realizing that wouldn't help.

"What do you mean they're there? What specifically are they doing?" Jackson asked.

"Lookin' about the yard right now," Bear said. "Four or five of them. One car is parked blockin' the end of the driveway."

"What about the shed? Have they spotted Ray's Lincoln?"

"No, not yet."

"We can't let that happen, Bear."

"Exactly what I was thinking."

"Do they have a warrant to search?"

"I don' know, but it doesn't look like it. They haven't even come up and knocked on the door yet."

Jackson took his foot off the gas and slowed down, thinking. That the police didn't have a warrant was a good thing. It meant they didn't have concrete evidence. They were running down leads hoping to find something. They couldn't go into the house without permission, but it didn't matter—if the house was on the police's radar, it was too hot. One way or another, they had to get out of there.

"You have to tell them off," Jackson said. "Like a redneck—"

"—*Rural Lifestyle Enthusiast,*" Bear corrected.

Jackson rolled his eyes. Bear was a character, but Jackson didn't always have time for it.

"Just make a big show of it," Jackson said, "you not liking the police on your property. Play it up. You're not hiding anything and you're pissed off they're there in the first place."

"That may get 'em to the street, but I'd bet a good chunk of change they'll sit on the house from where they can," Bear said.

"At least one car, you're probably right," Jackson agreed. "Doesn't matter—you've got to get them gone and then you guys get out of there yourself."

"And if they sit on the house? Going to be hard to explain how I'm here alone and then leave with the two people they're looking for."

"No, Bobbie and Ray are going to have to get out some other way."

Jackson drove by an open field and thought he could see headlights across the way. He was maybe 200 yards away if it were a straight shot, but the road continued north before bowing back. Still, the line of sight gave him an idea.

"The driveway is the only way in and out of your house, right?" Jackson asked.

"Only way," Bear said.

"There's no other way? Even on foot?"

"No, not really."

"Come on, Bear, think. There's *no* way to get away if you really had to? Like, say, now?"

The line went quiet for a moment.

"Well, if you head south and hump it through the woods a bit," Bear said, "you'd probably end up on Route 57. It hugs the Smith River."

"Perfect. Do you think you can tell them how to get out down there?" Jackson said.

"Sure, you walk in a straight line until you hit a road or the river. It ain't rocket science. But you want them to do this when the cops are here? They've still got to cross open space by the pond."

"On a moonless night like this they'll be damn near invisible. Especially if you're causing a scene on your front porch. You get the idea now?"

Bear chortled.

"Oh yeah," he said, "I got this."

"Make it like you've got somewhere to be and they're in the way. After you get them away, head out but head away from Route 57. You tell Ray and Bobbie to go through the woods to the highway. Then, when they're near, you have them call me. I'll find them."

"Sounds like a plan, brother. Just one question, though. Where we all goin' when you get them?"

Jackson paused. He didn't have a good answer. He looked at his phone's screen and double-checked Special Agent Bailey hadn't called. She hadn't.

"Let's just get you guys out of there," Jackson said. "We'll worry about that if this works."

14

Jackson drove past the turn for Bear's house and followed the winding roads to Highway 57, his mind going faster than the old Dodge could ever hope to. How had the police ended up at Bear's place? Had they already been to Ray's? Had they discovered Mason's car?

There were too many variables and not enough hard information. Not knowing was how people got in trouble, and Bobbie Casto was already in plenty of it.

Turning onto 57, Jackson pulled over and killed his headlights. The road was dark and deserted, a slow-bending arc of asphalt slicing its way through the woods of southern Virginia. Jackson could hear the Smith River gurgling somewhere on the other side of the foliage. He was listening to it when his phone buzzed.

It was Special Agent Bailey.

"Tell me you've got something.," he said answering the call.

"I do," Bailey said. "Like I told you, I didn't dig too deep, but you might have reason to look sideways at these Franko and Bragg guys. Their whole unit is a little shady, to be honest. The two men are part of the Hopewell County Sheriff's Vice Task Force."

"Why does a rural county have a Vice Squad?" Jackson asked.

"The West Virginia governor. His whole thing was declaring a new war on drugs in the wake of the opioid epidemic," Bailey said. "He promised pork barrels for any department that would step up to combat it. It was a blank check to create jobs. Just about all of them took the free money. Hopewell County Sheriff's Office more than most, though. You thought them having a Vice Squad was a lot, it turns out they bought their department an MRAP."

Mine-Resistant Ambush Protected was the term for an array of armored tactical vehicles originally designed for the military, but Jackson knew many police departments were now procuring them for SWAT teams and the like.

"Terrific, so what makes Hopewell County Vice shady?" Jackson asked.

"A laundry list of complaints. Everything from excessive force to planting evidence. Just about every member has something in their file, looks like," Bailey said.

"So how are they still on the street?"

"Accusations tend to stay just that. Also, their numbers. They make more arrests than almost the rest of the department combined."

"But how many of those arrests are without complaints?"

"It's a good question. Like I said, you might have good reason to avoid these guys. Luckily for you, you may have another option. It looks as though the State Police have a man on the investigation, as well. A First Lieutenant Colton Sayre. I haven't heard of him, but there aren't nearly the number of complaints in his file as the vice guys."

"He's not getting handed over to anyone without a lawyer, though."

"I've got something on that, too. I talked to a lawyer buddy of mine. Harper & Rhodes are one of those $1,000-an-hour type places specializing in criminal defense. Mostly they get mining execs out of DUI's and hit-and-runs. Things of that nature. But they also do pro bono work for the 'underprivileged'. Their way of balancing out the bad PR their firm gets for keeping rich assholes out of prison. The guy I know plays golf with Liam Harper. He said just drop his name – Ethan Johnson – and Harper should be able to help you out. I just sent you an email with the lawyer's contact info."

"That's a huge help, Bailey. Thank you."

"That might be the first time you've thanked me."

"Might be. Got to go."

"And he's back."

Jackson killed the call and opened up the email on his phone. He found Liam Harper's phone number and called it.

"This is Liam," a professional and polished voice answered on the second ring.

"Mr. Harper, my name is Jackson Clay. Ethan Johnson said you might be able to help out a friend of a friend in a jam."

There was a chuckle on the other end of the line that felt rehearsed, as if it'd been practiced and utilized dozens of times.

"Well, more than I can help his handicap, sure," Harper quipped. "What can I do for you?"

"I'm helping out a kid that's in some trouble," Jackson said. "He could use a good lawyer, but he's just a kid, so he's not exactly swimming in cash."

"Well, how much do you have, Mr. Clay?" Harper asked.

Jackson was silent, caught off guard by the question. Harper gave another perfected chuckle.

"I'm kidding, of course," he said. "I'm guessing Ethan didn't pass along my name for my hourly rate. It's true, we do some pro bono work at our firm, assuming the case is a good fit."

Good fit was probably code for "helped the company look good"— and whether or not the case was winnable.

"I'm not sure what kind of fit this would be," Jackson said.

"Okay," Harper said. "What's his story?"

Jackson was quiet again. He wasn't sure how many cards in his hand he wanted to show to a lawyer he didn't know. Harper cleared his throat.

"Mr. Clay, while you and I are not protected under attorney-client privilege," he said, "I can assure you I did not get where I am today outing people's business. Just lay it out for me. If it's not a good fit, we'll pretend this conversation never happened."

Jackson was still apprehensive, but he knew Harper was likely Bobbie's best bet.

"His name is Bobbie Casto," Jackson said, "you might've seen his story on the news. He's wanted, but trust me when I tell you the news doesn't have the whole story."

"*You* are with Bobbie Casto?" Harper asked.

The polish was gone from his voice now. He sounded surprised. And, more importantly, he sounded intrigued.

"I'm trying to help him out," Jackson said. "I'm telling you there's more to the story. I'm not asking you to get an attempted cop-killer a minimum sentence. I think the only thing Casto might've been guilty of that night is having some beer and weed on him while being at the wrong place at the wrong time."

Jackson heard papers shuffling furiously on the other end of the line. For whatever it was worth, it sounded like Liam Harper was all in.

"That's good, that's real good, Mr. Clay," Harper said. "Uh, when can we meet? You shouldn't hand him over to the authorities before we've met first."

"I wasn't planning to, but that's kind of the problem," Jackson said. "He – we don't have anywhere *to* go right now. And with the police—"

"My house," Harper said. "My house in Charleston. South of downtown. How soon could you make it?"

"Charleston? We're probably 200 miles from there. That's a long way to go with probably the most wanted kid in the area."

"Well, where are you, exactly?"

"South central Virginia. Near Martinsville."

The line went quiet. Jackson assumed Harper was thinking.

"What about White Sulphur Springs, just over the state line? I have a weekend house there. I could meet you in, say, a couple of hours probably."

It was still far, but Jackson didn't have a better idea. As far as the police knew, Bobbie had no connection to Liam Harper. If Jackson could get Bobbie there, they'd all be safe. Jackson was about to speak when his phone chimed with an incoming call. He didn't recognize the number, but it was local. Must be Ray or Bobbie, he thought.

"It may be a little longer than that, but that sounds good," Jackson said to Harper. "Text this number the information, and I'll do my best to get him there. I have to get on it, though."

"No problem, Mr. Clay," Harper said. "Hopefully I'll see you two—"

Jackson switched the call over.

"Jackson," he answered.

"Hey," Ray said, "It's us. I think we're near the highway."

"Did you get away clean?" Jackson asked.

"Near damn sure. Bear was raising hell with the local cops. I could hear him hollering still from across the pond out back."

"Good. Do you know where you are on the highway?"

"Nah. We crossed a railroad track, but other than that everything looks the same."

Jackson didn't know about a railroad, so what little information Ray had didn't help. Still, he was nearly certain Ray and Bobbie had to be somewhere ahead of him, since he hadn't gone too far down the highway yet.

"I'm pretty sure I'm north of you," Jackson said. "There haven't been any other cars headed my way. Stay on the line. I'm going to start driving. I should be the next car coming from the north."

"Got it, okay."

Jackson flicked on his headlights and headed down the road. After a quarter mile or so, he put the phone back up to his ear.

"Anything yet?" he asked.

"No. Wait – yes, I think I see you," Ray said.

"I'm flashing my high-beams," Jackson said.

"Yes, that's you. Keep coming, we're another hundred yards or so."

As Jackson put his phone down, he saw two shadowy figures emerge from the woods. He took his foot off the gas and coasted to a stop in the middle of the road. Ray and Bobbie hurried across the road – Bobbie limping – and climbed into Jackson's truck. The door wasn't shut yet before Jackson punched the gas.

"Are you guys good?" Jackson asked.

"Yeah," Ray said. "I'm worried about his leg, though."

"I told you it was fine," Bobbie said, wedged in between the both of them.

Jackson picked his phone back up and called Bear.

"Yhello," Bear answered.

"You get rid of the cops yet?" Jackson asked.

"Oh, they're gone brother," Bear said. "Made a real fuss of it. Yelled at them about how it was League Night at the lanes and they were holdin' me up. Told them unless they had a warrant they best get off my property before my lawyer shows up. Not sure they bought the lawyer bit, but they left."

"Did they *leave* leave?"

"There's a cop car out on the road, but they ain't doin' shit. I'm filling my bowlin' ball bag now with some essentials. You know, sellin' the story. I'll be on my way here in a minute. You got Ray and Bobbie?"

"Yeah, I've got them. We're already on the move. I'm going to have Ray text you an address with my phone. Meet us there, but make sure no one tails you."

"You got it, buddy."

Jackson ended the call and handed his phone over to Ray.

"Do you know how to text him with that?" he asked.

"I'm old, I ain't obsolete," Ray said.

Jackson gave Ray the address Harper had given him, and Ray began punching away at the phone. They followed Highway 57 another mile or two before taking a left and heading back north. From Collinsville, they'd head toward Roanoke and then on toward the West Virginia state line.

Bobbie leaned over and looked at the phone's screen as Ray typed. He squinted, confused, when he saw the address.

"What's in White Sulphur Springs, West Virginia?" he asked.

"Your lawyer," Jackson said.

15

Mia Parsons kicked her head back and let the shot of Evan Williams slide down her throat, warming her body from the inside. She lingered there, pushing the world around her away. In that moment it was just her, Evan Williams, and Luke Combs serenading her from the speakers around the bar.

She leaned forward, coming back to reality. The bartender, Joe, stood in front of her with an expectant look on his face.

"Another?" he asked.

Mia shook her head.

"Not right now. Thanks," she said.

"Whatever," Joe grumbled.

He slid the bottle of gutter whiskey back underneath the bar and walked away to tend to other patrons. Joe's Bar & Grill sat on the edge of Rion and was much more a bar than it was a grill. With peeling red paint, a sticky linoleum floor, and more burnt out lights than working, it was the kind of dive only a local could love. Joe, for that matter, took such a fact to be a badge of honor.

"He don' let on, but he wants to fuck you," her friend said from the barstool beside her. "You know that right?"

Bony and light-toned, Jimmy Green could be mistaken for a

walking skeleton if one had poor enough vision. His hoodie and jeans, covered in dirt and grease stains, hung off his frame the way they might hang from a closet hanger. In fact, the two biggest things on Jimmy were his mop of brown hair and the wad of cash he'd amassed from selling everyone on this side of Rion whatever a pharmacy wouldn't give them. Were his sleeves rolled up, the other bar patrons would've seen Jimmy used as much as he dealt.

"Leave Joe alone, he's harmless," Mia said.

"He's twenty years too fuckin' old for you is what he is," Jimmy countered.

Mia put her elbows up on the bar and scanned the array of bottles on the back wall. They all had names. Friendly names, like Jack and Jim and Evan. Friendly names because they were her friends more than she'd like to admit. Her other friends, her real friends, tended to let her down. Jack and Jim and Evan would never dare.

She had other friends, too, but they didn't have real names—they had more ominous aliases like dope, black rock, and crank. The truth was, if it was something that helped her escape her reality, even for a minute, she was well-acquainted with it.

Mia reached back and put her long, wavy brown hair into a ponytail. As she turned, revealing the front of her pink halter top, Jimmy couldn't help but to stare. Neither could the few other men on that side of the bar. Mia was slim and tawny and strikingly beautiful. She knew it, and the little world around her knew it. It was the one thing she had going for her in this godforsaken life.

She smiled at Jimmy.

"Watcha lookin' at?" she asked.

Jimmy smiled back, admitting he was caught before reaching over the bar and grabbing the bottle of Evan Williams from underneath.

"Fuck it, I'm having one more," he said.

Joe saw him and began to object when a figure stepped in between him and Mia and Jimmy.

"Now, Jimmy, you know that'd be theft unless you're payin' for it," the figure said.

Jimmy looked up as the figure brushed back his greasy long hair to reveal a pair of dark eyes that pierced through the lanky 22-year-old.

"H-Hey, Franko," Jimmy said, his voice wavering.

"How's it going? What would that make for you? Arrest number four? Five? If the judge had half a mind, he'd lock your useless ass up and throw away the key," Franko said.

"I—I was going to pay for it."

Franko flashed a smile of cracked, yellow teeth and slapped Jimmy on the shoulder.

"Don' I know it." He replied

"Hi, Ronnie," Mia said in little more than a whisper.

"Hey yourself," Franko said, his flaxen grin stretching wider. "I was hopin' to find you here. I wanted to talk to ya about that thing. Maybe we could go somewhere. Y'know, to talk."

Jimmy faced the bar, his head down. He knew very well they weren't going to talk, but he didn't dare raise an objection. Mia looked at him, disappointed that her real friend — not Jack or Jim or Evan — had let her down again.

"Sure, Ronnie," she said. "Let's talk."

A single streetlight illuminated the alley behind Joe's Bar, casting an array of trash cans and refuse in long, distorted shadows. Mia reached for one of said trash cans and braced herself as Franko pushed up against her and entered her from behind. Her jeans and panties around her ankles, Franko pinned her against the brick wall of the bar and did what he pleased. Mia could smell his rancid breath and held her own in an effort to avoid getting sick. There was nothing to do, really. She didn't want to—couldn't, truthfully—fight it and certainly wasn't going to enjoy it. So she stood there, waiting for it to be over.

Less than a minute later, it was. Ronnie stepped away and took his hand off her breast, letting it lay against the cold bricks with the rest of Mia's chest. She reached down, not daring to turn around, and began clothing herself.

"That was great, babe," she said, lying.

Franko laughed as he buttoned his own pants. Mia knew that laugh. The cop was smitten with himself.

"Gave you a good time, right?" he said.

"Every time, babe."

Mia fished the pack of Marlboros out of one of her pockets and patted the others in search of her lighter. She was about to give up when she heard a metal flick next to her. Franko held out his own lighter and offered its flame to her.

"Thanks," Mia said, and lit her cigarette.

In the long-cast light, Mia could see the pistol sitting loose on Franko's hip. He was always careless with it after he was done playing with a different gun. Time and time again Mia had thought about taking that pistol and blasting a hole in Franko. No one would blame her, right? Wasn't it self-defense? Like, technically? She didn't know. Not enough to ever act, anyways. And so, the gun and escape from Ronnie Franko remained an elusive dream.

Franko's phone buzzed in his pocket. He fished it out, looked at the screen, and shook his head.

"Work calls," he said.

"I'm sorry you've gotta run," Mia lied.

"Gotta pay the bills," Franko said.

He flashed his off-color smile again and leaned in for a kiss. Mia braced her queasy stomach and gave him what he wanted. She always did.

"I'll see ya," Franko said.

He fished a twenty-dollar bill out of his pocket and slid it inside the top of her jeans, moving his hand over and groping her as he pulled it out. "Have a drink on me. Maybe pay for that dipshit boyfriend of yours, too."

Mia took her open hand and clenched it in a fist. Her back against the wall, she slid down and sat on the cold cement beneath her. A part of her wanted to cry. It always did after Franko was done with her. She hated what she let him do. How he used her. She hated herself more than she hated him. It's why she had those friends like Jack and Jim and Evan. And those others with cruder names.

16

Just before midnight, Jackson, Ray, and Bobbie pulled up to an impressive timber-frame resort home that sat on a mountain ridge just outside White Sulphur Springs.

Ray climbed out of the truck, taking in the whole building.

"This is someone's *weekend* home?" he asked.

"When you bill four figures an hour it is," Jackson said.

He'd told Ray and Bobbie everything he'd learned from Special Agent Bailey as they drove to Harper's house. Ray seemed more excited than Bobbie that he would have a good lawyer. Jackson wondered if somewhere in Bobbie's mind he thought getting help meant avoiding legal trouble altogether.

Jackson looked over at the Mercedes S Class parked near the garage, its brilliant wax job reflecting the home's exterior lighting.

"I'm guessing he's here," he said.

Together, the three of them walked up to the door, which Harper opened with a warm greeting.

"Hello there," he said. "Liam Harper. Please, please, come in."

Harper was trim and smaller than Jackson expected – maybe a hair under six feet – with graying black hair and a rosy beige complexion that seemed like it might've been helped along by a couple visits to the tanning salon.

Inside, the resort home was an impressive open-plan home. Large, pristine windows ran from the floor all the way up to the cathedral ceiling, framing what Jackson presumed must be a spectacular view in the daylight.

"Why don't we all have a seat at the table here," Harper said. "Can I get everyone drinks? Water or coffee, or perhaps something harder?"

Ray and Bobbie both politely asked for water. Jackson passed, shaking his head, but Harper grabbed three glasses anyway.

"I have this great volcanic water from Waiakea, it's wonderful. Please, please, have a seat," Harper said.

He motioned to a gargantuan gray stone table that had to weigh somewhere near half a ton.

"This is, um, some table," Ray said.

Harper poured the glasses of water.

"Thank you," he said. "It's custom molded using concrete with local West Virginia shale. It came in one piece just like that. We had to have a crane lift it in before we put the roof on the house."

Jackson was getting the idea Liam Harper liked to talk about the things he had.

"Anyways," Harper said, bringing the waters to the table, "I had a couple of assistants put together what they could find in the news about your case, Bobbie, so I have some idea of what happened. But of course, their story is not your story. So why don't you tell me in your own words what happened."

"Okay, sir," Bobbie said.

"And as of now, I am your attorney," Harper continued. "So if I ask these two gentlemen to step out, everything you tell me will be protected under our attorney-client privilege. All I ask is that you tell me the whole truth. I have heard some bad things in my time, I promise you you're not going to scare me and I'm not here to judge anyone. It's my duty to represent you, even if you tell me you committed a crime. But if I don't know the truth, I can't protect you. Do you understand?"

Bobbie nodded. Jackson could tell he was nervous.

"It's okay, Bobbie. I know it sounds serious, but he really is here to help you. You just have to help him help you," Jackson said.

Harper flashed a big smile and patted Jackson on the shoulder. Jackson didn't appreciate the tactile interaction.

"That's exactly right," Harper said. "We're all just here to help you out. Now, like I said, I'm going to ask your uncle and your friend here to step out. Gentlemen, if you don't mind, I have a wonderful deck out back with a space heater."

"Not a problem," Jackson said.

"There's a bar out there, too. Please, help yourself," Harper added.

Jackson and Ray ignored the last part, but scooted back from the table and headed for the deck. The two were beginning to feel the wear and stress of the day, but as they stepped out onto Harper's deck they found the brisk autumn breeze reinvigorating. Ray walked to the edge, staring out into the night, and took a deep breath in before letting it out slowly.

In the moonless night, the valley below the house was a darkened canvas save for the tops of a few sycamore trees catching the light flooding out from Harper's house. Jackson posted against the house, watching Ray as he leaned against the deck's banister.

"That lawyer fella sure likes you to know he has money," Ray said.

"Seems like it," Jackson said.

"I think he'll be good for Bobbie, though. Lord knows he's more than I could've afforded."

Jackson didn't say anything back. Ray turned and looked at him, as if trying to figure him out; this man who had appeared seemingly out of nowhere and whisked them all to this vacationer's château at the edge of the Allegheny Mountains.

"I never did get a chance to thank you, by the way," Ray continued. "For doing everything you've done for Bobbie. He won't say it, but it means a lot to him, I'm sure. And to me."

"Don't mention it," Jackson said.

"No. No, I'm serious. It's not nothing. Truth be told, when Bobbie showed up on my doorstep, I didn't know what the hell to do. But you, you've had a plan for us all along. I don't know that I could've done this much on my own."

Jackson went quiet again. Ray was starting to understand that it was the man's default state. He was still watching him, trying to decipher Jackson as if he were a wall of hieroglyphs.

"I mean, if you don't mind me asking, why *are* you helping? It's not that I'm not grateful. Just, most folks wouldn't stick their neck out like you have."

Now a small grin formed on Jackson's face. He snorted, amused by the thought that came to him.

"It's funny, you say it like that," Jackson said. "I met Bear a little more than a year ago. I was looking for this missing girl when I followed these goons to a dive bar. I got in a fight with them, and that's where I met Bear. Next thing I know, we're at an Applebee's and he's laying out everything he knows about the guys I got mixed up with, helping me, and I didn't get it. Why he had just dropped everything to jump on what I was doing."

"I'm guessing you asked him," Ray said.

"I did. He looked at me like I had offended him or something. He asked who wouldn't want to help find some missing girl. That was it. For him, it was as simple as that," Jackson said.

"That's Bear for you. Always willing to give you the shirt off his back."

"That's right."

Ray smiled, realizing Jackson's answer to his question was the same as Bear's was to Jackson in that restaurant. He turned away so Jackson couldn't see the tear forming in the corner of his eye.

"He's a good kid, Bobbie is," Ray said. "That's how I know it isn't like the news says it is. Bobbie wouldn't do that. Get into all that mess."

Jackson stood upright and slid his hands into his pockets as he walked up to Ray, pretending they could see anything but the black of night in the world below. As he came up alongside him, Ray noticed the tattoo on Jackson's forearm. It was a snake wrapped around a sword behind a shield, the insignia of the US Army Rangers. Over the top, a furled banner was emblazoned with 75 RANGER RGT.

"You were a Ranger?" Ray asked.

"I was," Jackson said.

"75th Ranger Regiment by the looks of the ink," Ray said, nodding at Jackson's arm. "Hardscrabble boys."

"Did you serve?" Jackson asked.

"Marines in Desert Storm," Ray replied nodding. "Didn't do shit but secure burning oil derricks."

"Every soldier's got orders to follow."

"Ain't that the truth. But you boys, you boys are some serious ass-kickers."

Below the Ranger insignia, Ray noticed two words inked in curling, old-timey style.

"*Sua Sponte*. That's the 75th's motto, right?" he asked.

"Yes, sir."

"I assume you were in Iraq."

"Afghanistan and Iraq. Kosovo before that."

"When did you get into the Middle East?"

"October '01."

"Damn, you must've been one of the first pair of boots in-country. Wait, you weren't at Takur Ghar, were you?"

"I was."

The glass door to the deck slid open and Bobbie and Harper's conversation echoed off the cavernous walls of the house and drowned out the last bit Ray said to Jackson. Bear stepped onto the deck and closed the door behind him, preserving the nighttime quiet.

"What's good boys? How're y'all doing?" Bear asked.

"Fine, fine," Ray said. "How come you never told me you were friends with a bona fide badass?"

Jackson winced at the title.

"What do you mean?" Bear said.

"Jackson here fought in some real shit in Afghanistan. Takur Ghar. Bunch of Rangers and SEALs and other special ops types got in one serious fucking firefight. Dudes crash-landed on a mountain and kept on fightin'. Real American badasses."

Bear turned to Jackson.

"I din' know this. Why din' I know this?" he asked.

"It was war, it happened. Nothing more to it," Jackson said.

Jackson rubbed his arm. He saw Bobbie and Harper stand up from the table. Harper patted Bobbie on the shoulder with one hand and extended the other one open. Bobbie took it and shook it.

"Looks like they're about done," Jackson said, happy to change the subject. "You sure you weren't followed here, Bear?"

"C'mon, brother. Give me a little credit. This ain't my first rodeo," Bear said. "You of all people know that."

Harper stepped away, came to the sliding door, and joined the three of them on the deck.

"So, what do you think?" Jackson asked.

"Well, if it all went down the way he said it did," Harper said, "we certainly have some stuff to work with. This is heavy what we're talking about, though. It's a good thing you guys called me. Some public defender wouldn't know how to attack this."

"So, we're going to fight this, right?" Ray said

"We are. But the way you come at this is in the courts. I'm glad we got him out here and were able to circle the wagons, but he can't stay on the run now. He's got to turn himself in."

Jackson shifted his weight and crossed his arms. He'd already figured as much, but he was worried it hadn't dawned on Ray yet.

"We're concerned the County Sheriff's Office might have a chip on their shoulder and might be looking for retribution," Jackson said, trying to address what he knew Ray was worried about. "To them, Bobbie is just some kid that tried to kill one of their own."

"We can explore options about his surrender, but he's got to go in," Harper said.

"I have a law enforcement contact that says the State Police have an investigator on the case," Jackson added. "A Colton Sayre."

"I've never heard the name, but if you're implying we could deal with him instead, it's definitely a possibility. We can call him first thing tomorrow. Tell him Bobbie wants to come in but he's afraid for his safety and we would need assurances, yada, yada, yada."

"And medical. I did what I could for his leg, but he needs to see a doctor."

"Best not to leave that to the health care the Bureau of Prisons provides. I've got a guy."

"Is your guy going to turn around and report a gunshot wound?"

Harper laughed as if Jackson said something amusing.

"Mr. Clay, my people are discreet. Professional and discrete," he said. "And, lucky for us, they make house calls. I'll have him come out and look at Bobbie. Then Bobbie needs to get some rest. We'll hit the ground running with this Lieutenant Sayre in the morning."

Everyone nodded in agreement and filed inside. Jackson replayed his conversation with Ray over in his head about how he'd met Bear and his time in the Rangers. He ran his fingers over the *Sua Sponte* on his arm. It meant "Of Their Own Accord". It spoke to a Ranger's ability to take initiative and served in recognition that a Ranger volunteers three times: first for the US Army, then Airborne School, then service in the 75th.

Rangers of the 75th didn't wait to be told to fight. They saw the fight before them and jumped in it. Jackson didn't know Ray or Bobbie even six hours ago, but that didn't matter.

The fight was before him now.

PART II

CAPIAS

17

J ackson awoke to the sound of steam whistling from an espresso
machine rivaling that of most gourmet coffeehouses. Harper was
working the various levers, already dressed and freshly shaven.
He looked back over at Jackson and smiled.

"Oh, sorry, I didn't wake you, did I?" he asked, knowing full well
he had.

"No, I was just resting," Jackson lied.

"Can I get you anything? Latte? Cappuccino? Macchiato?"

Jackson shook his head as he sat up and stretched. Harper looked
away for a moment but did a double take when he noticed the
mangled crosshatch of scars across Jackson's upper torso.

"Woah, I'm guessing by the looks of those scars you've done some
service for this country," Harper said. "You weren't SEAL Team Six,
were you?"

"Army Rangers," Jackson answered, slipping on a tank top.

"Well, thank you for your service."

Jackson ignored the hollow gratuity and sat down at the gigantic
concrete table.

"When are we calling Sayre?" he asked.

"I was just about to ask you. The other guys are up, taking in the morning sun on the deck. Breakfast is on the way. My firm reps a nearby resort. Their kitchen is bringing over some stuff."

"I guess sooner rather than later."

"Excellent. I have the phone set up here. Speakerphone for all of us to hear. I'll get the guys."

Harper walked over to one of the large windows, knocked on it, and motioned for the others to come in.

Bear waddled in first holding an espresso cup that was comically small in his oversized paw of a hand.

"Jacky boy, you've got to try this stuff," he said. "Only thing is it makes you shit bricks."

Harper choked on his coffee.

"Oh, I'm sorry, boss," Bear said. "I mean, it, um, gets your body really going."

"No lie there," Ray said, walking in behind him. "I'm wide awake after just one."

"Help yourselves to another. I've brewed it, so you just have to pour it yourself. I'm going to get things going here," Harper said.

He sat down and turned on the speakerphone, then punched in a number.

"Harper & Rhodes," a woman answered.

"Hi, Cheryl. It's Liam," Harper said. "Are we ready to go?"

"Yes, sir. Just one moment. I'll send the call through," Cheryl said.

The line went quiet. Liam put his tiny cup and saucer down and addressed the group.

"We're routing the call through our offices in Charleston," he said. "Just in case the police want to get cute and try and run a trace. Jackson, it's your contact that found this guy, why don't you start. Then I'll come in. Maybe Bobbie already having legal representation will catch them off guard."

Jackson thought there was a lot of game-playing going on for a kid's life being at stake, but agreed nonetheless.

The line was quiet for another moment before a click followed by a man's voice.

"This is Sayre," said the man.

"Lieutenant Sayre," Jackson said, "my name is Jackson Clay. It's my understanding you're looking for Bobbie Casto."

"We are," Sayre said, "Do you have information to his whereabouts?"

"You could say that. He's sitting right next to me," Jackson said.

There was a shuffling of papers followed by what Jackson thought sounded like an office chair creaking under the stress of someone shifting their weight in it.

"You're saying Bobbie Casto is with you right now?" Sayre asked.

"That's right," Jackson answered.

"Well, you know the best thing for him is to come in. He's only making this worse on himself."

"We want to find a solution here, but there are concerns. This has to be done the right way. A way that works for us."

"Mr. Clay, you said it was? Mr. Clay, the fact of the matter is we already have a *capias* for Bobbie Casto. Do you understand? A bench warrant for his arrest. So, you can turn him in, or we can come get him. It's your choice."

Harper held up a hand to Jackson and leaned toward the speaker phone.

"Lieutenant, this is Liam Harper with Harper & Rhodes," he said. "Mr. Casto is my client. He wants to turn himself in, but like Mr. Clay mentioned, we have some concerns. Concerns that need to be addressed ahead of time."

"Like what?" Sayre asked.

"For one thing, my client is fearful of retribution from the Hopewell County Sheriff's Office. His account of the night in question will charge two of their men with behavior that, at best, was negligent, and probably more accurately, downright criminal. He's just a teenager. We need assurances that his well-being and safety can be guaranteed. That's why we are contacting you and not Hopewell County."

"No one is going to do anything to your client, Mr. Harper," Sayre said. "But you have to bring him in. You're worried about his well-being. I can assure you nothing is more dangerous for him than being wanted by the authorities."

"Like I said, Lieutenant, we plan on coming in. But this has to be done right. Let's talk about surrender in Charleston. Perhaps Troop 0, your state headquarters," Harper said.

"That's not going to happen, Mr. Harper. The charges against Mr. Casto are local to Hopewell County. I'm only tasked to the case because there are two department-involved homicides. These crimes are local—he has to surrender to Hopewell County."

"That's not good enough, Mr. Sayre. We need to come up with a solution that works here. Another option is we could simply go to the papers and my client can talk about how he's being forced to surrender to the police department that tried to kill him just the other night."

"Mr. Harper, this is ridiculous—No one is trying to harm Casto."

"He has a gunshot wound that begs to differ."

"Which happened as the Sheriff's Detective returned fire after being shot at. Should we talk about the gun he took from one of the detectives?"

"All done in self-defense. Look, we're talking in circles here. Like I said, our intention is to come in. But we need assurances."

"Let him turn himself in to the Hopewell County Sheriff's Department. You called me because you obviously see me as some sort of third party here. You bring him to Hopewell County I will escort him through myself. Make sure everything is done by the book."

Harper paused and looked around the table. Ray and Bear looked at Jackson. Seeing them, Harper turned, too. Jackson remained quiet as he thought. It was still too dangerous. Even if they trusted Sayre — which he wasn't sure about — the man was not going to be with Bobbie 24/7 until his court date. Bobbie would sit in a jail cell alone. Or worse, with a real criminal. If this Franko or Bragg or anyone from the Hopewell County Vice Squad wanted retribution, they'd have their chance. Jackson locked eyes with Harper and shook his head.

"Uh, Lieutenant, give me just one minute to talk to my client, here," Harper said.

He sounded annoyed. He pushed the mute button on the speaker phone and gave Jackson a look demanding an explanation.

"It's not good enough," Jackson said. "This Sayre guy isn't going to be Bobbie's personal bodyguard. He'll have to leave eventually. It's too much of a risk. Bobbie won't be protected."

"Look, you called me, right? You call a firefighter when you have a fire, you call a plumber when you have a leak, and you call a lawyer when you have a legal battle ahead of you. That's why I'm here. This is what I do," Harper said.

"It's only a legal battle if we make it one. He only goes to court if we allow him to go," Jackson countered.

"And what other option do you see for him, exactly? Go on the run? How long do you think that will last? It's only a matter of time before you'll be caught. And then you'll be in even more legal trouble and with less of a say on how things are handled."

"We can go to the papers, like you said. Blow this story up."

"Mr. Clay, quite frankly, that's a shortsighted answer. I know it and this investigator here on the other end of the line knows it. You'll get your fifteen minutes of fame, and then people will go back to their TV dinners and you'll still be fucked."

Jackson had to admit what Harper was saying made sense. Harper took a deep breath and sighed. When he spoke again, his voice was calmer.

"Mr. Clay," he said, "if you want to take Bobbie and Ray and Bear here and run, I won't stop you. I'll say you got cold feet and up and left. But then I can't help you. And more importantly, I can't help Bobbie. You want to fight this. Well, I do, too. But this is how I fight this. In court. Not in the papers, and not on the run or anything else."

Jackson was quiet. His mind raced for a better idea, but none came. This storm was coming whether they tried to run from it or not. Maybe Harper was right. It was better to face this thing head-on.

"Alright," Jackson said.

Harper looked around the table again. Ray and Bear nodded their heads solemnly. Harper hit the mute button again and conjured up his professional voice. "Okay, Lieutenant, that's fine. It can all be done this afternoon. Let's say three o'clock. Where should we meet?"

"Hopewell County Courthouse," Sayre answered. "The Sheriff's Office and jail are connected. I'll walk you guys through myself."

"Very well. Three o'clock at the County Courthouse. See you then."

Harper ended the call with the push of another button and took a long sip of his coffee.

"Well, that's that," he said. "Come on, we'll eat when the food gets here. Then we'll get ready to go. It should take us about three and a half hours to get up there."

Bobbie looked as though he was holding back tears as his lower lip trembled.

"I'm not that hungry," he said.

"Bobbie, you've got to eat something," Ray said.

"You don't think I'm coming out, do you," Bobbie said. "Out of jail after I go in."

"No, it's not that. But you are going to have to be in there for a while. At least while we get things sorted. Trust me, you're going to wish you ate before you got in there. We got this nice breakfast coming, and then we can find you some lunch on the road somewhere. Someplace you want to stop. Right, Mr. Harper?"

Harper nodded.

"How is this all going to work logistically?" Jackson asked, looking at Harper.

"I'd like to have you and Ray with us when we go—the optics are always better if there's a team around him. Ray is family, obviously. We can call you a family friend," Harper said.

"I can handle that."

"Are you armed?"

"I can be."

"Let's see how things look when we get there. We'll drive to Rion together. It'd be best if Bobbie is with me from now on. You take your car, Bear takes his. Ray, you can ride with whomever you'd like."

"Straight to the courthouse?"

Harper shook his head.

"No," he replied. "Only one car should go to the courthouse. Mine. We'll stage at a public spot nearby. You'll ride in the front to the courthouse with me. Ray and Bobbie in the back. Bear, sorry to say, I don't think there's room for you."

Bear shrugged his shoulders as he carefully refilled his espresso cup.

"Works for me. I can watch the cars," he said.

"Done and done," Harper said as the doorbell rang. "Ah, that must be breakfast."

He trotted across the house to the front door as Ray sat down next to Bobbie. Bear walked up and down the kitchen looking for some more cream or sugar. Jackson went to him and pulled him aside.

"I know I said okay, but I still don't like this," Jackson said. "I want to have options if something happens."

Bear flashed a boyish smile. He was being put in the game.

"What'd you have in mind?" he asked.

"After we leave in Harper's Mercedes for the Courthouse, set yourself up somewhere nearby in the Suburban," Jackson said. "A block or two away on the same street."

"Sure," Bear said. "And do what?"

Jackson patted him on the shoulder as he answered him.

"Pray I'm being paranoid."

18
_____

W olfe stomped down the marble corridor, his chagrin evident in every step he took. He trudged through his secretary's office, grabbed the soy latte with a spoonful of agave nectar waiting for him, and continued into his office.

"No calls and I'm not here until I tell you otherwise, Lydia," he growled, slamming his office door shut behind him.

Imbeciles. He had to deal with imbeciles all day. Every day. Imbeciles that not only gave him headaches but threatened to undo everything he was building.

He walked to the window, too mad to sit down, and pulled out his cell phone. He punched in a number and put it to his ear. After a couple of rings, the line went live with the rustling of what sounded like wind blowing. Great, Wolfe thought, this mouth breather is answering from his car.

"Starcher," said the man on the other end.

"Yeah, it's Lane Wolfe. So, Bobbie Casto, this kid you were supposed to find, he's going to turn himself in this afternoon."

"I just heard that myself, yes."

"Yeah," Wolfe said. "Tell me why my paper-pushing contact at State alerted me before the fucking Vice Squad I told to get on it. It's on the fucking news already, Starcher. How is it you managed to get to where you are with your head so far up your own goddamn ass?"

"This lawyer the kid's got called the State Police investigator, Colton Sayre. That's probably why whoever you've got over there heard about it first."

"Did I sound like I was fishing for a fucking excuse? How did this fuckwit land a lawyer like Liam Harper anyway?"

"Beats the hell out of me."

Wolfe turned and walked to the corner of his office furthest away from the door. He placed his hand on the molded mahogany wall, taking in the warmth coming up from the heating vent below him. When he spoke again, his voice was a low hiss.

"It doesn't matter," he said. "Listen to me, you've all fucked up enough. This ends today. I don't care how you do it, but it gets done. And it doesn't get back to me or the business."

Starcher went silent for a moment on the other end of the line before he answered.

"What exactly are we talking about here, Mr. Wolfe?" he asked.

"*Whatever* it takes," Wolfe said. "But this doesn't get back to *me* or the *business*."

"O-Okay," Starcher said.

Wolfe couldn't tell if their connection was getting weak or if Starcher's stomach was.

"I don't think I have to remind you," he said, "but bridges will burn before any of this gets back to us in Charleston. You understand me?"

"Yes. Yes, sir."

"Handle it."

Wolfe hung up and slid the phone back into the breast pocket of his coat. He took a sip of his coffee but grimaced as the caffeinated brew hit his tongue. It was cold. Not to the touch, obviously, but far colder than he could be expected to drink. He dropped the mug and saucer with disgust onto the granite credenza next to him and headed back out to apprise Lydia of her latest fuck-up.

Imbeciles, he thought. Imbeciles every day.

19

Mia was half-awake on her air mattress in her basement studio apartment when she heard the truck rumble to a stop outside. She didn't need to peak out the tiny window near the ceiling to see who it was. She already knew by the sound.

Cocky footsteps clopped down the sidewalk and descended the stairs to her unit just as they always did, followed by the usual ridiculous knock.

Rap-tap. Tap-tap-tap-rap.

She opened the door for Franko, flashing his usual smarmy grin in between locks of hair that framed his face like dirty drapes.

"Hey, sugar," Franko said. "Can I come in?"

Everything in Mia wanted to slam the door shut, but she opened it wider as she tried not to look at him.

"Sure. Can I get you something?" she asked.

Franko leaned in for a kiss. When Mia didn't offer it, he pecked her on the cheek, reaching down and cupping her backside.

"Yeah. Some coffee would be swell," Franko said.

Mia hurried for the pot, trying to stave off her rising nausea.

"Um, I can cook up some breakfast, if you'd like," she said.

She preferred to spend whatever this visit was at her table rather than the sofa or her bed. Or the shower as sometimes Franko preferred.

"Nah, sugar, not today," Franko said, leaning back into a chair. "Busy morning. I just popped by to see how you were doin'."

Liar, Mia thought. Franko never just popped by. He always wanted something. The only question was, was it her or something else? She turned, putting on her best smile, and brought him his mug of coffee. Franko took it from her before she could set it on the table and downed half of it in a couple of gulps. Mia sat next to him, waiting. Franko came up for air and wiped his mouth on his bare arm.

"So, listen," he said. "I need you to do something for me."

Mia didn't say anything. Franko reached behind him and grabbed a paper bag. Mia had noticed it when Franko walked in, but assumed it was a sandwich or something. Post-sex meals were his favorite. Now, though, she realized this was not that. He reached into the bag and pulled out a gun. Not a big, bulky, official-looking gun like his, but a little one. A grubby-looking one. The kind bad things were done with. Her heart thumped like a bass drum in her chest.

"You know that kid on the news? The one that's wanted?" Franko asked.

"Y-Yeah, I saw," Mia answered, her voice shaky.

"He's coming to the courthouse in Rion today to turn himself in. I need that not to happen."

Franko patted the gun and slid it over. Mia grabbed her chair with one hand feeling as though she might fall off it.

"W-What do you mean?" She asked. "I...I can't kill someone!"

"Jimmy, then," Franko said. "Get Jimmy to do it."

"I...I can't—Why would Jimmy do that for me?" Mia asked. "He wouldn't. I can't get him to just k-kill someone."

"Oh, c'mon. You know what guys will do for some good pussy. And you've got it. I should know."

"Franko, I—"

He flashed another smirk that would make even the most hardened orthodontist cringe. Mia was sure she was going to be sick this time. The room was spinning. The world was spinning.

"You *can* do it, Mia," Franko said. "Remember all those things I did for you? Now, I need you to do this for me. That's how this works."

"I'm telling you," Mia said as she began to sob, "I *can't*."

Franko looked down and huffed in frustration. He stayed that way for a moment before looking back up at her. When he did, the smile was gone.

"Listen to me," he seethed. "I know you're not fucking dumb. Dumb enough that your whore ass got caught under my thumb, sure, but not *dumb* dumb. And I know you know what goes on out there. So I know you're smart enough to know exactly what the fuck happens if you and your little shithead boyfriend *don't* do this."

Mia's head was in her hands. Her body shook as she cried.

"He's not my boyfriend—please don't make me do this," she said.

Franko moved to put an arm around her, but she flinched at his touch. He gave it a moment before trying again. This time, she acquiesced.

"C'mon now, just get Jimmy to do this," he said. "The little twerp he's going to shoot is no good, anyways. The second he pulls the trigger, all hell will break lose. Anyone trying to catch him will lose him in the chaos. All he's got to do is put the dirtbag down and he's done. Both of you are done."

Mia remained silent. Franko rubbed her back. Mia dry-heaved.

"Just do this, okay?" Franko said.

No, Mia thought. Not okay. She was no angel and Jimmy was no saint, but neither of them were fucking killers. Murderers. That's what he was talking about here. Murder. But Franko was right—she knew enough. She'd heard the stories. The people that disappear. She understood. Those things happened to people that said no to people like Franko.

Mia wiped at her eyes and nodded slowly.

"Okay," she said. "He'll do it. I'll make sure."

"You can't back out on me now," Franko said.

"I won't. We won't. I'll get him to do it."

Franko grinned once more and leaned in to kiss her on the cheek again. As he pulled back, he spoke softly into her ear.

"That's my girl."

20

The convoy of Jackson, Bear, Bobbie, Ray, and Harper pulled into Rion. They drove to a public park and slid into three parallel spaces beside the sidewalk.

Bear hopped out eagerly with a Ziploc bag.

"I got change to feed all the meters," he said. "Don' you guys worry."

No one did.

Jackson climbed out and stretched. Ray and Harper climbed out of Harper's Mercedes and walked over to Jackson.

"Are you gentlemen ready?" Harper asked. "It's ten 'til three."

Jackson and Ray nodded.

"Good. Mr. Clay, you said you have a firearm?"

"I have an M9 Beretta and Sig Sauer P320," Jackson said. "I have a thigh holster and a concealed carry holster for my waist."

"West Virginia is a constitutional carry state," Harper said. "Grab one of your guns and carry it in your concealed carry. We'll tell the officers there you're armed. If they won't let you in with it, we'll leave it in the glove box."

Jackson reached into his truck and grabbed the Sig Sauer. He double-checked it was loaded and the safety was engaged and slid it into the concealed carry holster in the small of his back.

"How's Bobbie?" Jackson asked.

"Still working on that sub we got him from Subway," Ray said. "Hasn't said two words the whole way up."

Jackson couldn't blame him. He wasn't personally much of a conversationalist on a good day—he imagined he'd be even less talkative facing multiple felony charges.

"All the meters have three hours on them," Bear said, trotting up to the group. "That should be enough time, right?"

"Well, you'll certainly be able to watch the cars," Harper said.

Bear glanced at Jackson, then back to Harper. Harper clapped his hands together.

"Alright," he said. "If we're ready, let's get on with it."

"Good luck, boys," Bear said. "Tell Bobbie I said good luck, too."

Ray smiled kindly as everyone but Bear headed for Harper's Mercedes. Jackson opened the passenger door but before he climbed in, he looked back at Bear, who nodded at him.

Harper fired up the Mercedes and pulled out onto the road. The courthouse was less than five minutes away. Ray looked over at Bobbie—he was looking out his window, hoodie pulled over his head.

"It's going to be okay, son," Ray said. "Your mom and stepdad are going to meet us there. I talked with Mr. Harper—we're going to see if you can maybe see them tonight before or maybe shortly after you go in."

Bobbie didn't say anything. Harper looked up and studied Bobbie through the rear-view mirror.

"Remember, Bobbie, this is just the beginning," he said. "None of us are going anywhere. We're all going to fight this. Together. We're going to make sure the truth gets out."

He turned to Jackson.

"We're about to turn onto the street," Harper said. "Do you want to call Lieutenant Sayre?"

Jackson nodded, pulling out his phone and pulling up the number he'd saved.

"Sayre, Jackson Clay," he said. "I'm with Bobbie. We're about to be at the courthouse. Are you out front?"

"Yes," Sayre answered. "I've got a dozen deputies working crowd control."

"Crowd control?" Jackson asked.

But as they neared the courthouse, he saw what Sayre was talking about. Underneath a pair of sugar maples turned brilliant gold with the season, a group—no, a *mob*—had gathered in the plaza in front of the courthouse.

"Christ almighty," Ray said. "Doesn't anyone have anything better to do on a Friday afternoon?"

A wave of fear washed over Jackson. Not fear of the situation, but fear that they'd made a horrible mistake. He thought about what he'd told Bear back at Harper's vacation house—he hadn't been paranoid. This was happening.

"I...I don't want to go in there," Bobbie said. "I can't."

"It's okay, Bobbie," Harper said. "We'll walk you through. Jackson, tell them we're here."

"Sayre, we're here. Black Mercedes coming from the south," Jackson said.

"Pull up to the front—the walkway up to the courthouse is barricaded," Sayre said.

Harper did as Jackson directed and pulled the Mercedes forward, the sight of which only further fueled the crowd's anger. A couple of people reached out and slapped the car before deputies moved in and pushed them back.

"Go ahead and keep that gun on you," Harper said to Jackson.

Together they stepped out. Harper stepped back and opened Bobbie's door. Jackson came around the car and stood in front of them, scanning the crowd. The men and women were a medley of judgment and vitriol. Picket signs bobbed up and down in protest. An older man with a gray ponytail held his sign out in front of him.

KILL ALL DRUG DEALERS

These people didn't even know what they didn't know, Jackson thought. He heard a car door shut behind him, followed by a tap on his shoulder.

"Let's go," Harper shouted over the crowd.

Jackson moved forward, but the crowd pushed to get closer. The metal barricades began tilting as the people surged as one, reaching for and yelling at Bobbie. The deputies struggled to keep everyone back. Jackson wanted to move faster and get everyone inside, but he couldn't risk separating from the others.

He walked slowly, remaining calm. Panic wouldn't help any of them. He looked through the crowd on either side of him, searching for anyone that might try do something. It was a wall of angry faces. Shouting and snarling. Ahead, Jackson saw a man standing atop the three concrete stairs that led to the front doors of the courthouse. A black suit sat perfectly on his athletic frame, a gold badge with blue lettering clipped to his belt. Lieutenant Colton Sayre, Jackson presumed.

They were almost there. Twenty more feet, and they'd be inside. Bobbie wouldn't be safe – he'd still be at the mercy of a Sheriff's Office who employed two men that had already tried to kill him – but at least he would be out of all this. Jackson took it a step at a time, counting down the distance in his head.

19 feet. 18. 17.

That's when he saw the man.

A man, or possibly even a kid, by the looks of him. With a mob clamoring for Bobbie's head on a spike, this person stood where he was, motionless. He was wearing a pair of jeans and a plaid flannel coat that was much too big for him. A gray hood came up from underneath the coat and covered what looked to be a full head of brown hair. A large pair of sporty sunglasses concealed most of his face.

He didn't fit. Something about him wasn't right.

Jackson watched him out of the corner of his eye.

16 feet. 15.

He couldn't be sure with everything moving around him, but Jackson thought the guy was shaking. Trembling.

14 feet. 13.

The man stepped forward and pulled a snubnosed revolver out of his coat pocket. Jackson turned and put himself between the gunman and his target, then reached for Bobbie and pulled him to the ground.

The gunshot cracked loud, like thunder.

The angry shouting of the crowd turned into screams of terror. Jackson could feel feet hit him as people began to run. Something—someone—landed on his legs. He heard a second gunshot. Then more —but fired from the opposite direction.

"Shooter! Shooter!" someone yelled.

Jackson turned, saw the gunman was now tucked into the corner of the building where it met the front stairs. The man continued firing, even as deputies fired back at him. Jackson looked down, found a dark lump of a human body slumped over his legs. He slid one leg out and used it to kick the other free. The body rolled over—Liam Harper's lifeless face looked up at Jackson, blood flowing from the wound just above his left eye.

"We've got to go," Jackson yelled at Bobbie underneath him. "Are you hit? Are you okay?"

"I...I think so," Bobbie yelled back.

More gunshots kicked off. Jackson looked around for shelter. A deputy reached down to grab them, but a round hit him in the side. The officer fell to a knee and returned fire before being shot again.

A second deputy ran over to the fallen officer, yelling into his radio. "10-1! 10-1! Officer down, get me backup to the courthouse!"

Jackson was pushing himself off of Bobbie when he felt a large hand grab him and help him up, then Bobbie.

"C'mon, let's go!" Ray yelled.

Jackson put an arm around Bobbie and ushered him forward into the sea of panicking people. He pushed him and Ray away from the gunfire, maneuvering them through the mayhem and away from the courthouse.

"Keep going, keep going!" Jackson yelled. "Harper's gone. Make for his car. Go!"

Together, the three of them worked their way back toward the street. As they got to the curb, the crowd was thinning. Jackson could see the Mercedes, but it was now blocked in by police cars responding to the shooting. It wasn't going anywhere.

"Keep moving," Jackson said. "Move! Go."

There was a loud, metallic crash as they moved further away from the courthouse. Jackson whipped his head around to see a red Suburban demolish a metal barrier in the street behind them.

Bear leaned out the driver-side window of the Suburban and beckoned for them.

"Someone call an Uber?" he asked.

Jackson, Ray, and Bobbie ran for the truck. Jackson climbed into the passenger seat as the other two dove into the back.

"Go, go!" Jackson said.

Bear kicked the truck into reverse, backing over the mangled fencing. When he was clear, he gave the Suburban some gas, revving in reverse, slamming on the brakes and jerking the wheel. In one swift move, the nose of the truck whipped around and straightened out pointing away from everything that had just happened. Bear shifted it into drive and took off down the road.

"What the hell happened? Where's Harper?" Bear asked.

"Dead," Jackson said. "Shooter in the crowd shot him."

"They shot his fucking lawyer?"

Jackson turned around and looked in the back seat. Bobbie had his arms wrapped around himself; he was shaking. He looked up at Jackson.

"I don't think they were aiming for Harper," Jackson said.

21

Bear pressed down on the gas and the Suburban roared to life with all the energy it's 30-something-year-old engine could muster. Jackson shifted his gaze from Bobbie to the rear windshield—no police appeared to be following.

He sat back down in the passenger seat and looked at Bear.

"We've got to get off this road," Jackson said. "It's too major of an artery. We've got to get lost."

"Where do you want to go?" Bear asked.

"Take the next turn, that right up ahead," Jackson answered.

"No, that road doesn't go anywhere," Bobbie said from the back-seat. "Take the one after that."

Bear looked at Jackson who looked back at Bobbie, then nodded. They took the turn and followed the road deep into the West Virginia wilderness. Bear continued driving fast, the Suburban ripping red and brown foliage off the trees as it flew by.

Jackson pulled out his phone.

"I don't have service," he said.

"Whatcha need?" Bear asked.

"To figure out where we're going," Jackson said.

Bear reached over and punched open the glove box. He stuck his large hand in and fished around until he came up with a handheld GPS. He handed it to Jackson.

"Thanks," Jackson said.

He booted up the GPS and zoomed in on their area. Their position pinged on the tiniest of white lines. This road they were on seemed to barely exist. That was good, Jackson thought.

"Alright, this looks like it continues to wind its way south for a bit," he said. "There's other major roads that way, so if they're looking for us, we might be okay on here."

"Where are we headed?" Bear asked.

"That's what we need to figure out," Jackson said. "We've got to get off the road. We need a place to go. Or another vehicle to switch to."

Ray leaned forward from the backseat.

"You said there were more major roads south, like not a lot of a reason to be on this one?" he asked.

"I guess. Why?"

"Because that little car's been on our ass for a good bit now."

Jackson and Bear glanced at the rearview mirror. A small gold sedan was, indeed, behind them.

"Don' think that's a cop," Bear said. "That's some piece of shit. Look at it. It can barely keep up with us goin' uphill."

"I don't know," Jackson said, looking at the GPS. "Take the next turn, see what they do."

Bear did just that. The car behind them continued to follow.

Jackson looked at the GPS again.

"There's a right in three-tenths of a mile," he said. "Take it."

"Wait, I've been down here before. There's a dead end," Bobbie said.

"Exactly," Jackson said.

Bear turned onto the road. Jackson leaned forward again and watched the little sedan make the same turn behind them. It looked like a Chevy Cavalier or some other small domestic economy car.

"Still followin'," Bear said. "I still don' think they're cops."

"I can't see through the windows if there's more than one of them," Jackson said.

"Looks like we're about to run out of road, Jacky boy. What's the play?"

"You got a gun on you?"

"Do I shit in the woods?"

"When I say to, hit the brakes. Get out gun up on the driver side. I'll cover the passenger. Swing wide and close in. Ray, you and Bobbie get down in the back."

No one said anything; Jackson took their silence as compliance.

"Alright hit it," he said.

The body of the Suburban bucked forward as all four tires screeched to a stop. Jackson and Bear came out of their respective doors fast, weapons drawn and moving around the sedan in a wide arc.

"Do not move!" Jackson shouted.

He could see a slender silhouette in the driver's seat moving about but still couldn't tell if there was a passenger.

The sedan's transmission made a rickety clank as the car began moving backwards. Jackson fired two rounds into the pavement near one of the wheels. The car stopped abruptly.

"Next one's in your engine block. Do. Not. Move!" he ordered, waiting to see if they would make another move. "Turn off the car and get out."

The car's engine rattled off and the driver-side door slowly opened. A slim young woman with wavy brown hair stepped out nervously. She was sobbing so hard her thin frame shook as she stood there holding herself.

"Why are you following us?" Bear asked.

"I...I," the woman stuttered, trying to form words.

Nothing coherent came. She stepped awkwardly away from the car, as if she were disoriented.

As she came around the open car door, Bear spotted a revolver in her hand. He raised his gun higher and squared the sights on the woman's chest.

"Drop the gun, lady," he said. "I don' want to shoot you but I will if you make me."

The hairs on the back of Jackson's neck pricked up at Bear's words.

He moved toward the front of the sedan until he, too, could see the revolver in the girl's hand. He looked at her face, saw fear there. She looked as though using the gun was the last thing she wanted to do.

"It's okay," Jackson said, his voice softer. "No one's going to shoot anyone here. Just put down the gun."

Still sobbing, the young woman bent forward, lowering the gun until it was just a few inches off the ground. Finally, she let it go.

"That's good, that's real good," Jackson said. "Is there anyone else in the car?"

The woman shook her head, but Jackson still had to check. He looked at Bear.

"I got you, brother," Bear said.

Jackson swept around, stepping behind Bear and moving further until he could see straight through the open door. There was no one in the front. He then walked toward the open door, pointed his gun inside, and looked. No one in the back, either. All clear.

As he stepped away, Jackson picked up the woman's revolver, opened the cylinder, and dumped out the ammo.

"What's your name?" Jackson asked.

"Mia," she said in between sniffles. "Mia Parsons."

"Okay, Mia," Jackson said. "What are you doing following us with a loaded gun?"

"I don't know. I...I'm so sorry. I never meant to—"

"Well, you obviously meant to do something. No one just leaves their house with a loaded gun and follows a car full of people down a dead-end road."

"The guy back there. He..."

She trailed off. Jackson stepped forward and cupped her arm reassuringly.

"It's okay," he said. "What guy? The shooter at the courthouse?"

"Yeah," Mia said, "At the courthouse back there. We were...the one who tried to kill...him."

Tried, Jackson thought. Not killed, *tried* to kill. Harper was the one dead. He had a feeling his suspicion about Bobbie was right.

"Bobbie Casto," Jackson said. "That's who he was trying to shoot?"

Mia looked down, wiping at her nose.

"I guess," she muttered. "The boy on the news."

"That'd be Bobbie," Jackson said.

"This is all my fault," Mia said, wiping at her eyes, "I...I..."

Mia looked away but Jackson grabbed her gently and tried to get her to focus. He'd seen enough users in his time to know she was high on something.

"Why?" Jackson asked. "Why is it your fault?"

Mia held herself tighter as she shook her head, kicking at the ground with one of her feet. Her voice wavered as she answered Jackson.

"I...I told him to do it."

22

Lieutenant Sayre crouched over the body of Liam Harper, still trying to break down in his mind what had just happened. Everything had turned to shit so fast. The crowd had been pushing at the barricades, the sheriff's deputies doing everything they could to hold them back. And then, suddenly, gun shots.

Sayre had run headlong into the crowd when he saw Bobbie Casto go down, fearing the young man had been hit, but he never made it to him. A stampede of panic-stricken people knocked him about like he was in a mosh pit at a metal concert. When he realized the shooting wasn't over, Sayre turned back to try and help the other officers. By the time he'd gotten clear of the crowd, though, a deputy had flanked the shooter and shot him twice in the chest.

Now Liam Harper, the shooter, and two others were dead. A woman in her 40's had caught one of the shooter's rounds to a subclavian artery and bled out in the havoc. Nearby, an elderly man was found literally trampled to death. Six dead in total, Sayre thought, stemming from something as innocuous as a traffic stop. He wanted to know why.

"You look like you could use this," said a voice.

Sayre turned around to see his partner, Sam Hall, extending a cup of coffee toward him. He stood up and took the coffee.

"I thought the lieutenant said I was running this one solo," Sayre said.

"I was on my way to Morgantown when I heard the call go out," Hall said. "Figured I'd check in on you."

"What's in Morgantown?"

"In-laws. My niece is getting married. Now, my wife's at a motel down the road not talking to me."

"Sounds like you might be the one that needs backup."

Sayre took a sip of the coffee. It was instant-made garbage, but he appreciated the jolt of caffeine. He glanced over at two criminalists photographing the body of the shooter.

"You have an ID on him yet?" Hall asked.

"Not yet, running prints," Sayre said. "We'll find out soon, but I'm guessing it'll make even less sense than it does now. And that's saying something."

"How do you mean?"

"Look at him, the shooter. He can't be more than 25, and he's got needle marks up and down his arm. What's a junkie doing here, waiting to off someone in front of the courthouse like a hardened hitman?"

"Maybe he had a beef with the lawyer? Prior conviction he blames him for? Are you sure this lawyer fella was even the target?"

"No. Only a few people knew he was coming with an attorney. My guess is Bobbie Casto was the target."

"Didn't this all start with a traffic stop that produced meth and weed? So, the junkie is a dealer worried this Casto kid would name names. Tried to put him down," Hall said.

"Maybe," Sayre said.

But he had his doubts. Something about this all felt wrong.

"Occam's Razor," he said.

"What?" Hall asked.

"Occam's Razor," Sayre repeated. "Entities should not be multiplied without necessity."

"Okay, are you going to clue me into what that means?"

"The simplest explanation is most likely the right one. Casto was going to come in. His lawyer said he wanted to tell his side of the story. Then, the shooting happened and Bobbie Casto still isn't in custody."

"Right. Like I said, the tweaker over there was a dealer. A dealer who tried to shut Casto up."

Sayre took in a deep breath and sighed.

"That, or someone sent the shooter," he said.

Someone who isn't dead, he thought. Someone still pulling the strings.

23

W olfe was fifteen minutes into his cycling session when he saw his phone flash to life in the bike's cup holder. He'd decided taking his pent-up energy out on the stationery was a better idea than his first instinct—which was to go on a shooting spree in front of a courthouse himself. But instead of some rich dirtbag lawyer and some dumb middle-aged lady, he'd take out every dipshit cop on his payroll in Hopewell County.

He hopped off the bike and stepped away to answer the incoming call. The Nazi bitch on the bike's screen was still yelling at him to keep up the pace. Fuck her, he thought.

"Nice of you to return my call," Wolfe said. "What the fuck happened?"

"It went sideways," Starcher said.

"Yeah, there seems to be a lot of that fucking going on this week. The problem is, I'm paying you to get shit done—not fuck it up."

"You said make sure it couldn't be tied to us. That limits our options. I can't exactly send out a SWAT sniper to off the little shit."

"Who was he, anyway? The shooter they killed."

"A nobody. My guy barely knows him," Starcher said. "Set him up through an informant he leans on from time to time."

"I'm starting to see where the room for fuck-ups comes in. What about this informant? Are they a problem?" Wolfe asked.

"*She* is under my guy's thumb. And more to the point, she's scared shitless. She'll do what she's told."

Wolfe walked into his kitchen and grabbed the workout smoothie he'd prepared beforehand. He opened it, took a gulp, and winced. The stuff looked like rabid saliva and tasted even worse, but he was in it for the nutrients. The satisfaction of taste was temporary and fleeting. That was for the weak—he was about results.

"So now the fucking kid is back in the wind," Wolfe said. "How are you going to handle it?"

"It's complicated now. The courthouse shootout made national news. We've got the governor's office now calling over to headquarters and asking what's going on. Plus, there's still this asshole from State. We've got a lot of eyes on us. Maybe you could call off some of the dogs over there."

Wolfe almost flung the bile he needed to drink across the kitchen.

"For someone fucking up left and right this week you sure have no problem asking me to fix everything for you," he said.

"Look, we both want the same thing here," Starcher said. "I'm just saying it would go a long way if you could get *him* to pull back."

"You want me to work over things at the state level when this State investigator up there apparently is closer to getting Casto than your unit is? Maybe I have the wrong cops on the business' payroll."

"The kid knew Franko and Bra—"

"No names," Wolfe said.

"The kid knew...my two guys were Hopewell County Sheriff's Office," Starcher said. "He was worried about surrendering to us. That's how State got the call first."

"Imagine fucking that."

"Yeah, well, now I know we've got to keep an eye on this prick. That won't happen again."

Wolfe forced down another swig of smoothie and then reached for a bottle of water as a chaser. He downed the whole thing before wiping his mouth on his arm. "None of this—and I mean none of this bullshit —happens again. You understand me?"

"I got you," Starcher answered. "The kid is on the run again. Things happen when people are on the run. This is good for us. We just need to manage the situation."

"Get it done," Wolfe said.

He hung up.

Fuck-ups, Wolfe thought. They reminded him of Basil Lyle. Lyle was a piece-of-shit private from his Army days. The cretin could barely tie his own boots. The rest of the unit couldn't count on him for anything. Wolfe had decided enough was enough. Before their next patrol outside the wire, he switched Lyle's rifle magazines with ones carrying training blanks and put him on point. An hour later, they crossed paths with two Taliban sitting on their route. Wolfe could still see Lyle get lit up as he tried to return the two gunmen's fire. The subsequent investigation concluded Lyle had made a mistake that had ultimately cost him his life. What a jackass. But dead men no longer got in the way.

Wolfe polished off the smoothie and grabbed a glass for some scotch. He poured himself two fingers of Macallan 30, daydreaming of replacing Starcher's magazines with blanks.

24

Jackson took the keys to Mia's Cavalier and together he and Bear drove the group to an abandoned gas station where they could stay out of sight as they figured things out.

There, Mia told them about everything. About Franko and her arrangement with him. How he had pressured her to kill Bobbie and, when she'd refused, pushed for her to get Jimmy Green to do it. Jackson didn't move or make a face as she told them her story, but anger simmered in him as he listened. He'd spent the latter part of his life chasing predators. These guys – Franko and Bragg – were a different kind of predator, but predators still the same.

"So, why'd you chase us down, gun in hand?" Bear asked.

"I don't know, to tell you the truth," Mia said. "I wasn't thinking. I just...I wanted this to all end."

"You were desperate. Desperate people do desperate things," Jackson said.

Bear looked at him and shrugged, conceding the point.

"All of that doesn't change our situation, though," Ray said. "As nice as the back of this old gas station is, we can't stay here forever. And the search for Bobbie – us – is only going to get more serious."

"We could go back to Harper's weekend house," Bear suggested. "It's not like the guy'll be comin' 'round to use it."

Ray shot him a look. Bear held his hands up.

"No, Harper is now connected to us, so his properties and his offices are connected to us. We need some place they can't connect dots to. Some place off the grid," Jackson said.

"What about your place, in the mountains?" Bear asked. "Does it exist? Like officially, I mean?"

"I used my name with Sayre. I'm as connected to this as Harper or anyone else. Besides, that's much too far to go with two cars full of West Virginia's most wanted. We need someplace closer than that. Someplace not connected to *any* of us."

The group fell quiet.

Bobbie looked around anxiously.

"I, um, I actually might know a place," he said.

"Yeah? What's that?" Jackson asked.

"Well, we were headed down Highway 10 before we turned off into here. Further down the highway, there's this person, Fraggie."

"Okay. Who's this Fraggie?"

"She's like one of those, what do you call them? Preppers. She keeps to herself, mostly. Her and her girlfriend. I've been up there before. They let us blow some fireworks up on their land. They'll know me."

"How far away is she?"

"Maybe an hour or so."

"On the map it showed Highway 10 ran on for a good bit in this valley. There wasn't a whole lot on there. Even an hour away."

"Yeah. I'm telling you, their place is in the middle of nowhere," Bobbie said. "We told Fraggie once the stuff we brought was going to make one hell of a bang. She said her closest neighbors would barely hear it."

"And you know how to get there?" Jackson asked.

"Yeah."

Jackson scratched at the stubble on his jawline, thinking.

"Wait, we're really considering this?" Ray asked.

"Do you have a better idea?" Jackson said.

"No, but we're just going to trust some backwoods prepper with Bobbie's life? There's no way."

"We'll literally be off the map. People who live like that value their privacy. That's what we need right now."

"And we're supposed to drive up on these people unannounced? Don't you think we've gotten shot at enough today?"

Jackson turned his palms toward Ray.

"If you've got another play, I'm all ears," he said. "But like you said, we can't stay here forever."

Ray didn't say anything back. He still didn't like the idea of it all, but he knew Jackson was right.

"What do we do with Annie Oakley over here?" Bear asked.

Jackson looked at Mia. She'd taken a seat on the curb and pulled her knees to her chest, watching the group that would judge her fate.

"We leave her," Ray said. "She ain't coming with us."

"Please, no. Franko. You don't know…he'll kill me," Mia said, her eyes welling up.

"Lady, you just tried to get my nephew killed and followed us down here with a six-shot. You've got to be dumber than you look if you think we're going to help you out," Ray said.

Jackson held out an arm, pushing Ray away from Mia.

"That's enough," he said.

The tears in Mia's eyes spilled over and streamed down both of her cheeks.

"We bring her with us," Jackson said.

Ray slapped his hands at his sides and walked away in protest.

Bear took Jackson by the arm and pulled him aside.

"Jacky boy, I'm all for keeping her out of the hands of those pecker-heads back there," he said. "But Ray's right. We just stopped this girl followin' us with a loaded gun not an hour ago. We can't trust her, and we sure as shit can't bring her with us. I've got a hundred and fifty bucks on me. Now, I say I give it to her and we tell her to get lost."

"Where's she going to go, Bear?" Jackson asked. "That buys her what? Three nights in a shitty motel? Maybe a pizza or two? Look at her. You want to help Bobbie out? There's not a difference between the two of them. Except Bobbie has us and she doesn't have anyone."

Jackson's point quieted Bear. Jackson looked around once more at the group. Ray had gone over to a tree across the way and leaned against it, still shaking his head, but Bobbie had sat down next to Mia and offered her a balled-up tissue to wipe her face. Mia nodded in thanks, but didn't take her eyes off of Jackson. He'd seen that look a dozen times on the faces of people just like her—desperation. Pleading for help without having found the words to say it. Jackson had been there to help all the others. He wasn't going to turn Mia away.

"We bring her with us," Jackson said again. "We're all in this together now."

25

Lieutenant Sayre grunted as he moved a stack of boxes off the desk and tossed them onto the floor. He'd requisitioned an abandoned workplace in the corner of the Hopewell County Sheriff's Office and quietly claimed squatter's rights. The entire workplace had not seen its interior updated since its creation in the 70's — all wood panels and burnt orange walls. Single-paned windows framed by metal beams separated his area from the offices beyond.

No one seemed to mind him moving in unannounced, and he got the feeling he was going to be there a while. He'd even checked into the same motel his partner's wife was stuck at. He waved when he saw her. She'd waved back with only one finger.

There was a knock on the open glass door and Sayre turned around to see said partner, Detective Hall, standing in the doorway with a stack of papers.

"ID came back on the shooter," Hall said. "James 'Jimmy' Owen Green. Age 22 from right here in Rion. He's got a nice list of priors."

Sayre took the paper and flipped through it. "Doesn't look like anything violent, though. It's mostly simple possession. Only one Intent To Distribute."

"Yeah," Hall agreed.

"It doesn't fit," Sayre said. "What kind of hardened, shoot-em-up drug dealer has no violent convictions and only one sale charge?"

"Maybe he's an up-and-comer. Everyone starts somewhere."

"Yeah, but to go from this to shooting it out with police in broad daylight on the courthouse steps?"

Hall shrugged and stuffed his hands in his pockets.

"What do you want me to say? That's your shooter," he said. "Died with the gun in his hand. There's no second person on the grassy knoll on this one."

"Were they able to run the gun?" Sayre asked.

"Yeah, second packet there. Someone tried to file off the serial number but did a shit job."

Sayre read to himself as he flipped through the papers again.

"Used in an armed robbery at a CVS in Rion five years ago," he said. "Found on a suspect dead at the scene. What's it doing in the hands of some kid? Why isn't it in an evidence locker somewhere?"

"Beats me," Hall said. "I guess you have some, you know, investigator work to do."

Sayre nodded, acknowledging the joke. Hall looked at his watch.

"Listen, I've got to run for real," he said. "If I don't get the missus to family soon it'll be my murder you'll be looking into."

"Won't be much of a whodunnit there," Sayre said.

Hall chuckled. He slapped the door frame and waved as he turned to leave.

"Hey, wait. One last thing," Sayre said.

He motioned for Hall to step back in his office and lowered his voice.

"What do you know about these small county Vice Squads?" He asked. "Like the one here in Hopewell."

"Not much," Hall said quietly. "I mean, I've heard they've gotten results. Narcotics busts are up something like 35% in the departments that created them. Hopewell here was the poster boy for the governor's initiative."

Sayre nodded.

"Thanks," he said.

"No problem. You know how to reach me," Hall said.

Sayre nodded again and Hall walked out. Photos – stills pulled from the security cameras outside the courthouse – showed the mayhem at the courthouse as it played out like a flip book, moment by moment. Sayre studied the first few as the shooting began. Bobbie Casto, Liam Harper, another man, and this Jackson Clay were making their way toward the courthouse. Then Jackson Clay turned and lunged for Casto. He'd spotted the threat before anyone else— including the deputies working crowd control.

As Clay jumped on top of Casto, the back of his shirt came up. Sayre could clearly see the grip of a pistol protruding from Clay's waistline. The man had been armed but his first instinct had been to preserve life, not take it. With six dead bodies in 48 hours, that was as unusual as anything else in the case.

Sayre twirled the photo between his index and middle finger.

"Who are you, Mr. Clay?" he asked himself.

26

The drive to Fraggie's place was unremarkable. With Jackson driving Ray and Bobbie in the Cavalier, and Bear following behind them with Mia in the Suburban, the two-car convoy could count on one hand the number of other cars they saw. Highway 10 was virtually deserted. And more to the point, no police were patrolling it.

"The turn is just up ahead," Bobbie said from the backseat. "That gravel road on the left."

"Gravel road on the left, quarter mile," Jackson echoed.

"Got it," Bear said through a staticky phone connection.

Jackson had kept a line open with Bear since only Bobbie knew the way. Cell service was touch-and-go as they wound their way in-between the mountains of the Potomac highlands, but Jackson managed to get them all there together.

He turned onto the gravel road and looked in the rearview mirror, watching as Bear did the same. The road was a straight-shot up a large mountain, where trees bordered a large clearing all the way to the summit.

"Fraggie is up here?" Jackson asked.

"Off this road, yeah. Just a ways," Bobbie said.

Jackson drove up the road slowly, if for no other reason than to take it easy on the economy sedan, since it wasn't built for that kind of terrain. They passed an elderly man loading wood onto a log splitter; Jackson nodded and waved, being friendly. The man broke his stare only long enough to spit a wad of dip onto the ground next to him.

"Friendly guy," Jackson said.

"He probably hasn't seen this many black folk since he was fighting at Gettysburg," Ray said.

"There's two of you."

"Exactly."

As they drove on, the trees gave way to the clearing on the right. Jackson saw a large fenced-in field with the top of a camper-trailer laying in the middle of it. Two goats stood atop keeping sentry over their pen.

"Their drive is just up ahead. On the right," Bobbie said. "By the no trespassing sign on the post."

"Do I have to reiterate what a bad idea this is?" Ray asked.

"You're welcome to hitchhike back to the courthouse," Jackson said.

He relayed the upcoming turn to Bear and Mia and reminded them that their arrival could be unwelcome.

"Don't do anything to instigate," Jackson said. "Do you understand?"

"You mean like call them lesbos?" Bear asked.

"That. Exactly," Jackson said.

The two-car convoy turned onto the drive slowly. About 50 yards ahead was a bulldozer parked facing them. In front of it, the dirt drive split in two. Jackson drove slowly toward the fork when a booming gunshot thundered through the air. He slammed on the brakes hard enough that Bear nearly rear-ended him with the Suburban.

A woman on an ATV came tearing down from the left-hand drive. She had a pistol twice the size of her hand pointed just in front of Jackson's sedan.

Jackson put his hands up. Ray and Bobbie followed suit.

"Fraggie," Bobbie said.

"She seems friendly," Ray said.

Fraggie approached on the ATV and positioned it between the

group and the fork in the drive. She killed the engine, hopped off, and walked toward Jackson and his driver-side door, all while keeping the gun pointed out in front of her.

"Don' know if you can' read, but the sign back there says no trespassin'," she said.

Fraggie had a thick accent, one Jackson couldn't place. A mixture of Southern and something else. He sized her up to be a few inches under six feet. She was fit, with toned muscles and washboard abs that showed themselves underneath her short plaid shirt and tank top. Her hair was dyed a bright violet and shaven on one side with shoulder-length locks brushed over to the other. In the middle of the shaved side of her head was a scar and gray hair in the shape of a chevron.

"We didn't mean to come up on you unannounced," Jackson said calmly. "I've got Bobbie Casto here with me. I think you know him? He's in a lot of trouble. We could use some help. He thought of you."

Fraggie bent down and looked into the back of the car. Bobbie waved shyly. Fraggie smiled at him and winked before returning to Jackson, keeping the business end of her scoped revolver pointed in his direction.

"From the sounds of it, the police are lookin' for him," she said.

"They're looking for all of us now, technically," Jackson said. "Bobbie just tried to turn himself in. Someone shot into the crowd. His lawyer was killed. I got him out of there before anyone else got hurt. But now, you can imagine, things are only kind of worse."

Fraggie lowered her cannon of a pistol and sighed. With the barrel not pointed at his face, Jackson thought it sort of looked like Han Solo's blaster from the Star Wars movies. Fraggie looked around. Jackson guessed she was thinking.

"Aight, follow me up to the house," she said finally. "We'll talk."

Jackson watched as Fraggie hopped back on the ATV, turned around, and headed back up the drive.

"If she's gay, I'm a woman," Bear said over the open phone line.

"Bear," Jackson admonished.

He put the sedan in gear and followed Fraggie up the drive with Bear following him in the Suburban. Fraggie pulled up next to a modest modern American farmhouse with white siding that showed its age. The yard in front of the house was fenced off with what looked like two furry beasts patrolling the edge of it, eyeing the newcomers.

Ray looked at them nervously.

"Are those dogs or wolves?" he asked.

"Dogs. Dutch shepherds to be precise," Fraggie said. "Don' worry, they're not a threat to you unless you're tryin' to fuck with our live-stock. That's Argos closest to you. The other one is Maera."

Fraggie hopped off the ATV. Her pistol was now holstered and a shotgun was slung around her shoulder.

"Hey, Fraggie," Bobbie said as he climbed out of the back of the sedan.

"Hey, bud. You okay?" Fraggie asked.

"Yeah, I'm okay," Bobbie answered.

"He's got a gunshot wound that could use a redressing if you've got the supplies," Jackson said.

Fraggie looked down at the leg then back up at Jackson.

"I thought you said someone *tried* to shoot him," she said. "Sure as shit looks like they succeeded."

"*Tried* to shoot him *today*," Jackson said. "Actually shot him two nights ago."

Bobbie and Ray proceeded to tell her everything that had happened to Bobbie and his friends at the highway overlook. Jackson finished with the shooting at the courthouse and Mia following them. When Jackson told Fraggie about Franko, Mia began to sob again. Fraggie walked over to her and put an arm around her as she wiped Mia's face with her sleeve.

"That's when Bobbie suggested you might be able to help everyone lay low until we can figure this thing out," Jackson said.

"So Ray's his uncle, but who are you two?" Fraggie asked.

"Ray and Bear run a store together. We're friends," Jackson said. "We just want to help. Something about all of this isn't right. And we need to figure it out. But we need some place safe. If that's not here, I understand, but then we've got to get on our way. Things are only going to be getting worse for us."

Fraggie took a deep breath and sighed.

"No, that's here," she said. "Y'all can sleep here tonight. Tomorrow, we'll get you fixed in the smokehouse."

"Smokehouse? Lady, I don't mean to turn away hospitality, but I ain't sleepin' in the middle of a bunch of dead meat," Ray said.

Fraggie chuckled.

"We call it the smokehouse because that's what it used to be," she said. "Now, we're fixin' it up into a cabin of sorts. Not that anyone comes out here."

"You mean you and your prepper girlfriend?" Ray asked.

The door on the side of the house swung open and out stepped a woman with cherrywood skin and flowing black hair.

"Everything all good out here?" she asked.

"Yes, Maggie and I," Fraggie said to Ray before turning back to her girlfriend. "Everythin's all good, hon."

Bear coughed like he'd choked on something.

"I'm sorry, Maggie?" he asked. "And you, you're Fraggie?"

"Ain't no stupider than some man callin' himself Bear," Fraggie answered.

This time even Jackson chuckled. The tete-a-tete between Fraggie and Bear seemed to only draw more of their accents out of each of them.

"It's short for Magdalena. Magdalena Lynch," Maggie said as she walked over to the group. "Maggie's just easier."

Maggie had no accent, making Fraggie all the more difficult to decipher.

"I just call her hon, though," Fraggie said.

"Magdalena, that's what? Spanish?" Ray asked.

"Greek, actually," Maggie said. "But my parents are both full Shawnee."

"Indian?" Bear asked.

Fraggie turned to Bear.

"That's Native American-Indian, not India-Indian, big boy," she said.

Bear uncrossed his arms and presented her with his middle finger in response. Fraggie laughed. Maggie elbowed her in the ribs, rebuking her.

"We prefer native or indigenous American, but yes," Maggie said smiling. "Please, come on in. We're smoking some goat out back and our neighbor up the road, Joshua, just dropped off a fresh batch of mead he brewed. It's wonderful."

"I dunno about all that but if you've got a cold High Life, I'll take one of those," Bear said.

Maggie laughed. She didn't know Bear wasn't kidding. Together, the group walked around Fraggie's ATV and headed for the door on the side of the house. Jackson and Fraggie brought up the rear.

"Thank you, again," Jackson said. "None of them may want to admit it, but we were growing desperate out there."

"Don' mention it," Fraggie said. She stepped away from the door just long enough to flip a large switch.

Jackson heard a subtle buzz stir up around them in the distance. "What was that?"

"Tripwire system," Fraggie said. "Rigged it myself. Runs around the whole inner perimeter here. From the drive to the livestock pens and all the way behind the house here. Anyone trips it, we'll know about it."

Jackson gave a look somewhere between astonishment and fear.

Fraggie chuckled again.

"Welcome to the farm," she said.

PART III

THE FARM

27

The next morning, Jackson found himself on the front porch of Maggie and Fraggie's house cleaning his M9 Beretta as the sun struggled to climb over the mountaintop behind him. The gun was pristine, having been cleaned a week ago and unused in the time since, but for Jackson it was a matter of habit. He needed to keep his hands and mind busy; to have something to take his mind off the present.

Ray pushed open the front door of the house with his backside and stepped out with a cup of coffee in each hand, steam swirling off the top of them in the chilly forenoon air.

"Saw you out here," he said. "Fraggie's up and made a pot of coffee. Thought I'd bring you some."

Ray placed the coffee on the table next to Jackson and sat down in the porch chair opposite him.

"Thanks, appreciate it," Jackson said.

"Fraggie said you were up before her. Couldn't sleep?"

"No, I slept fine. Just didn't need much, I guess."

Ray watched him work on the barrel of the pistol as if he were whittling a stick. Jackson felt the man's eyes on him.

"So, where do we go from here?" Ray finally asked after a sip of his coffee.

"Not sure. It'd help to know who was shooting at us at the courthouse. Then we might have a clue as to just what kind of a mess we're in," Jackson answered.

"What about that Sayre guy? He might know."

"He may also be the one that put the shooter in play."

"You think so? It could've been anyone, really."

"That's the problem. Until we know who we can't trust, we don't know who we can trust."

"So how do we figure all that out?"

"I have a contact. I'm going to have to call in a favor for some info. Just waiting until it's a bit later."

Jackson put the cleaning tools back in their case and reassembled the Beretta. He finished by reinserting the magazine. The slide on top snapped forward and the gun once again resembled itself.

"That's some piece you got there," Ray said. "M9?"

"Yep," Jackson said, "I'd left it in my truck. Bear grabbed it before he came and rescued us all."

"The grip looks custom."

"It is."

"Mind if I take a look?"

Jackson held the Beretta by the barrel and handed it to Ray. The pistol was silver with black accents and a black compensator. The grip was wood with an ebony stain. A circle of small stars encompassed the letters *ERC* in a script font.

"Who or what is ERC?" Ray asked.

"Evan Randolph Clay," Jackson said. "My son."

"Oh. Didn't know you have a son."

Jackson nodded. He hated this part.

"I did," he said

"Oh, I'm sorry, I didn't—"

"No, you're good. We lost him when he was just a toddler. Disappeared at a park one day. He was there one minute, gone the next."

"God. I'm sorry," Ray said.

"Yeah. Me too," Jackson said.

"And he was never found?"

"No. I did find the person who took him, though."

"You? You found the person?"

"I did."

Having seen Jackson in action, Ray feared where this was headed. He didn't say anything, though Jackson saw the consternation on his face.

"I didn't kill him," Jackson said. "Wanted to, but I didn't."

"So, what happened?" Ray asked.

Jackson paused, debating whether to give Ray the Cliff's Notes and end the conversation as quickly as possible or just tell him. He didn't know why he'd told Ray what he had already or even why he'd told him about Bear helping him track down the missing girl. There was an easiness to Ray, Jackson supposed.

"I went to confront the man, but when I got there, he had another kid with him. He'd taken another one. When I saw the kid, I couldn't kill the guy. Not in front of that little kid. So, I called the authorities."

Ray took a long sip of coffee, digesting the story.

"You gave that boy a life," he said. "You may very well end up helping do the same for Bobbie."

"I guess. Evan would be about Bobbie's age now. Probably getting into trouble just the same," Jackson said.

Ray smiled sadly.

"He won't say it – teenagers are like that – but I know Bobbie is grateful you're doing all this," he said.

Jackson nodded, unsure of what to say. Instead, he took a sip of coffee and let the silence linger. In another life, Evan could've been Bobbie, needing the same kind of help. Jackson hadn't been able to help his son—not when he'd needed it most. That dark truth had fueled much of how he'd lived his life every day since. It'd brought him to Bear. Then to Bobbie. And now into the crosshairs of some unknown enemy.

That part Jackson wasn't used to.

It was time to do something about that.

28

Special Agent Bailey was standing taking in what was now a totaled BMW Z4 when her phone rang. She looked at the number but didn't recognize it.

"Bailey," she answered.

"You got a minute?" Jackson asked.

Bailey looked for a quiet spot, recognizing his voice. She walked over to the light pole the convertible smashed into and stepped behind it.

"Jesus Christ, are you okay?" she asked. "I saw you on the news at the courthouse."

"Did the news ID me?"

"No, of course not. But holy shit, what the hell happened?"

"That's what I need to find out. I didn't wake you, did I? I know it's a Saturday."

"No, it's fine. I'm working. A state senator's daughter drove her birthday beamer into a family of four. It's a shit show. What about you, where are you?"

"It's probably best I don't say."

Bailey turned to see two uniformed officers walking toward her. She waved them off and stepped further away.

"Jesus, it's that bad?" she asked.

"You saw the news, you tell me," Jackson said.

"Yeah, it didn't look good. They said three dead plus the shooter."

"One of them was Bobbie's lawyer. The guy your friend referred."

"Yeah, I caught that. My friend is...not happy."

"I'm sorry about that, but I don't think the shooter was gunning for him. I think Bobbie was the target."

"Which is why you're back on the lam."

"I don't have a choice until I figure some things out. We tried to do this right. It almost got Bobbie killed."

"No, I've got you. I'm just putting pieces together aloud."

Jackson was quiet for a moment. Bailey waited for him to speak.

"Listen," he said finally, "I need to know which way the wind is blowing here. Someone wants Bobbie dead and if I go to the wrong people, next time they won't miss."

"You think it's that Lieutenant Sayre?" Bailey asked.

"The thought crossed my mind," Jackson said. "He was there. Near the shooter, even."

"I can dig deeper, but when I checked him out the first time, he looked clean. Virtually spotless."

"Then I have to know if I can trust him."

"Let me get into it and see what I can find. Call you back on this number?"

"It's probably best I call you. Noon enough time to get started?"

"Yeah, this DUI is going to get held up with red tape. Let me get into it. I'll see what I can find out before noon."

"Thanks," Jackson said. "One other thing: It sounds like this whole thing starts with the Hopewell County Vice Squad."

"Yeah, you told me that. Franko and Bragg. I told you there were some red flags with them, remember?" Bailey said.

"I do, but they weren't at the courthouse. I saw it online. It said they were placed on paid administrative leave."

"Either that, or they weren't supposed to be at the courthouse but were."

"I guess. Either way, though, I get the feeling it's more than two bad apples."

"I'll see what I can find from my end."

"I appreciate it."

"Keep your head down out there."

She smiled when the line went dead without a reply. The classic Jackson Clay farewell. The two uniformed officers were standing by waiting for her. Bailey took a deep breath in, composing herself, before waving and approaching them with her best professional smile. The truth was she was a little bit nervous.

Not for Jackson—she knew he could handle himself.

No, she was worried for whomever she turned Jackson loose on.

29

Lieutenant Sayre sat at the desk in his requisitioned Hopewell County workspace reviewing information from the courthouse shooting. He could feel Starcher's eyes peering at him from the man's own desk clustered across the way with the rest of the Vice Squad but ignored him. He was used to ruffling the feathers of locals that felt their toes were being stepped on. He even enjoyed it in the instances where he felt he was a better officer than them. When it came to Detective Red Starcher, Sayre particularly relished it.

A deputy stepped into his open door and knocked on the frame. Sayre waved him in.

"This came for you, sir," the deputy said, handing Sayre a folder thick with papers.

Sayre took it and thanked the officer as he left. Sayre opened the folder—it was the ballistics report from the highway overlook. He skimmed over the findings.

Mason Westfall had, in fact, been killed by a round fired from Detective Franko's gun. The shot fractured a rib on entry before piercing the left ventricle of his heart. Mason Westfall could've been shot in an operating room surrounded by the best surgeons in the country and still wouldn't have survived.

Emma Miller had died from a gunshot wound to the head, a round that splintered upon hitting her left cheekbone. The shards mushroomed outward, causing immense damage, even severing her brain stem. She'd died instantly. The report couldn't conclusively tie the gunshot to Bragg's gun without having it to compare, but the bullet was the same type of ammunition as Franko's and hadn't been fired from Franko's gun. Sayre looked over the autopsy report until his eyes hit three words written in red ink.

Pregnant – Eleven weeks

"Christ almighty," he muttered.

Several more shots had been fired by both Detective Franko's gun and the one using identical ammunition. Most of the shots had been fired in the direction of the pickup the three teenagers had driven in. A third gun was found near Mason Westfall's body, a Ruger LCR revolver that had fired four of the five shots in its cylinder. Two shots had struck the detectives' truck's windshield before smashing into the interior body of the cab. A third shot had hit the pavement near where Mason lay and a fourth shot was unaccounted for, but that didn't surprise Sayre. With the other two shots fired from the overlook back toward the highway, it was reasonable to assume the unaccounted-for shot had missed completely into the woods across the road.

Sayre flipped through his papers again to find the file on Mason Westfall. From the beginning, the notion that he'd come out guns blazing on two police officers didn't jive with who Mason was on paper. He had never had any run-ins with the law, and his school record showed exactly one disciplinary note: a detention for being late to three classes. It didn't add up.

He looked for a number for the Westfall's house and called it.

A woman picked up on the second ring.

"Hello?" she said.

Sayre thought the voice sounded tired. As if it had been up for days on end.

"Hello," Sayre said, "my name is Colton Sayre. I'm an investigator with the West Virginia State Police. Is this Mrs. Westfall?"

"Please," the voice said, sounding even more strained, "I've answered all of your guys' questions. I just want to bury my son and be left alone."

"I understand that, and I'm sorry for your loss. I really am. But I'm not, in fact, actually with the Hopewell County Sheriff's Office, who I'm sure are the ones who've talked to you to this point."

"I've had all sorts of police here the last two days and you all think the same thing. That my son tried to kill two police officers. So, I don't really care who you're with."

"Mrs. Westfall, I promise you the only thing I want to do is find out what really happened. You clearly don't think your son tried to shoot anyone. I would really like to hear what you have to say."

The line was quiet.

"Please, Mrs. Westfall," Sayre said. "Let me hear your son's story. From you."

"Okay," she said.

"Thank you, Mrs. Westfall. Really, thank you. Would it be alright if I came by your house now? I can be there in twenty minutes."

"That's fine, I guess."

"Great. Thank you. I have your address here, and I'll be there soon. Thank you again."

"You're welcome."

Sayre hung up and grabbed his suit coat before hopping to his feet and trotting out of the office. Starcher rotated his desk chair slowly, watching him the whole way. Sayre passed by an inbound Detective Bragg at the doors for the lobby. The two passed looking at each other without saying anything. Bragg walked over and plopped down in the chair next to Starcher and lit up a cigarette.

"There's no smoking in here," a nearby uniformed officer said.

"Fuck off, Fisher," Starcher said.

Bragg took a deep drag from the cigarette and blew the smoke upwards.

"Where is golden boy off to?" he asked.

"I don't know. But it looked like he had something to go after and I don't like that," Starcher said.

"Might want to keep tabs on him. You know?"

Starcher nodded slowly as he thought about it.

"Might be right. Where's Franko?" he asked.

"Runnin' down that Mia girl about the thing," Bragg said.

"Call him," Starcher said. "Let's get someone on Sayre."

30

Mia opened the side door to Maggie and Fraggie's house and stepped out to light a cigarette, her hands shaking and unsteady. She knew the drugs were leaving her system and that realization made her anxious and queasy. She saw Ray and Bobbie further down the property helping the two women feed their various animals. Jackson and Bear sat atop Bear's suburban watching them, each with a gun by their side.

Struggling to actually light the cigarette, Mia walked over to them.

Jackson turned as he heard her approach.

"Good morning," he said.

"You din' shoot us in the middle of the night, which was nice," Bear said.

"Bear," Jackson said.

Bear raised his hands, signaling he was stepping off.

"I'm sorry about that again," Mia said. "I really am. Do you think one of you could help me with a light?"

"Sure," Jackson said.

Jackson and Bear both noticed her tremors as she struggled to hold the cigarette over the flame.

"Are you going to be okay?" Jackson asked.

He took the lighter and kept it lit for Mia until she'd taken several drags and got it started. She held her arms by her side, trying to hide the shaking, suddenly embarrassed the two men understood what was going on. She nodded earnestly, trying to convince herself as much as the two of them.

"Yeah. I'm sorry," Mia said. "I just…I'm okay. I'll be okay."

Jackson and Bear looked at each other. She wasn't convincing anyone.

"We're safe here. Franko can't get you here. And if he tries, he's got us to worry about," Jackson said.

Mia blew the smoke from her cigarette into the air as she tapped on it, knocking off the ash.

"He kept me out of the system when I got in trouble," she said. "All he said I had to do was flip on the guy that had given me the meth they found on me. But then one favor turned into more and more."

Mia took another drag from the cigarette.

"It wasn't long before I was letting him do god knows what to me to stay out of prison," she said.

The burgeoning anger inside Jackson was invisible to Mia and Bear.

"Don't get me wrong, I'm thankful for what he did," she said. "Here—"

"No," Jackson interrupted.

"What?" Mia asked.

"Do not be thankful for him. Him and everyone like him. They're preying on you. Exploiting you. I don't care what you did, you don't deserve that."

"I'm just saying. I'm glad to not be in the system. You get picked up on a drug offense here, your choices are prison or NRIP. One takes your freedom, the other takes your money. What little I have, anyway."

"What is NRIP?"

"Narcotics Rehabilitation something Program. Something like that. They give you that choice if it's your first bust, but it costs a lot. Most people 'round here can't afford it. The program offers you payment plans or something, but it just ends up costing you more. I had a friend, Ava, go into it. She ended up having to start dealing to keep up with payments. Then got busted again. In jail and still owing money. It's fucked up."

Jackson and Bear didn't say anything else. They watched as Maggie, Fraggie, Ray, and Bobbie finished up the chores and walked back up to them. As they got close, Fraggie nodded at the pistol on Jackson's thigh.

"You can put that BB gun away," she said. "We got plenty of tools like that on this farm. You know what I mean?"

"Pfft, you got some balls calling that Beretta a BB gun," Bear said.

Fraggie pulled out the massive scoped pistol she'd had on her yesterday.

"Holy fuck, is that an XVR?" Bear asked. "Can I see it?"

Fraggie engaged the safety and twirled the gun around so the handle was pointed toward him. Bear took it from her and handled it with an impressed look on his face.

Mia burned her cigarette to the filter, before dropping it and stepping on it with one of her pink flip flops.

"Jesus, it's fucking freezing out here. I'll be inside," she said.

Maggie and the group smiled politely as Mia turned and scurried for the house. When the door shut, Fraggie turned back to the group.

"Sweatin' an awful lot for a girl that's supposedly cold," she said. "She's jonesin', ya know. Damn thing's shakin' like a li'l dog."

"The question is from what," Jackson said. "Meth? Heroin? Alcohol, even, maybe."

"Or all of the above. I've seen a lot of fiendin' in my day. Next 24 hours are gonna be a bitch for her," Bear said.

Jackson checked his watch.

"It's almost noon," he said. "I better call my contact back."

"We still need to get your truck back, too," Bear said.

"Assuming the police haven't found it and are sitting on it," Jackson said as he walked away.

He walked over to the fence penning in the farm's cows and called Special Agent Bailey. She answered almost immediately.

"Hey, yeah," she said. "I've got some stuff for you. One sec."

"Sure," Jackson said.

He put his arms up on top of the fence and leaned against it. A large brown cow standing in the middle of the small herd stared at him as it rudely chewed its grass with an open mouth.

"I emailed it all to you," Bailey said. "Basically, you're right. Every detective in the Vice Squad has notes in their files. It's almost like having a dozen complaints against you is a prerequisite for being on the team. The interesting thing is their boss, a Lieutenant Red Starcher. The guy looked to be a shit cop. Shot an unarmed elderly woman, wrapped a cruiser around a tree drunk. He'd been assigned to office duty before he magically landed the Vice Squad shortly after it was formed."

"So how do they keep operating if they're so much trouble?" Jackson asked.

"Well, for one thing, they account for about two-thirds of the department's arrests. Almost all of which are narcotics-related. The governor over there has this whole New War on Drugs initiative. Hard to pull your best players off the field when they're producing, you know?"

"Even if they're bad actors. What about Sayre?"

"Sayre is a different story," Bailey said. "A couple of complaints but for far less malicious stuff. He told a woman who confessed to smothering her children that the world would be better off if she killed herself. I called a colleague of mine over in Charleston, and he said the guy is known to not play well with others. I guess he can be overly honest and doesn't hold back. My guy called it Asperger's but that's probably just my guy being an ass."

"Doesn't sound like the type to set up a murder-for-hire, though," Jackson said.

"No, it doesn't. Still, might not be the best thing to approach him. It sounds like the guy has one gear. He's police and you're abetting a fugitive."

"Maybe, but maybe he's in it for the bigger fish."

"Like who?"

"Like whoever really killed Emma Miller and Mason Westfall and put that shooter in play at the courthouse."

"I don't know, Jackson. But, speaking of, I've got his ID, too. His name is—"

"Jimmy."

"James, but yeah, goes by Jimmy. How'd you know?"

"I've got a friend of his here. She says Franko gave her the gun and told her to kill Bobbie. When she refused, he told her to get Jimmy to do it."

Bailey snorted in frustration as the line went quiet. Jackson knew she was annoyed now.

"Somehow you forgot to mention all that when you had me run this information down," Bailey said sharply.

"I'm sorry," Jackson said. "I wanted independent verification. The truth is we caught her following us with a loaded revolver. Didn't know how much we could trust her story."

Bailey sighed.

"You're really up shit's creek on this one, huh?" she said.

"It would seem that way," Jackson said.

"Alright, well, it's your call on Sayre, I guess," Bailey said. "I'll see what else I can find out. Keep your head down in the meantime."

"While you're at it, maybe you can check something else for me. No games this time."

"Shoot."

"NRIP. The girl said it's some alternative to prison here for first time drug offenders, but it sounds sketchy."

"Yeah, I've heard of it. Narcotics Rehabilitation and Intervention Program. From what I understand it's supposed to be a bone thrown to civil liberty-types worried about non-violent criminals being incarcerated."

"Well, the way she tells it, they're much less altruistic than that."

"Let me see what I can find out."

"Thanks. I'll check in tomorrow."

Bailey acknowledged that and he killed the call. Fraggie was on the ATV coming up the drive. When she saw Jackson put the phone away, she veered left and climbed the small hill up to him.

"Your friend have any info?" she asked.

"Yeah," Jackson answered, "it's not great news for Bobbie. Sounds like the guys that busted him aren't exactly on the up and up."

"You know how you find a crooked cop in Hopewell County, don' you?"

Jackson shook his head.

"Find one with a badge," Fraggie said.

Jackson smiled and allowed himself to laugh for the first time in what felt like forever.

"C'mon," Fraggie said. "You wanna get your truck back?"

"I want to try, anyway," Jackson said.

Fraggie nodded back and to her right.

"Meet you at my truck over there," she said. "You and I, we'll go to town."

Jackson nodded. The ATV growled as Fraggie put it into gear and headed back down the hill toward the others. In just a couple days it'd come to this. Holed up on a remote farm with two survivalist types, helping Bear and his business partner hide a kid and a young woman from a unit of shady police officers.

Special Agent Bailey was right. He really was up shit's creek on this one.

31

Lieutenant Sayre knocked on the front door of the Westfall's home and stepped back to take in its exterior. It was a modest-sized Cape Cod, sage green with white accents, all of which was well maintained.

The door opened just a couple inches. A pair of eyes—red, with large bags beneath them—peered out at Sayre through the opening.

"Mrs. Westfall?" Sayre said. "I'm Lieutenant Sayre. We spoke on the phone."

She opened the door a little more, still wary of what else might be outside. Days of police officers and reporters hounding her had probably ingrained this behavior into her, Sayre thought.

"It's just you?" Mrs. Westfall asked.

"Yes, ma'am. Just me. Like I said, I was wondering if we could talk."

She opened the door the rest of the way to let Sayre in, and closed it as soon as he stepped through.

"It's Amelia," she said. "May I take your jacket, officer?"

"That's alright, I'll keep it, thanks," Sayre said. "You can just call me Colton. Or Sayre if you'd rather."

"Okay. Would you like some coffee?" she asked.

"That's okay, thank you. I just wanted to speak with you briefly."

"Then why don't we sit here in the living room."

She led Sayre to a pair of armchairs facing opposite a sofa. Sayre sat on the arms of one of the chairs as Amelia centered herself on the sofa.

"I know several police officers have already asked you a bunch of questions," Sayre said, "I'd just like to ask a couple more. To understand for myself what exactly happened the other night."

"They all think my boy tried to shoot two cops," Amelia said.

"I'm guessing you told them that doesn't sound like your son," Sayre said.

"Why, is that something mothers of cop killers say?"

"No, I'm just saying. From what I've seen in his file, Mason wasn't a violent kid. Unless his home life was a different story?"

"Of course not. He was a great kid. Kind and sweet. And funny. He was happy. Happy kids don't do what those cops say he did."

"What about a gun? Does he have one? Or know how to use one?"

"It's West Virginia. Everybody knows how to use a gun. He didn't have one personally, though, no."

"Is there any reason why he would go get a gun? Even just for recreational shooting?"

"No, and these are just the same damned questions everyone has asked."

"I'm sorry, Amelia. I'm just trying to make sense of it all. What about Bobbie or Emma? Would they have a reason to have a gun?"

"Emma definitely not. She was an angel. And I don't think Bobbie would, either. He could get into trouble here and there, sure, but nothing like that."

"What kind of trouble would Bobbie get into?" Sayre asked.

"I'm not saying anything against that boy," Amelia said. "As far as I'm concerned, they're all lying about him just the way they're lying about Mason."

"I understand. You meant like, what? He would get in trouble for little stuff, right? Things kids normally do," Sayre said.

"Yes. They were all still kids. He'd go and shoot his stepdad's beer cans off trees out in the woods. Stuff like that."

"Did Mason ever do this with him?"

"Yes, but that doesn't make them cop killers. Because they shot a couple of aluminum cans."

"I never said it did."

Amelia placed her head in her hands for a moment before rubbing at her face. A part of Sayre felt bad for her. This all must be a nightmare. Only these kinds of nightmares don't end when the sun comes up.

"I have to ask, Amelia," Sayre said. "Did you know Emma Miller was pregnant? My understanding is she and Mason were dating."

At that Amelia began to weep. She buried her head back in her hands as her shoulders shook. Sayre looked around for a tissue box. He spotted one on an end table and grabbed it. Behind it was a photo of Mason. He grabbed that, too, handing the tissue box to Amelia.

"Thank you," she said in between sniffles.

"Of course," Sayre said.

"I'm sorry," Amelia added. "She came to me before Mason. I was so touched. She thought I would be mad. At what? That they were going to have a life together?"

"So Mason knew. What'd he think?" Sayre asked.

"He was over the moon about it. One night I picked up his laptop after he fell asleep with it. He was looking at onesies online," Amelia said.

"Would he have been protective of her, maybe? If someone did something to her?"

"Why do you all keep looking for a reason to peg my boy as some killer? Yes, he shot guns with his buddies. Yes, he would've protected Emma. Wouldn't you protect the mother of your unborn child? That doesn't make him a killer—that makes him a good and decent young man."

"Amelia, please. Please believe me when I say I'm not looking for an angle here. I'm just trying to make sense of what happened that night. I want to know who Mason was. What he was like."

Sayre looked down at the photo of Mason. He was in a baseball uniform, splayed out as he threw a pitch off the mound. One leg and one hand charging forward as he held the ball back in the other, prepared to sling it. He looked every bit the part, Sayre thought. Tall and lean—he had a pitcher's physique. Though, the longer Sayre studied the photo, the more something seemed off about it. Then it struck him.

"Mason was left-handed," Sayre said as he flashed the photo toward Amelia.

"Yes," she said. "His dad coached him until he died. The man loved baseball his whole life. As soon as he figured out Mason would be a lefty he was trying to make him into a pitcher. Two fastest ways to the majors, he would joke: a catcher and a southpaw pitcher."

An uneasiness burned in Sayre. He couldn't be sure, but something felt off with that fact and what he'd read in the police report. He tried to recall specifically what, but couldn't. It bothered him now. A red flag waving in his face.

"Well, thank you for letting me talk to you," Sayre said, standing up. "I hope I can call you again if I need to ask some more questions."

"Sure, I guess that'd be fine," Amelia said.

"You have a nice day, ma'am," Sayre said.

He left quickly, trotting down the front stairs and hopping into the driver's seat of his unmarked police car. As he got in, he reached for the files in the back seat and began flipping through them, looking for Franko and Bragg's account of the incident. A moment later, he found it.

Franko had stated he'd returned fire from Mason Westfall, eventually striking Mason in the chest. Then, according to Franko, he had proceeded to move toward Westfall's body, confirming he was down, and then Franko had kicked the gun out of Mason's hand. That's what Sayre recalled. So what was bothering him?

He opened up a separate file with photos of the crime scene and flipped through them until he got to those of Mason. As he looked at one, Sayre realized what was off. The realization gave him goosebumps. After being shot, Mason had come to rest on his back, but his left arm had bent awkwardly behind him. In essence, he'd landed laying on his left arm. The gun, meanwhile, had been photographed several inches away from Mason's outstretched right hand.

If he had shot at the officers the way they said, there was no way he'd done so with his dominant left hand. Why would he use the gun with his non-dominant right hand? Sayre couldn't think of a plausible reason. Which left the obvious and more troubling conclusion: he didn't.

Sayre flipped back to the statement given by Franko and Bragg, double checking what he read was right. Yes: shot him, walked up to him, kicked away the gun. It all supposed Mason fired the gun with his right hand. Another thought occurred to Sayre and he flipped to Mason's autopsy report. The gunshot wound to his chest had what medical examiners called tattooing, discoloration on the skin caused by burning gunpowder. Mason had to have been shot at near point-blank range, not several feet away like the detectives stated.

My god, Sayre thought. They're lying about the whole thing. He pulled out his phone and called his supervisor, Captain Levi Smith. The call went to voicemail.

"Captain, it's Sayre," he said, leaving a message. "Call me back when you get this. I may have a problem here."

Sayre ended the call and tossed the phone onto the passenger seat. He was looking out the far window at the Westfall's house when there was a knock on the driver side door next to him. Sayre jerked around, one hand grasping instinctively for his service weapon.

Detective Ronnie Franko stood outside his car. He smiled and blew a cloud of cigarette smoke in Sayre's face.

"You're a bit jumpy, huh," he said.

Sayre didn't say anything but kept his hand on his pistol. Franko chuckled and put the cigarette back between his lips for another draw. Sayre heard the crackling of tobacco and God-knows-what-else burning. Lungs full of smoke, Franko let the cigarette drop from his mouth and snuffed it out on the pavement.

"So," he said, blowing the smoke as he spoke. "What kind of problem do we have?"

32

Lieutenant Sayre forced himself to smile politely at Franko.

"Good afternoon, Detective. Checking up on me?" he asked.

"Something like that," Franko said.

The stench of stale tobacco wafted off of Franko and into Sayre's open window, making it even harder for him to hold his smile.

"So," Franko said, "what was that problem?"

"Oh, just Amelia Westfall isn't being as forthcoming as I'd hoped," Sayre said. "That's all."

Franko stared at him, as if trying to gauge the validity of his answer.

"Forthcoming," Sayre said. "It means 'to come forth with.' It means she didn't talk."

Franko chuckled. He grabbed his pack of cigarettes and smacked it in his hand.

"That's good. Funny," he said. "Well, I'll tell you what. Why don't you leave all the question asking to us, and if anyone isn't as *forthcoming*, as you said, as we would like, then we'll take care of it."

Sayre's hand squeezed the grip of his holstered pistol tighter, imagining it was Franko's neck. Restraint was not one of Sayre's strong suits—it took all he had within him not to lose his cool.

"If it's all the same to you, detective," Sayre said, measuring his words, "I'll keep doing my job, worrying about me. You do your job, and worry about yourself."

Franko pulled another cigarette out of the pack and lit it. He took it in between his fingers and leaned forward.

"That's a good idea, lieutenant," he said. "Worry about yourself."

Sayre and Franko locked eyes. They stayed like that as Sayre's hand slowly slid off his pistol and turned the keys in the car's ignition.

"Anything else, detective?" Sayre asked.

He looked down at Franko's elbow, leaning against the car, before looking back up at the man. Franko grinned and stepped back, brushing his hair away from his face before gesturing to Sayre that he was welcome to leave. Sayre put the unmarked police cruiser in gear and took off.

Franko stood there, in the middle of the road, watching Sayre, then turned and looked at the Westfall's house. Mrs. Westfall was peeking out from behind one of the curtains. Franko smiled and waved at her as he pulled out his phone. She drew the curtain shut quickly. Franko punched in a number and put the phone to his ear.

"You find him?" Starcher asked on the other end of the line.

"He was at the Westfall house," Franko said. "Looked like he'd just talked to the mom when I caught up to him. I overheard him call someone and say they had a problem."

"Any idea what that problem is?"

"He said somethin' about the mom not being cooperative."

"You buy it?"

"Not for a second."

"Well, she's probably scared. Maybe she really wasn't all that talkative."

Franko played with the lit cigarette between his fingers. He watched as Mrs. Westfall slowly pulled back the curtains again just enough to see if he was still watching the house.

"Maybe she's not scared enough," Franko said.

33

The hour-long drive back to Rion was as quiet as the trip out had been—quieter, even, if you counted everything that happened with stopping Mia on the road. Jackson sat quietly, content to not make small talk, before Fraggie spoke up.

"I'm guessin' by that tattoo you were in the Rangers," she said.

"I was," Jackson said. "You did some work somewhere, too, right?"

"What makes you say that?" Fraggie asked.

"The way you drew your pistol earlier, bringing your gun to your chest before extending out. That's tactical training. They don't teach you that at the local gun club."

Fraggie grinned and shook her head.

"All that and brains, too, huh?" she said. "Yeah, I've seen action before."

"Is that where you got that shrapnel scar on your head? And I'm guessing your nickname, too?"

"Two for two. Don' tell me you're some kind of detective, what with all these problems we're havin' with cops."

"No. Just a few tours abroad. You get to know what shrapnel does when it finds people. And your nickname isn't exactly a riddle."

"Well I din' come up with it. Guys I worked with did."

"Armed forces?"

"Nah, I was out back here long before those fuckers were lettin' women see combat. I wanted to fight, so I joined up with security contractors. Mostly ferryin' suit-types around. Oil execs and whatnot."

"That's where you got the scar?"

"On a job, yeah. Al Qaeda had been kidnappin' European business types for ransom. We were supposed to protect this German energy exec when we got lit up. Had to fight our way out. Lost four guys and the German."

"Sounds like shit."

"It was. We got out to return fire when a frag grenade landed next to the truck I was behind. I was lucky, obviously. Only permanent damage is the scar and the fact it fucked up the way my hair grew. I decided, fuck it, and just shaved it."

"And then you were known as Fraggie."

"Really shoulda been a detective."

Fraggie took a left onto the highway that went through the heart of Rion. They were just a few minutes away.

"So what's your real name then?" Jackson asked.

"Frances. Frances Conway."

"I like Fraggie better."

"Me, too."

"So is that where you met Maggie? In country?" Jackson asked.

"No, Maggie's never done anythin' like that," Fraggie said. "Don' get me wrong, the woman knows her way around a gun. She can put a .223 Remington through a buck's heart from a hundred yards out, but she never served or nothin'."

"So then where'd you two meet?"

"Met her at the Food Lion outside Rion here couple years back."

"That's cute."

"You might want to shut up before your lip is as purple as my hair."

Jackson grinned. They rolled into town, driving by the courthouse. Yellow police tape still lined the front plaza, winding its way around street signs on either corner before coming back around to the large columns at the front of the courthouse. The crime scene clashed with the stoic aesthetic of the building's colonial revival architecture, a blight on the area's small-town charm.

Fraggie continued through town on the main road until they got to the street where Jackson's truck was parked. There, she slowed down and pulled over at the corner. The truck was still in the metered parking spot next to the park, a bit covered in fallen orange and brown foliage, but no worse for the wear. Both of them studied it from a block and a half away.

"Still there," Fraggie said. "You think they're watchin' it?"

"Only one way to find out," Jackson said.

He reached into the pack he'd brought along and pulled out his FLIR monocular. He scanned the area for heat signatures.

"What're you doin'?" Fraggie asked.

"Looking for anyone watching from their cars," Jackson said.

Fraggie pursed her lips, admitting she was impressed. Jackson moved the monocular slowly left-to-right. The frames of the cars were black on a dark blue backdrop. If there were people in them, they would've shown up bright yellow or orange. He lowered it from his eye.

"Looks clear," Jackson said.

"Did you really think they'd make your truck?" Fraggie asked.

"Lieutenant Sayre, at the very least, saw me at the courthouse and knows my name," Jackson said. "All it would take is someone running the registration on the truck to come back to me. I'd be watching it if I were them."

"Sounds a bit paranoid to me. And I think the world is endin'."

"Yeah, well, last time I thought I was being paranoid, four people died."

Jackson quickly scanned the cars once more before putting the FLIR back into his pack. He drummed two fingers on his chin, thinking.

"I think we're good," he said, "but let's make it fast anyway. Circle the block and come up behind the truck. Drop me off right at it. I'll hop in and we'll go."

Fraggie nodded and put her truck into gear. She drove down a block to circle back, taking the turn without slowing down and speeding down the adjacent street. A squirrel narrowly avoided an untimely demise beneath Fraggie's tires and chattered its displeasure as the two flew by.

"Easy, easy," Jackson said.

"You said fast," Fraggie said.

She turned the corner onto the back street, and then once more onto the street with Jackson's truck, tearing down the road. Fraggie slammed on the brakes just fifty feet away. Jackson hopped out and jogged over to his truck. An elderly couple watched the two with suspicion from a nearby park bench.

"Quick nooner with the husband," Fraggie yelled to them. "Hafta go get the kids now where we left 'em."

The elderly couple shook their heads in disapproval. Jackson got into his truck and fired it up. The familiar roar was soothing to him.

"We good?" Fraggie asked out her open window.

"Good," Jackson said. "Let's roll."

Together, they got back on the main road and headed back toward the farm.

34

W olfe sat on his company's private jet, staring out the window at the West Virginia state plane across the tarmac. The Beechcraft King Air was a twin-engine propeller plane. This one, painted midnight blue with a gold trim and white belly, was used by the governor to travel.

What a piece of shit, Wolfe thought to himself as he drank his cactus water. A propeller plane? In this day and age? It wasn't an airplane so much as an eyesore. Lane Wolfe would almost prefer flying commercial. Almost. It should be embarrassed to be at the same airport as his Bombardier.

The two planes were parked at Yeager Airport, a single-runway airport plopped atop a 300-foot mountain three miles from downtown Charleston. Situated in the general aviation part of the airport, away from concourses and major airlines, Wolfe took pride in the fact that his was easily the nicest jet parked there.

Seeing the governor's motorcade approach the state plane, Wolfe got up and headed for the door. He descended down the stairs attached to his plane and walked hastily toward the convoy of black SUVs that had parked in a semicircle.

Two members of the governor's security detail moved to intercept Wolfe before a third yelled at them.

"Stop," he ordered. "What are you, crazy? That's our boss."

The two stopped and returned to their positions. They were State Police troopers that Wolfe supposed weren't read-up enough to know who he was. The third man, the one that had stopped them, was a contractor supplied by Wolfe's company, VigilOne. Good man, Wolfe thought. He trotted past them and waved at the governor.

"Governor," he shouted over the airplane engines, "good afternoon."

Governor George Law was a large man in every way. Tall enough to play basketball professionally but probably twice the ideal weight, he had jowls that rivaled some bulldogs. The smile he'd had on his face faded when he saw Wolfe approaching.

"Mr. Wolfe," the governor said. "I was just on my way to Morgantown. The Mountaineers play on national TV tonight."

"Is that so? I didn't know that," Wolfe said. "I've always been more of a *futbol* fan myself."

"I wouldn't say that here. Not liking football is damn near a sin in West Virginia," Governor Law said.

"I'm not one for church, either, so I guess I'm okay."

"I'm running late, Mr. Wolfe. What is it that I can do for you?"

"I was wondering if we might have a quick word. In private."

Governor Law stared at him as if his portly scowl might persuade Wolfe to rescind his request, but Wolfe simply returned the governor's gaze with a smile that told the man he didn't have much of a choice. The two of them both knew Wolfe's generous campaign contributions came with the understanding he'd have access to the governor and the powers of his office should the need ever arise.

"Sure, why don't we step on my plane here and we'll have ourselves a quick chat," Governor Law said before turning to his aides. "You folks wait here. It'll just be a minute."

Wolfe made his insincere smile even bigger and motioned for the governor to go ahead first. He waited until the man was all the way in the plane – something about having that lard ass's rear near his face made Wolfe sick – before jogging up the stairs himself.

Inside, Governor Law had wedged himself into the one seat on the nine-passenger plane he sort of fit into. Wolfe looked around the inside of the plane, taking in the interior with a face that said he wasn't impressed.

"This is, um, homey, I guess," Wolfe said as he took the seat opposite the governor.

"Cut the shit, Lane," Governor Law said. "What do you want?"

"I'll make it quick, *George*. I'm on the way out myself. Not to Morgantown, but Napa Valley. I have a dinner reservation at The French Laundry. You know how it goes."

The governor gave him another scowl.

"Anyways," Wolfe continued, "there's this mess up in Hopewell County."

"Where I've got four dead a day after two were shot by county police? Yes, believe me, I'm aware," Governor Law said.

"My understanding is the state police are assisting on the investigations. And federal agencies may even come in."

"That's what happens when cell phone video of a crowd running for their lives makes the six o'clock news."

"Well, truth be told, that doesn't really work for us. It'd be better if this were kept a local matter."

"And why would we do that?" Governor Law asked.

"Out of discretion," Wolfe said.

The governor pulled a white handkerchief from his pocket and wiped at his liver-spotted forehead.

"Discretion," he echoed.

"Yes. This, quite frankly, would all work better if the feds and, for that matter, the state authorities were kept out of it," Wolfe said.

"The same locals that have already royally fucked it up so far," Governor Law said.

"From what I understand, there's a state police investigator down there rubbing people the wrong way. That's as much to blame for the problem as anything. And it's only going to get worse if we let the feds in."

"Do you know what, exactly, you're asking for here, Lane? It's not like I haven't done right by you. I know this is about the side business you've got going on. I've been willing to look the other way, but this is pushing it."

"That's right. So far our arrangement has worked. One hand washing the other. But let's not pretend your hands haven't needed cleaning from time to time as well. I imagine that's the sort of thing that could come up again. That is, unless you've quit Thai hookers and cocaine cold turkey."

Governor Law sighed and folded his kerchief over, this time dabbing his upper lip. Little droplets of spittle blew in and out of his mouth as he huffed. Wolfe tried not to pay attention.

"You're one hell of an asshole, you know that?" the governor grumbled. "I'll talk to my police superintendent, explain to him how...*we*... would prefer to keep things local on this one."

Wolfe smiled again. This time it was even somewhat genuine. He held out an outstretched hand for the onlookers on the tarmac. Governor Law grasped it and shook it.

"Go fuck yourself, Lane," Governor Law said as he tried to stand up.

"Just as long as you don't fuck me, George," Wolfe said.

Wolfe climbed out of the plane and walked back over to his own, shaking his head. He was always putting out fires. Doing other people's jobs for them. If he knew the morons fucking shit up could be replaced, he'd have no problem putting the next guy who fucked his day up in a six-foot hole.

35

It was just past five o'clock when Fraggie and Jackson pulled into the drive for the farm. When they got to the split by the parked bulldozer, Fraggie took a right instead of a left toward her house. Jackson followed and she led the two of them to the smokehouse.

The building was little more than a typical single-story home. Most of the exposed wood siding had been replaced by simple vinyl, and the stairs leading up the front door were just loose cinder blocks. A small yard had been carved into the woods surrounding the house with a wire fence separating a small, manicured lawn from the untamed nature surrounding it.

As Fraggie and Jackson pulled up, Bear emerged from a large shed surrounded by various vehicles and appliances in disrepair. A large boyish smile stretched across his face when he saw the Dodge D100.

"You got it back," he said as Jackson hopped out.

"It was clear," Jackson said. "I guess local law enforcement hadn't made it yet."

"Their loss. It's good to have it with us," Bear said.

"Where's everyone else?"

"Oh, Ray's inside there. He's been tryin' to see what he could find on the Internet. Bobbie and Mia have been followin' Maggie around pretty much doin' whatever. Mia's been strugglin', though."

"No other trouble, though, while we were gone?"

"Nope, we're groovy, brother."

Fraggie had turned her truck around and was now waiting for Jackson to come over.

"I'm gon' head up to the house, check on Maggie," she said. "You good here?"

"Yeah, we should be. Thanks again," Jackson said.

"No problem. Dinner'll be in a few. We'll holler."

With that, Fraggie put her truck in gear, kicking up dirt and rocks on the unpaved drive. Jackson waved her off and then headed into the smokehouse to see Ray.

The inside of the smokehouse was much like the outside, with little of its original elements still intact. Drywall now made up the walls. Most of the floors were either lined with linoleum or wall-to-wall carpet. Two sliding glass doors looked over a small deck facing the woods behind the building.

Ray was hunched over a table next to the doors, studying something on a laptop. He looked up as Jackson walked in.

"You get your truck back?" he asked.

"I did," Jackson said. "What are you working on?"

"I figured I'd make myself useful and see what information I could dig up for us," Ray said.

"I'm surprised they have internet."

"I was, too. Apparently, it's satellite based. Maggie offered me a computer and their Wi-Fi password."

"Bear mentioned Bobbie and Mia have been helping Maggie out."

"Yeah, I think it's actually been good for them. Gives them something to do to take their mind off of everything. I've seen Bobbie smile today for the first time since all this nonsense began."

"That's good. Is there a place I should put my stuff?"

"The bedroom right there. Bobbie and Mia are going to couch surf. The den over there has two cots set up for Bear and me. We left the bedroom for you. It doesn't look like much, but it's a place to lay your head."

"I'm fine on a couch."

"Don't even try to object. You're in the bedroom."

Jackson tried to think of something to say but conceded and dropped his pack just inside the doorway. He took off his coat and pulled out the gun holstered in the small of his back and placed it on the table before sitting down across from Ray.

"So, did you find anything?" he asked.

"A bit, yeah," Ray said. "A couple articles on this so-called Vice Squad. Mostly talking about what this New War on Drugs initiative from the governor is and how it'll affect people locally. Said it gave the department funding for the squad and some other stuff. Did you know they bought some armored vehicle?"

"My contact mentioned something about that," Jackson said. "Can I see the story?"

Ray nodded and clicked away on the laptop before sliding it across the table. Jackson skimmed the article.

The initiative offered a huge influx of money to any law enforcement agency within the state willing to combat what the administration perceived to be as a "spike" in drug-related crime. For Hopewell County that had meant the new Vice Squad and a revamping of their SWAT team. One sentence in particular caught Jackson's attention:

Both the SWAT Team and newly-formed Vice Squad will be provided both special training and tactical weapons and equipment by VigilOne, a private military contractor headquartered in Charleston.

Jackson was familiar with private military contractors from his tours abroad—particularly Iraq. In his experience, on their best days, they were soldiers-for-hire that got paid twice as much for half the danger. On their worst days, they were goons with no real rules to hold them in check.

"Do you have a piece of paper handy?" Jackson asked.

"Yeah, hold on," Ray said, "I've been jotting notes on this pad of paper."

Ray tore off a piece and slid it over to Jackson. Jackson noted the private military contractor and then Googled them. The website hardly looked like that of a company that loaned out mercenaries and military-grade equipment. In fact, it looked like any other standard corporate website. Stock images of people at an office working together. An engineer in a lab coat. Two men watching a bank of television screens with headsets on. Throughout it all were generic business buzz-phrases like *Solutions For a Global Future* and *Meeting Real Demands in Realtime*. Jackson closed out of the window. He wasn't going to find anything useful there.

Fraggie came through the front door with a large sack of rice under each arm. Ray immediately stood with hands out.

"Can I help you there?" he asked.

"I'm good, bud," Fraggie said. "Just got to put these away. We keep the extra supplies down here."

Ray and Jackson looked at each other, wondering what kind of stockpile of rice deemed two 20 lb. bags "extra". They heard two dull thuds followed by a door shutting before Fraggie came back out.

"Hey, Fraggie, who did you work for overseas with the security contract work?" Jackson asked.

"Endure," Fraggie answered. "Endure Security Services. Why?"

"This article here says the SWAT Team and Vice Squad of the Hopewell County Sheriff's Office were trained and supplied by a contractor called VigilOne. Have you ever heard of them?"

"Heard of, sure. There's only so many companies out there. But we never worked with 'em or nothin' like that."

"Do you have any idea how they work? When I was in-country some of these companies were known to be bad news."

"Nah, I never heard anythin' like that. Din' hear one thing one way or the other. Sorry."

Jackson nodded as Fraggie headed out the door. He turned back to Ray.

"What about the Vice Squad, specifically?" Jackson asked. "Did you find anything on them? My contact said the detectives that make up the squad had a bunch of red flags in their files."

"There were a couple stories like that," Ray said. "I mean those weren't the main story. They were about big drug busts that went down. But when I read them, there were people in it saying how they didn't do stuff and were innocent. Stuff like that."

"What do you mean? Like give me an example."

Ray reached over and took the laptop, typing away for a minute. He slid it back over to Jackson.

"Like there," Ray said. "This guy crashed his car because he OD'd behind the wheel. Heroin. The crash wasn't bad and the paramedics took him to the hospital, but that Vice Squad searched his house on reports he was dealing and found two bricks in his apartment. His folks say in that story, though, that he may have used, but there was no way he was a dealer. They said their son even had to ask for money and sometimes took things from them and pawned it."

Jackson read the article quietly to himself. It was as Ray described. The parents' names were Wyatt and Sophia Anderson. Their kid was Hunter. Jackson wrote the names down on his sheet of paper.

"What are you thinking?" Ray asked.

"I'm thinking if they tried to push stuff on Bobbie, they've done it to others," Jackson said. "Maybe this family knows more than we do."

"But why would these cops do all this?"

Jackson leaned back in his chair, thinking.

"That's a good question," he said. "My contact said their arrest numbers are big. They could do half as much and still be pacing the rest of the department in busts."

Ray frowned at Jackson's answer and the two fell quiet. Jackson continued to think. It really was a good question. Unless they simply got off on locking people up on trumped-up charges – which he supposed was possible – there was something else at play here.

Figuring out what, though, was the key.

36

As the sun set over Rion, the number of people in the Sheriff's Office headquarters had thinned out considerably. Being a Saturday, the place was less crowded than usual anyways, but now there were only a couple deputies along with Starcher, Sayre, and a sergeant manning the front desk.

Starcher had been in most of the day—only leaving to take a generous two-hour lunch break—posted up at his desk in the Vice corner of the office. Anyone who asked was told he was there because Vice was running a bust near the county line. His real mission, though, was to keep an eye on Sayre.

Sayre had returned to the office after talking to Amelia Westfall and his subsequent run-in with Detective Franko, shutting himself in the workspace he'd requisitioned and closing the decades-old blinds that dropped down over the windowed portions of the walls. After his run-in with Franko, he was ever more suspicious about prying eyes.

He began to look more into the background of Detectives Ronnie Franko and Arsen Bragg. The story they'd laid out had been smooth. Almost perfect, even. That made Sayre wonder if this was the first time they'd covered something up, and he wanted to see how many other suspicious incidents they had on their record.

He was scrolling over a file on Franko when his phone began to buzz on the desk. It was his boss back in Charleston, Captain Smith, calling.

"Cap," Sayre greeted. "Thanks for getting back to me."

"You said you had a problem," Smith said. "What is it?"

The Captain's tone was tense and agitated. Sayre knew him to be a levelheaded person, even when Sayre had rubbed him the wrong way, making any fluctuations in his mood unusual.

"The boy who was shot, Mason Westfall," Sayre said. "I interviewed the mother and noticed something off. I think there might be more to this shooting than the officers involved are letting on, sir."

"Jesus Christ, Sayre," Smith said. "Is this why I'm catching shit over here?"

"Sir, Westfall was – wait, what? What do you mean?"

"I just got called on a Saturday, a *Saturday*, by the Director of Field Operations asking what sort of shit you were stirring up in Rion. Do you know what it takes for a Lieutenant Colonel to call you up and chew you out on a weekend?"

"Sir, but I never—"

"Never what? What exactly is going on up there?"

"Sir, just listen. I have evidence suggesting the detectives involved in the shooting are lying. They said Mason Westfall was shot about thirty feet away, and that after he was down they kicked the gun out of his hand. Mason Westfall is – was – left-handed, but the gun was lying near his right. His left hand was tucked up underneath his body."

"Lieutenant—"

"And the gunshot wound to Mason Westfall had tattooing around it. Tattooing from a shot that was supposedly fired thirty feet away. That's not me saying that. That's the medical examiner's official report."

"And?" Smith asked.

"And what?" Sayre said. "They lied about the whole shooting. The whole thing is fucked."

"Are you fucking kidding me, Sayre? This is what I'm getting my ass chewed out for? You don't have two officers lying, you have two discrepancies you haven't fully looked at. Hell, it's not even circumstantial."

"Sir, why would—"

"No," Smith said. "Sir, nothing. Do you understand they want me to pull you off the case entirely? *Put his ass in a car tonight.* That's the Director's words, twenty minutes ago."

"But you talked him back, right?" Sayre asked.

"I talked him out of taking you out of town. But listen, you are observation-only. You sign off on *their* investigation, and then you get your ass back to Charleston."

"Sir, if I could—"

"It's either that, or you're in the car, driving back tonight. Your choice."

"I'm telling you there is something profoundly fucked up here. And if you let them, these guys will sweep it under the rug."

"Even if you were right, which you're not, what do you want me to do? Let you open up an investigation on the whole county sheriff's office? Because that's what you're getting at here. You do realize what you're alleging, right? That the whole department is complicit in some cover up."

Sayre gripped his cell phone so hard, he thought he might break it. His other hand, no cell phone in the way, was balled up in a fist.

"With all due respect, sir," Sayre said, "I'm out here to investigate this shooting. It's literally my fucking job. I'm telling you something stinks on this one and you're pulling the rug out from under me."

"Listen to me," Smith said. "It *will be* your literal fucking job if you don't stop rocking the boat out there."

"Sir, think about it. I haven't said anything to anyone. How do you already know about this? Someone is trying to shut this down."

"And if it's someone over my head, then shut down it's going to get. Shit rolls downhill, Colt. You're a little fucking old for me to have to explain that to you."

"What if Mason Westfall didn't shoot anyone? What if we've got two dead innocent kids?"

"I'm done with it, Sayre. No more, you understand me? Now, you figure out if you're going to play nice up there or come back to Charleston. Good night, lieutenant."

The line went dead. Sayre held the phone in his hand, talking himself back from throwing it across the office. He dropped it onto the desk and paced the room trying to expel his rage. It didn't work. He came around the desk and kicked the rolling chair into the door.

"Fuck!" he yelled.

Outside, the noise caught the attention of the few people still there. Even the sergeant at the front desk poked his head around the corner to see what had happened. Starcher chuckled as he picked up his phone and punched in a number. An irritated voice picked up on the other end.

"You better be calling with solutions and not more problems," Lane Wolfe said.

"I assume you did something, because that Sayre fella from State is throwin' one hell of a hissy fit," Starcher said.

"So is he handled?" Wolfe asked.

"I'd say so."

"I don't think I need to remind you that was just one loose end. You've still got a lot of fucking work to do."

"And we're on it."

"Where are your boys? The two that started all this shit?"

"Bragg is at home laying low. And Franko—"

Starcher looked at his watch as he finished answering Wolfe.

"—Franko should be tying up another one of those loose ends right about now."

37

Amelia sat on the couch in the living room of the house she now lived in alone. Her husband, dead from cancer twelve years ago, and now her son, shot and killed when he was just nineteen, were gone. She'd always known Mason would leave eventually, and maybe to a point she'd even prepared herself for it—but not like this.

She sat there, her slight frame sinking into the crevasse between two oversized couch cushions. The television was on, but she wasn't watching it. She stared blankly at her cup of tea on the coffee table as her mind wandered. She took herself on a torturous ride, replaying everything that had happened the last two days, wondering what others must think of her now. Amelia Westfall, mother of a dead drug dealer.

Yes, in her heart, she knew that wasn't true, but she also knew it didn't much matter. People were going to think whatever they wanted. Right now they thought her dead boy meant one less criminal out there prowling their country roads.

The television was white noise, voices in the background to trick herself out of feeling so alone. A group of friends talking at a bar on some nameless sitcom. Jokes followed by laughter followed by more jokes. She had it up so loud she hadn't heard the two men enter her house.

Dressed in all black with ski masks, they approached her in the living room from opposite sides, leaving her nowhere to run. A flicker of movement took Amelia out of her trance and she looked up at one of the menacing figures. She went to scream but the man's large hand grabbed her mouth and squeezed it, muffling her. With the same hand he stood her up and moved her away from the couch before pressing her head against the wall.

With his other hand, the man unholstered a pistol and brought it up to Amelia's face, making sure she could see it. She tried to scream again but the man pressed even harder against her mouth. Amelia felt as though the man might break her jaw in his grip.

"You like to fucking talk, don't you?" the man said.

Amelia tried to shake her head but couldn't.

"Mm mm," she managed to mumble.

"Could've fooled me," the man said. "You were talking with the police again, weren't you? That state cop today."

Amelia didn't say anything. Her body was trembling as she looked into the man's eyes. They were black pits. Not angry so much as dead. Lifeless. As if this was nothing to him. That only made her more terrified.

The man slid his hand off her mouth and grabbed the back of her neck.

"It's okay, you didn't know," he said, his voice gentler now. "You didn't know you weren't supposed to talk. You thought you were doing the right thing."

The man rubbed the back of her head gently. Amelia felt a wave of nausea come over her.

"It's okay, I get it," he said. "I really do."

But in a flash, the man's hand came around her throat and gripped it so hard Amelia choked. He raised the gun and pressed the barrel against her temple. Tears formed at the corners of her eyes.

"But I am here to tell you," the man growled, "that you are wrong. Dead fucking wrong. You're going to shut the fuck up and stop fucking talking."

The other man turned the volume up on the TV and then walked to a window facing the street, peeking out through the curtains.

The man with Amelia pulled the hammer back on his pistol. She began to hyperventilate.

The man shook her by her neck.

"Calm the fuck down," he ordered. "Now!"

Amelia tried desperately to reign herself in. Her breathing slowed just enough that she could understand the man as he spoke in a low tone.

"I am going make this so clear that even a dumb fucking cunt like you understands," he said. "If you talk to the cops again, we will come back here, and we will fuck you and kill you."

Amelia let out something between a shriek and a whine.

"Say it," the man said. "Say what I told you so I know you understand. If you talk to the cops…"

Amelia's voice was shaky.

"If I-I talk to th-the c-c-cops," she said.

"We will fuck you and kill you," the man said.

Amelia sobbed. The man used the hand around her throat to pin her even closer to the wall.

"We. Will. Fuck. You. And. Kill. You," he repeated.

"W-w-we will f-f-fuck you and k-kill y-you," Amelia said sobbing.

The man took his hand off her throat and replaced it with his forearm. Using his free hand, he pulled the slide back on his gun. The pistol dispensed a 9mm round like some sort of twisted PEZ dispenser.

"Open your mouth," the man ordered.

Amelia pursed her lips together and shook her head fervently.

The man grabbed her by the throat again and banged her head against the wall.

"Open your fucking mouth!" he barked.

Amelia slowly did as she was told. The man shoved the bullet into her mouth and then shut it.

"If I have to come back here," he said, "I'll put another fucking one in your mouth. But next time I'll just pull the fucking trigger."

Tears trickled down Amelia's face as she closed her eyes and whimpered. The man grabbed her by the back of her neck again and threw her onto the ground. Her body hit two chairs around her dining room table and she curled into a ball trying to protect herself. The other man left the front window and joined his partner standing over her. He nodded toward the back door. The one that had thrown Amelia took his boot and used it to tilt Amelia's face upwards until she was looking at him.

"Don't you even think about getting up until we're gone," he said.

The two men walked to the back door and left, leaving the door open behind them.

As he left Amelia Westfall's backyard, Ronnie Franko removed his ski mask and pulled out his phone. Starcher picked up almost immediately.

"It's done," Franko said.

38

B y noon the next day, Jackson had found just about all he felt he could online related to Bobbie's case, the Hopewell County Sheriff's Office, its Vice Squad, VigilOne, and Colton Sayre. He'd even found out more about Wyatt and Sophia Anderson and their son, Hunter.

Hunter Anderson had, in fact, been arrested by the Hopewell County Vice Squad, but in all the articles he'd found, Sophia and Wyatt had been vocal defenders of their son, proclaiming the boy's innocence to anyone who'd listen. Curious to hear what they had to say for themselves, Jackson had Googled them and found a phone number.

He knew he was due to check in with Bailey, but he wanted to try and call the Andersons first. After a few rings it went to an answering machine.

Jackson hung up. He looked again at the listing he'd found. It was a Martinsburg address, one of the larger towns in the eastern panhandle of the state. They weren't too far away, but showing up unannounced was risky. Mulling what to do, he called Special Agent Bailey instead.

"Bailey," she greeted.

"It's me," Jackson said.

"You managed to go 24 hours without any more shootouts it sounds like," Bailey said.

"It's a nice change of pace. You find anything else out?"

"Yeah, I've got some info on that Narcotics Rehabilitation and Intervention Program. It's basically a program open to first-time offenders. Offers them the poor man's version of rehab."

"From what I understand, there's nothing poor about what they charge. The girl here said they get you paying forever with interest charges."

"That may be, but it's not illegal for a business. Credit card companies are largely the same."

"Business? You mean this program isn't run by the government?"

"It's overseen by the government, but it's privately-owned under the umbrella of the privately-owned prisons out there,"

"I didn't know the prisons here were privately owned."

"Most aren't, but a new one was built to address overcrowding. This New War on Drugs initiative has led to a spike in incarcerations. The state didn't have money to build or operate the prison, especially after giving millions to local police departments, so they contracted the work out. This NRIP program was a part of that."

"Contracted out to who? Or what?"

"Hold on, I have it here."

Jackson could hear papers shuffling on the other end of the line.

"VigilOne Services, Inc.," Bailey said.

"Son of a bitch," Jackson said.

"What?" Bailey asked.

"I've been doing some information gathering of my own. VigilOne is the same company that armed and trained the Hopewell County Sheriff's Vice Squad, SWAT team, and, from what I read, a dozen other counties' special units created as a result of this thing with the governor. It's even become their main revenue stream in recent years and they're a multi-billion dollar private military corporation."

"Yes, it sounds like they're very much in the business of law and order out there."

"The question is, who are they really serving and protecting?"

"What do you mean?"

"Bobbie admitted him and his friends had weed, but swore the meth wasn't theirs. Meth is a big step up in terms of charges. And now you've got VigilOne, the company profiting from incarcerating these guys, tied to the police departments making the busts."

Bailey sighed.

"I don't know, Jackson," she said. "Make sure you're not seeing a boogeyman where there isn't one."

"You can't be so gung-ho blue that you think it's impossible for these guys to be dirty," Jackson said.

"Come on, Jackson," Bailey said. "You're not naive. You know how murky this shit is. Maybe it's fucked up, but that doesn't make it illegal."

"People don't plant drugs on others and then cover up a bad shooting for the hell of it, Bailey. There's a reason everything went down wrong that night. And it's a big enough reason someone tried to kill Bobbie before he could turn himself in."

"And sometimes bad things just happen to good people."

"That's a pretty pessimistic attitude for someone in the business of serving justice."

Bailey took a deep breath and exhaled. "I don't know what to tell you, Jackson. It is what it is. Anyway, I also found some more on your Lieutenant Sayre."

"I did some digging, too," Jackson said. "He made a name for himself in a shootout with a couple of heavily-armed meth cooks on the Ohio border."

"That's right," Bailey said. "After I got off with you I realized the name sounded familiar. He and his partner went looking for an informant that was MIA. Came up on a shack with three strung out meth heads armed to the teeth. His partner was shot and killed, but he went in without backup anyway. Saved the informant's life."

"Yeah. The articles I read were praising him for it all. He won some fancy award."

"The Superintendent's Award, yeah. It would explain why he's bounced around inside the department out there like I heard. Maybe he's hard to work with, but no one's going to fire a hero cop."

"Still doesn't answer whether or not he can be trusted."

"I guess that's for you to figure out."

Jackson fell quiet now. Bailey felt like she could hear his mind working the calculus of that problem.

"Are you good?" she asked.

"Yeah, I'm good," Jackson said. "I'll call if I need anything else. Thanks for the info."

"Anytime," Bailey said.

He ended the call and put his phone away. He was staring at the ground, thinking, when a gunshot rang out. Instinctively, Jackson reached for his pistol, but as he looked up, he saw Maggie, Fraggie, Ray, and Bobbie laughing. Maggie had placed a pumpkin on a fence post and was showing Bobbie how to shoot with her hunting rifle. Bobbie had missed horribly and clipped a tree branch several feet above. The branch fell and took out the gourd anyway.

Fraggie, seeing Jackson was off the phone, started walking over to him.

"Real bona-fide killer," Bear said, walking up behind him.

Jackson snorted.

"Yeah," he said. "Where's Mia?"

"Laying down in the smokehouse," Bear said.

"How's she doing?" Jackson asked.

"Sick to her stomach. Says she's got a headache and can't stop shaking."

"Withdrawal's no joke."

"Don't I know it. But the only cure is time and layin' off the shit. Maybe one good thing can come from all this."

"Still, it's going to get worse before it gets better."

Bear nodded in agreement as he posted up against his Suburban.

"What'd your cop friend have to say?" he asked.

"Nothing good," Jackson said. "This VigilOne company has their hand in a lot of the stuff out here. It's sketchy, but it might not be illegal. In which case, it doesn't really help us."

Fraggie came up spitting out a sunflower seed she'd been working on.

"This VigilOne company again, huh?," she said. "I still know some of the guys I worked with. I can see if they know anythin' more than I do."

"That might help, yeah," Jackson said. "In the meantime, I think I'm going to roll over to this Anderson family. See if I can talk to them."

"You sure that's a good idea?" Fraggie asked. "We don' know who's all lookin' for you."

Jackson climbed down from atop the Suburban and slid his phone into his pocket.

"I've got to risk it," he said. "We need to make a move."

"You want me to come along? Back you up?" Bear asked.

Jackson shook his head.

"The fewer of us out there the better," he said. "You stay here, keep an eye on everyone."

Fraggie took out her keys and tossed them to Jackson. He caught them, a confused look on his face.

"They might be lookin' for your truck," Fraggie said. "They won' be lookin' for mine."

39

Lieutenant Sayre started out taking the same route through Rion toward the Sheriff's Office headquarters he'd taken every other day, but when he got to the turn for the parking lot, he kept driving. Instead, he followed the main road across the river to the West and back to Mrs. Westfall's home just on the edge of town.

He'd spent the last twelve hours debating whether to pack up and return to Charleston or stay on as a rubber stamp to Hopewell County's investigation. Ultimately, he'd decided he was going to do neither. Sayre couldn't shake the idea that someone had gone to his superiors to stop him before he could dig further into what was going on. The last person he'd talked to before his boss called to chew him out was Franko. If Franko was trying to stop him, it probably meant the Vice Squad as a whole was trying to, as well. They clearly hadn't wanted him talking any more to Mrs. Westfall—so that's exactly what he was going to do.

When he got to Mrs. Westfall's block, he drove past and circled back, looking for anyone watching the house or tailing him. He went down one block and doubled back, coming around to the Westfall's street from the opposite side. From the intersection, he didn't see any unmarked police cars or the black trucks the Vice Squad used.

Sayre turned on the street and drove down it slowly, looking into each curbside car for anyone sitting and watching. When he got to the end of the street, he circled back the opposite way and came back from the other side. It looked like he was in the clear.

He drove up to the house and pulled all the way into the driveway, obscuring the view of his car as much as he could from the road. Hopping out, Sayre walked around to the front door and knocked. When no one answered, he knocked again. The house was still and quiet. He peeked through the adjacent windows. Nothing. After knocking one more time, he cupped his hands to the door's window to peer inside. Sayre could see straight down the hall to the back of the house. The back door was partially open.

Sayre followed the driveway to the back of the house. Attached to it was a modest deck with wood stairs leading down to the yard. At the top of those stairs was the open back door. He jogged up the stairs and knocked on the open door, leaning his head in.

"Mrs. Westfall," he called, "are you home?"

No answer. He pushed the door open more and it whined with reluctance. He leaned further in.

"Mrs. Westfall? Amelia? It's me, Lieutenant Sayre." he said louder. "Are you in here?"

From his vantage point, the house looked in order. The only thing out of place was the open back door. That, and no one answering him.

"Mrs. Westfall? Or anyone in here? If you can hear me, it's Lieutenant Sayre. Your back door is open here. I'm just coming inside."

Sayre's instincts and police training told him to call for back up and let a dispatcher know he was entering the house, but the backup that would arrive would be the sheriff's deputies. He was better off on his own.

He slid his standard-issue Smith & Wesson Model 4506 pistol from its holster and leveled it at the floor. "Mrs. Westfall? Lieutenant Sayre, West Virginia State Police."

Stepping off the kitchen, he moved toward the living room and front den. Still nothing. Anyone on the first floor who wasn't deaf would've certainly heard him by now. He moved toward the stairs he remembered seeing near the front door. At the base of them, he shouted up to the second floor.

"Mrs. Westfall? Are you upstairs? It's Lieutenant Sayre."

No answer. Something wasn't right. He started to treat the situation as such.

"West Virginia State Police," Sayre barked. "Anyone up there, come to the stairs now, make yourself known."

No response. He began moving up the stairs, repeating the same orders.

The top of the stairs connected to a narrow hallway with doors on either side. The door at the far end opened onto what he thought must be the main bedroom. The door just before that, though, was open only a crack. A light was on.

Sayre approached slowly, again announcing his presence.

He moved down the hall, stopping just short of the cracked door. From what he could make out through the slight space between the door and its frame, it looked like a bathroom. He leaned forward and listened closely. Water droplets dripped from somewhere and splashed one by one into a pool of something.

Sayre knocked on the door.

"State Police," he said again. "Anyone in there?"

Silence. With his gun out, Sayre pushed the door open wider. When he saw the blood on the floor, he kicked the door all the way open.

Amelia Westfall lay in the bathtub, submerged in water turned red by her own blood. A bloody razor blade teetered on the edge by her hand.

"Oh god," Sayre said.

He dropped to his knees and pulled her arms out of the bloody water. Both wrists had a number of lacerations on them, each one deeper than the cut next to it. Sayre grabbed a towel off the rack and squeezed it against both wrists as he pulled out his phone and dialed 911. When the operator picked up, he cut her off, immediately giving her information.

"This is First Lieutenant Colton Sayre, West Virginia State Police. I need an RA to 642 Stoney Lane for a suicide attempt. Multiple wrist lacerations. Severe blood loss."

"Okay, sir," the operator said, "I'm dispatching now. Apply pressure at the point of bleeding. Fire and rescue will be there as soon as possible."

"How soon?" Sayre asked.

"Maybe fifteen minutes, sir."

The amount of time hit Sayre like someone punched him in the chest. He remembered now most small towns like this relied on volunteer departments. In some cases, first responders had to go get the rescue vehicles before they could even start toward where they were needed.

"Not enough time," Sayre said.

The operator told him something about them doing the best they could, but he wasn't listening. He needed to move, and he needed something to keep pressure on the wounds. He grabbed another towel and, with his knife, cut it into strips. He wrapped a strip around each wrist where the cuts were, then pulled out his handcuffs and cuffed them over the towels to hold them in place and hopefully apply some pressure.

Sayre reached into the tub and picked Amelia up. Her naked body was wet and lifeless, like a slippery sack of meat and bones. He held his phone to his ear with his shoulder as he wrapped a third towel around her and carried her down the stairs.

"I'm taking her myself," Sayre said. "Where is the closest hospital?"

"The nearest hospital to you is Hopewell Memorial," the operator said. "It's across town behind the big shopping center."

"Okay, stay on the line. I need you to get me there."

Sayre carried Amelia Westfall's limp body out to his car. He slid her into the back and then hopped into the driver's seat, hitting his lights and siren as he backed out of the driveway.

The back wheels of the upgraded Chevy Impala screeched as it tore down the quiet residential street. Sayre got back to the main road, taking the turn at speed and just barely missing a car coming the other way.

"Okay, I'm eastbound on Highway 50, crossing over the river now," he said.

"You're going to go through town and out the other side. Stay on

50," the operator said. "I've notified surrounding units. Two sheriff's deputies are expecting you in town, they'll block traffic and escort you to the hospital."

Sayre's stomach churned at the thought of the sheriff's office. The truth was he didn't trust anyone there right now, but he had to believe these responding deputies were genuinely there to help.

"Got it," Sayre said. "I need you to alert Hopewell Memorial's ER I'm coming in with a suicide attempt. Like I said, multiple lacerations to both wrists. They're going to need whatever kind of trauma team they have ready."

"I'll pass that information along," the operator said. "Do you have any information on the victim?"

"White, female, middle-aged, maybe 40's. Didn't check for vitals. She's unconscious."

"Copy. I'll notify the hospital. Thank you, sir."

Sayre ended the call. As he got into town, he kept his speed up. He was just passing a drugstore when two Hopewell County Sheriff police cruisers pulled out in front of him. Their lights and sirens adding to his, they quickly accelerated taking turns blocking each intersection that came up. Sayre took a deep breath in and exhaled.

The three cars snaked their way through what little traffic the town had and continued on the mile or so to the hospital. When they got to the entrance for the ER, the two sheriff's deputies pulled over. Sayre sped through and drove into the ambulance bay. Before he was out of his door, a team of people in scrubs and face masks were wheeling a stretcher toward the car.

"Back door," Sayre said.

A nurse opened the door and grabbed Amelia under her shoulders. Sayre ran to the other side and lifted her legs as the nurse pulled Amelia out. The team slid her onto the stretcher and wheeled her through a pair of automatic doors. Sayre began to follow before the nurse that had pulled Amelia out stepped in front of him and stopped him with a hand to his chest.

"We've got it from here, sir," she said.

She patted Sayre on the chest and lingered a moment, acknowledging his effort, before jogging inside and rejoining the team of doctors. Sayre leaned on the open back door of his car, catching his breath. Amelia's blood had brushed drag marks across the seat. He couldn't be sure how much, but he knew it was a lot. Suddenly, he was painfully aware of how much blood she must've lost between his car and the bathroom.

He placed his hands on his knees and doubled over, panting. Someone in scrubs came out and offered him water, but he didn't pay attention. His mind was racing as fast as his car had been just moments ago. Dozens of questions swirled around in his head, but one more so than any other.

What the hell had happened?

40

J ackson pulled up to Wyatt and Sophia Anderson's home just a little after four that afternoon. The house was a quaint ranch-style near the end of a dead-end street, painted white with a maroon door and shutters. In front of it, a charming yard was centered around a massive oak tree that had already lost most of its leaves. Jackson parked at the curb and walked up to the front door.

Before he could knock, a woman opened the door and was startled to see him there. She chuckled as she doubled over and breathed a sigh of relief.

"I'm sorry, I didn't mean to scare you, ma'am," Jackson said.

"That's quite alright," the woman said, "I was just looking for the mail. What can I do for you?"

The woman was petite, almost frail looking, with cotton-white hair and warm amber eyes that narrowed as she smiled.

"Are you Mrs. Anderson? Mrs. Sophia Anderson?" Jackson asked.

Now the woman's smile faded.

"Last time I checked," she said. "What's this about?"

"My name is Jackson. Jackson Clay. I was wondering if I could talk to you about your son."

Sophia scowled.

"What are you?" she asked. "Police? A reporter?"

"No, ma'am," Jackson said. "I just wondered if you could help me understand a few things."

"Understand this, Mr. Clay," Sophia said. "The matter of my boy is not something to satisfy your curiosity. Please leave our family be."

"Mrs. Anderson, from what I understand, you believe the police or someone set your son up. I believe the same thing is happening again to another young man, and I'm trying to stop it."

"To someone here? In Martinsburg? My boy didn't live here; he lived—"

"In Rion. Arrested by the Hopewell County Sheriff's Office. Specifically, the Vice Squad. Like I said, ma'am, I think it's happening to someone else."

Sophia's expression softened. She opened the door and stepped back.

"Come in here," she said.

Sophia led Jackson into a cozy living area. A recliner and a sofa faced a television that had to be about thirty years old. An older man lay in the recliner, his spotted hands grasping the suspenders that extended over his beer belly. His hair—and impressive mustache--was as cotton-white as Sophia's, though much shorter.

"Wyatt, sit up, we have company," Sophia said. "This is Jackson Clay. He thinks some funny business happened with Hunter's arrest and is happening again with another boy."

Wyatt struggled to reach for the lever on the recliner. When he did grab it, the chair lurched forward, catapulting the man into an upright position. The movement of the chair was jerky and violent, but Wyatt seemed to be hardly bothered by it.

"Can I get you something to drink, dear?" Sophia asked Jackson. "Perhaps coffee or tea?"

"I'm okay, thank you," Jackson said.

"She brews a helluva sweet tea," Wyatt said, extending his hand from the recliner. "Wyatt Anderson."

Jackson shook his hand and returned the greeting. Sophia must've ignored Jackson or not heard him, because she stepped into the kitchen just long enough to fill the tea kettle and put it on the stove.

"I'm really okay, Mrs. Anderson," Jackson said. "I don't want to take too much of your time."

"Nonsense. We love to talk about Hunter. Just so long as it's the right people," Sophia said.

"Not those bastards looking to lock him up and throw away the key," Wyatt said.

Jackson sat down slowly on the couch and took off his hat.

"I'm not with the police, Mr. Anderson," he said. "Just a friend of someone in trouble."

"Do we know them?" Wyatt asked.

"I'd rather not say. Just easier for everyone," Jackson answered.

Wyatt gave Jackson a look like he didn't understand, but shrugged his shoulders and laid back in the chair.

"That's alright, dear," Sophia said. "You tell us whatever you feel comfortable with."

"Actually, I wanted to ask more about Hunter," Jackson said. "From what I understand, you believe someone planted the drugs in his apartment. Do you also think something funny happened with the car accident?"

"I don't think so," Sophia said. "Hunter is a wonderful boy, but he has his problems. He was working construction, paid under the table by his boss. I said I didn't like it, but he was earning twice as much as he could at a real job. But one day he got hurt. There was no worker's comp or anything for him. His boss told him don't even say it was at his job site. So, Hunter went to a walk-in clinic and lied and said he hurt himself doing yard work. The doctor there basically gave him a prescription for Vicodin and sent him on his way."

"You're saying he developed an addiction?"

"Yes, dear. At first just to painkillers like that. But then he eventually found that awful stuff to be easier to get a hold of, I guess."

"Heroin?"

"Yes. Ugh, just the thought. It makes me want to—"

Sophia shook her head, fighting back the tears welling in her eyes.

"Anyway, we tried to get him help several times," she said. "It just never happened."

Jackson nodded. He knew enough to know it was an all-too-common story, especially in blue collar communities like this one.

"So, then, if you don't mind me asking," Jackson said, "what makes you so sure the heroin in his apartment wasn't his?"

"Because we'd decided enough was enough," Wyatt said. "After the hospital, I went straight there and threw all that shit out. His pills, the heroin, everything. I even tossed all his beer and cigarettes."

"I assume you told the police this," Jackson said.

"I did. I told that sonofabitch Franko. He turns around and accuses me of making up the whole thing. Then tells me I should shut up if I want to stay out of jail. Says I could get locked up for destroying evidence or something like that. Goddamn bastard."

"So you didn't pursue it any further?"

"With who? About what? The man was a damn cop. The same cops that found the heroin in his apartment after. Literally. Him and that partner of his. Briggs or whatever."

"Bragg?"

"Yeah, that boy couldn't be a day older than Hunter. And for him and that asshole to do Hunter like that? I just couldn't believe it."

"You think they put the heroin there?"

"Who else would?"

"Someone looking to get Hunter in trouble, maybe? A dealer of his? Someone he might've thought was a friend? Was Hunter asked to testify against anyone?"

"No, nothing like that. They thought he was just another junkie. Treated him as much that way. They were going to charge him with a simple DUI before the heroin. Afterwards, everyone's walking around like they caught Tony Montana."

Jackson looked up at Wyatt. Something the man said sparked a thought in him.

"Detectives Franko and Bragg," he said. "Did you deal with them before they found the heroin in Hunter's apartment?"

"No," Wyatt said, "it had just been normal types of cops. You know like patrol cops. Uniform types and whatnot. Well, actually, there was another guy that wasn't in uniform. Wore a suit. Older guy, sort of fat and bald. The officers were talking to us outside Hunter's hospital room when the big guy waved them over and they started talking amongst themselves."

Jackson wondered who this other guy might be. Bailey mentioned Franko and Bragg and the rest of the Vice Squad had a superior officer, Lieutenant Red Starcher. Asking Wyatt and Sophia to give him a moment, he pulled out his phone and Googled the name. When a photo popped up, he held it up for Wyatt to see.

"Hot damn, yeah," Wyatt said. "Yeah, that's the guy. Who is he?"

"Franko and Bragg's boss," Jackson said, putting away his phone. "He runs the Vice Squad they're on."

"You think he and Franko and Bragg did some funny business?" Wyatt asked.

"I don't know. But I promise you, Mr. Anderson, I'm going to find out."

"If that sonofabitch set up my boy, you leave me and him alone in a room and give me five minutes."

Jackson stood up to leave.

"I'll keep that in mind, Mr. Anderson," he said. "I really should get going. Thank you both for letting me come talk to you. I appreciate it."

"Oh, it was our pleasure dear," Sophia said, standing with him. "Here, I'll walk you out."

Jackson nodded. He turned and waved at Wyatt, still reclining in his chair.

"It's that Bobbie Casto, boy, isn't it?" Wyatt said.

"I'm sorry?" Jackson asked.

"Your friend, the one you're helping," Wyatt said. "It's that one on the news, isn't it? That Bobbie Casto?"

"Like I said, Mr. Anderson, I'd rather n—"

"Okay, okay. You'd rather not say."

Jackson waited for him to say something else. When the silence lingered, Jackson waved and continued on toward the front door. He was almost out of the room when Wyatt spoke again.

"If they're trying to do that boy wrong like they did mine, you put a stop to all that. You stop them anyway you know how. You hear me?"

Jackson pinched the bill of his ballcap and tugged it up and down.

"Yes, sir," he said.

He thanked Sophia again by the front door and walked out to Fraggie's truck. The sun was dipping below the horizon, painting what few clouds there were in a brilliant golden-orange light.

Jackson fired up the truck. This whole time he knew there was something wrong about this Sheriff's Office Vice Squad, but he couldn't figure out why or what they were doing. Wyatt and Sophia Anderson gave him a theory. Their son's accident had been a routine DUI. Hunter might've not even served any jail time. The Vice Squad came snooping around and, all of a sudden, it was a big narcotics case. Special Agent Bailey had told him that the Vice Squad accounted for two-thirds of all the department's arrests. That'd be big business if each arrested individual doubled as a customer.

He looked down at the navigation screen. When Jackson had arrived at the Anderson house, he'd plugged in the coordinates to return to the farm – Fraggie and Maggie preferring not to have a street address. He canceled that now, and set directions for Rion.

41

Lieutenant Sayre sat in the ER waiting room, anticipating news on Amelia Westfall. He looked down at his hands—checking again he'd gotten all the blood off of them—before placing his head in them, then slowly combed his hands through his hair as he sighed.

He replayed everything over in his head, wondering if he could've gotten to her faster. What if he hadn't searched the house so slowly? What if he'd noticed the back door faster? Hell, what if he hadn't wasted half the day deciding what to do next?

His head was back and his eyes were closed, his mind prodding him with these questions when a nurse finally called him. Sayre popped out of the plastic chair and raised a hand, indicating he'd heard her. She motioned to the front desk and they buzzed the two of them back.

"Mrs. Westfall is in critical condition, but we've managed to stabilize her," the nurse said. "The attending doctor is in Mrs. Westfall's room if you'd like to speak with her."

"I would," Sayre said.

The nurse escorted Sayre to an ER room and pulled back a pale green curtain. A tall, thin woman with black hair stood over Mrs. Westfall, her hands tucked into a white doctor's coat.

When she saw Lieutenant Sayre, she pulled out one hand and extended it toward him.

"Hello. Dr. Avery Taylor," she greeted.

"Nice to meet you. Lieutenant Colton Sayre, West Virginia State Police," he said.

"Nice to meet you, too," Dr. Taylor said. "Usually it's someone from the Sheriff's Office I see in here."

"I'm assisting on a case," Sayre said. "I was looking to follow up with Mrs. Westfall when I discovered her in her bathtub."

"Her wrists already lacerated, I assume."

"That's correct. I called for an RA, but when they said it'd take some time, I decided taking her myself would be faster."

"You probably saved her life with that. Another five minutes and she might be on a slab down the hall."

The nurse scowled at the doctor's bluntness. Sayre didn't seem to mind.

"Unfortunately, I don't know when you'll be able to talk to her," Dr. Taylor continued. "Rest is key now. She lost a lot of blood. We went through nearly three quarters of our bank of O-negative trying to stabilize her. A small hospital like ours doesn't have the luxury of carrying a lot."

"That's alright," Sayre said. "She can rest. There are other people that need to answer some questions now."

"Speaking of questions," Dr. Taylor said, "can I ask you something?"

"Shoot."

"You said you found her with her wrists cut in the bathtub. Did you notice evidence of any other attempts?"

"What do you mean?"

"Like a rope or a cord strung up somewhere? Some form of attempted hanging?"

"Not that I saw. To be honest, the house looked pretty normal before I got to the bathroom where I found her. Why do you ask?"

Dr. Taylor leaned over and pulled the sheet away from Mrs Westfall's chest. She pushed some wires to one side to make her neck visible.

"There's bruising here. Signs of trauma. Seeing as she attempted to take her own life, I thought perhaps she might've tried that first and failed. Or maybe decided to do something else for some reason."

"Like I said, I didn't see anything."

"Did she live with anyone? A husband or a boyfriend? Even a son, maybe? The bruising could also be indicative of someone choking her. We see it all too often, unfortunately. Domestic abuse."

Sayre was quiet and still, but his mind was running at a dizzying pace. No, no one she lived with was still alive. So, who would hurt her? He flashed back to Franko questioning why he was talking with Mrs. Westfall the day before. Maybe he'd sent someone to scare her into not talking. Or perhaps he'd done it himself. Sayre looked down at Amelia, lying there with her wrists bandaged and wires running all over her. Her arms and legs were strapped to the bed, standard procedure for anybody that had attempted to take their own life. If someone had tried to scare her, they'd gone too far.

"She lives alone now," Sayre said. "Her son and husband are dead. Her son was killed in that shooting on the highway overlook earlier this week."

"That's, well, that's too bad. I'll document it in my notes, but I suppose you're the investigator. I guess it's up to you ultimately to explain how the bruising got there," Dr. Taylor said.

"It is," Sayre agreed.

Dr. Taylor nodded and stepped out of the room. Sayre lingered a moment longer, looking at Amelia Westfall. Something—someone—had pushed her to this. Her wounds may be self-inflicted, but he was sure someone had tried to kill Mrs. Westfall just as someone had tried to kill Bobbie Casto at the courthouse. And the more he thought about it, the more those things were connected with the deaths of Mason Westfall and Emma Miller. He felt himself tense up with rage.

Everything felt distant as Sayre left the ER room and walked down the hall. Voices muffled and mixed together with the ambient sounds of the busy hospital. His vision pulsed in unison with his elevated heartbeat, his head the lid on a pressure cooker with no release. As he exited through the waiting room and felt the cool, fresh air envelop him, he was momentarily relieved.

But standing there, against his pickup, a cigarette dangling from his mouth, was Detective Franko. He watched hospital visitors and patients come and go with a smarmy look on his face. Sayre steeled himself and tried to walk past, ignoring the man. But when Franko saw him, Franko flashed the same sinister smile he'd shown Sayre every other time they'd met.

"How's it going, lieutenant?" Franko asked.

Sayre ignored him. He just wants a reaction, he told himself. Keep walking. Just keep—

"What's wrong, Romeo?" Franko said. "Juliet try to check out early on ya?"

In an instant, Sayre was around Franko's truck and charging toward him. Franko moved to meet him but Sayre was faster. He grabbed Franko by the lapels of his denim jacket and slammed him against the pickup.

"Say it again!" Sayre shouted. "What'd you do? Tell me you did it! Give me a fucking reason!"

"Get your fucking hands off of me!" Franko shouted back.

Two sheriff's deputies standing by the front door of the hospital dropped their coffees and rushed over. But before they could get there, Sayre cranked back and planted a fist into Franko's jaw. He cocked back again, raising his arm—only this time, one of the deputies caught it and used it to pry him off Franko. The other deputy stepped in and wrapped up Franko.

"Get off me!" Franko said. "Hit me again, pretty boy! See what happens!"

"Let me find out you did something! I pray you, just let me! Let me find out this was you! I'll fucking kill you myself!" Sayre said.

As the two deputies struggled to separate Franko and Sayre, another unmarked black pickup rolled up and screeched to a stop, flicking its emergency lights on.

Starcher hopped out of the driver's seat and hurried over.

"That's enough!" he barked.

Franko and Sayre kept trying to wiggle free from the deputies and get at each other. Starcher stepped between them and shoved Franko back.

"You! Take a walk," Starcher ordered. *"Now."*

Franko pulled up and let the deputy handling him push him away. Starcher turned to Sayre.

"And you—you were already given a warning, weren't you?," he said. "You're done now. You hear me? I'm calling Charleston and having you pulled. You're fucking gone."

Sayre brushed the deputy off him and stepped back. He walked backward toward the parking lot, glaring at Franko every step of the way. He brought a hand up to his mouth and brushed it. His hand came away bloody.

"Fuck all you hillbillies," Sayre growled.

He continued backing up, still facing all of them, until he got to his car. Then he got in, fired it up, and left.

SAYRE'S DRIVE back to his motel was a blur. Truthfully, he wouldn't have been able to tell anyone how he'd gotten there. In the early night, the panhandle of West Virginia was cast in a dark blue light. All Sayre saw, though, was red. The red of Mason Westfall's hoodie with a bullet hole in it. The red of the gunshot wound below Emma Miller's right eye. The red of the blood pooling across the courthouse plaza. The red of the water in Amelia Westfall's tub.

When he got to the motel, everything was dark except for one light overhead the main office door and his room, Room #1. Sayre plodded along the cement walkway, down the open-air corridor of motel doors . He was reaching for his key when a man's voice spoke from the darkness.

"Colton Sayre," it said.

Sayre's hand shifted from his pocket to his pistol. But as the stranger stepped into the light, Sayre didn't draw it.

It was the man from the courthouse. The one who had saved the boy and fled with him.

"We need to have a talk," Jackson Clay said.

PART IV

NO WITNESSES

42

L ieutenant Sayre studied Jackson. He couldn't see the top half of the man's face, his ball cap and hooded coat casting a shadow over it from the light overhead. The bottom half of his face, though, was expressionless.

"You wouldn't happen to have Mr. Casto with you, would you?" Sayre asked.

"No, and you won't see him until I'm sure he's safe," Jackson said.

"The shooter at the courthouse," Sayre said. "You think I'm involved with that?"

"Someone is."

"If you think it's me, you're not as smart as I think you are."

"Give me something else to believe, then."

Sayre went quiet, thinking—deciding—what to tell Jackson.

"When you and the lawyer first contacted me," Sayre said, "you said Casto wanted to tell his side of the story. That the story from the Sheriff's Office wasn't true."

"That's right. The whole thing was a bad stop. And a bad shoot," Jackson said.

"What if I told you I think I believe you?" Sayre asked.

"It'd be a start. What makes you believe me?"

Sayre told Jackson everything he had that was wrong about the shooting. The gun being found near Mason's non-dominant hand and the forensic evidence that didn't jive with Franko and Braggs' statements. Jackson stood quietly as he processed all the information. Sayre felt as though he could've been talking to a statue.

"Do you have copies of those files?" Jackson asked.

"Not on me, no," Sayre said. "They're back at the Sheriff's Office headquarters."

"We're going to need those files," Jackson said.

"Take them to trial like you wanted to. It would all have to be turned over for his defense," Sayre said.

"Assuming the files didn't disappear,"

"You're a rather paranoid man, aren't you?"

"Someone already set up a murder-for-hire on the kid. I don't think shredding some papers is out of the question to these people."

Sayre nodded, acknowledging his point.

"The files are in an office I took at the headquarters," he said. "But I don't know if I'm going to be able to get back in there after tonight."

"What do you mean?"

"Let's just say I may have bought myself a one-way ticket back to Charleston."

Jackson waited for Sayre to elaborate.

"I told my superiors there was something off with the case," Sayre said. "They warned me to play nice and not rock the boat. Someone high up wants this to go away quickly and quietly. That was twenty-four hours ago. Then, tonight, I punched Franko. In front of his boss, Starcher, no less. Starcher said he was going to get me sacked. I have every reason to believe he will."

"Where was this?" Jackson asked.

"Outside the hospital up the road," Sayre said.

"This just happened?"

"Yeah."

"So, you have no reason to believe they're at the headquarters right now."

Sayre snorted and smiled.

"Should we take one car or two?" he asked.

43

Jackson, in Fraggie's truck, followed Lieutenant Sayre to the Sheriff's Office. They rounded the courthouse plaza—the Sheriff's Office was attached to the back of the building—where they'd first laid eyes on each other shortly before Jimmy Green opened fire. Two post lamps at the foot of the stairs leading up to the front doors cast the area in a warm amber light as yellow crime scene tape flapped awkwardly in the late-night breeze. The town was still recovering from the shooting in more ways than one.

Jackson and Sayre turned onto the next street where metered parking lined a sidewalk and a grassy lawn led up to the side of the courthouse. Sayre pulled over and motioned out his window for Jackson to pull up alongside.

"The office is on the other side of the courthouse," Sayre said. "When we get over there, you pull up short and wait on the street."

He reached out and tossed a business card into the Jackson's passenger seat.

"That has my cell number on it," he continued. "Call it and hang up so I have your number. If you see anything while I'm inside, call again."

Sayre took off toward the next intersection and Jackson followed.

They took the next two right turns and circled around to the Sheriff's Office until Sayre finally pulled into the parking lot filled with Hopewell County patrol cars. Jackson did just as he was told and pulled over outside the entrance. He turned off his lights but left the engine running.

From where he was parked, Jackson could see Sayre hop out and enter through the main doors. A uniformed police officer taking a smoke break just outside the entrance didn't pay Sayre any mind. Jackson took that as a good sign.

Just two days ago Sayre was telling Jackson and the others they had no choice but to turn Bobbie in. Now, unless this was all one big setup, the state police investigator was actively helping him elude detection of the local authorities. Something had changed. Something big. But what?

Two pairs of headlights appeared in Jackson's rearview mirror, but he paid them little mind—until those headlights turned into to two black pickup trucks pulling into the Sheriff's Office parking lot. Jackson sat upright and alert.

A plump fellow with a receding hairline and goatee climbed out of the first truck, while a young, fit man with a military buzz cut, and a taller, older man with shoulder-length blonde hair got out of the second. Based on Bobbie's description, Jackson figured the latter two men were Franko and Bragg; going off Sayre's account of what went down outside the hospital, he guessed the portly man was Starcher.

Jackson grabbed his phone. Sayre picked up almost immediately.

"I think the rest of your fight club is about to walk in," Jackson said.

"Fuck. Okay," Sayre said. "West side of the building. There's a window near the northwest corner. Get out and go to it."

Jackson hopped out of Fraggie's truck, slipping his Beretta into the concealed-carry holster on his waist, and trotted around the corner of the building. The back side, opposite the front of the courthouse with the plaza, was a dark alley. Jackson moved through it, invisible. When he got to the corner of the building, he peaked around the side—there was a window no more than a couple feet from him. A shadow in the window moved, silhouetted by the light of the office. Jackson made sure it was Sayre, then came around to it.

Sayre saw him and opened the window, handing Jackson a thick folder of files. "Here. This is everything I've got here that'll help. Take it and go. I've got your number."

Jackson didn't say anything as he took the files. He ducked back around the corner into the dark alley just as three figures eclipsed Sayre's office door.

"I thought I told you you were fucking done," Jackson heard a voice say.

"Kiss my ass. I'm not going anywhere until I'm ordered to," Sayre said.

Jackson didn't stick around for the rest of the conversation. He moved back through the alley and began crossing the small lawn to his car when a voice stopped him.

"Excuse me, where are you coming from?" a man said.

Jackson turned. The officer that had been by the front door was now shining a flashlight on him. He was an older man, with gray hair and a belly that said he couldn't run off the burgers like he used to.

Jackson raised his hand to block the light and nodded over his shoulder.

"Back that way," he said.

He caught a glimpse of the building that made up the other side of the alley. Brass letters above the door read Hopewell County Public Works.

"I work for transportation," Jackson added. "Just calling it a night."

"What do you got there in your hands?" the officer asked.

"Just boring civil engineer stuff," Jackson said. "I can show it to you if you'd like."

"No, no, that's alright. You need a hand carrying it?"

"Nope, I think I can manage."

"Alright then. Have a good night."

"You do the same."

Jackson walked leisurely back to the truck and put the files on the passenger seat before walking around and hopping in behind the wheel. The officer was still watching him. Jackson waved as he fired up the truck. The officer waved back.

He put the truck in gear and pulled out into the road. As he drove past the Sheriff's Office he could see Sayre being walked out of the building by two other uniformed officers. The older officer that had been talking to Jackson heard the commotion and trotted over to help.

Sayre looked up. Jackson met his eyes and Sayre nodded. He was empty-handed. Or at least, that's what the Vice Squad thought.

44

Lieutenant Sayre spent a restless night in his motel room anticipating the call that would order him back to Charleston. At three minutes after eight that morning, it came. He imagined his boss, Captain Smith, walking into his office at eight sharp and checking the voicemails on his phone. There, Starcher or perhaps even the Hopewell County Sheriff himself, William Davis, had left a message yelling about the fight Sayre had started and demanded he be pulled off the case. Smith, who particularly hated headaches caused by his own people, would be all too happy to oblige the request.

Sayre didn't even look at the Caller ID as he answered it.

"Yeah?" he said.

"Well, since I'm calling you, I'm guessing you already know what this is about," Captain Smith said.

"I do. And I'm guessing you don't want to hear the other side of it," Sayre said.

"Unless you have concrete—and by concrete, I mean fucking bullet-proof—evidence that the officers you're supposed to be working *with* are involved in some sort of criminal activity, you're right. I don't want to hear it."

"I have a sworn statement from the two detectives at the initial shooting that does not line up with the forensic evidence."

"And have you given them a chance to explain it? I'll save you the time. No, you haven't, because even the world's shittiest union rep lawyer could explain it away. Come on, Sayre, you're not this naïve."

"Then give me a few days to find harder evidence."

"Forget it. You have until check out time in whatever motel you're in to get your ass in the car and be heading back here."

Sayre grimaced as he shook his head. His free hand clenched the lip of the mattress in frustration.

"So, I'm done here then?" he asked.

"Yes, you're done." Captain Smith said.

"Then I request time off," Sayre said.

He could hear Captain Smith sigh on the other end of the line and mutter something under his breath.

"That's really how you want to play this?" Captain Smith asked.

Sayre kept his voice level. Official-sounding. Both he and Captain Smith knew what he was doing, but he played dumb.

"I'm not sure I know what you mean, sir," Sayre said. "You're pulling me off my current case. So, with that in mind, I'm asking to use some of my time off."

Captain Smith, on the other hand, did not keep his voice even and calm.

"And just how much time do you think you need, Sayre?" he asked.

"I don't know, sir," Sayre replied. "I could put in a call to HR and ask how much I have stored up."

A loud thump came from Captain Smith's end of the line. Sayre assumed his desk or a nearby table had just taken the brunt of his boss' frustration. Sayre was playing a game now and he was winning.

"Enough, Sayre," Smith said angrily. "That's enough. I'm giving you a week. You take a week to clear your head or do whatever and then you're back here. You hear me? You're back here next Monday."

"One week should be more than enough time, sir," Sayre said calmly. "I'll see you next Monday."

He ended the call and slid the phone into his pocket. In less than half an hour, he had all his stuff packed and loaded. He walked over to the motel office, returned the key, and left a tip for the housekeeping staff.

"Anything wrong with the room?" the gruff woman behind the counter asked.

"Plenty," Sayre said, "but that's not why I'm leaving. Have a good one."

The woman gave him a scowl as he walked with purpose out to his car. He got in, turned it on and pulled his phone back out. He scrolled through his call log, selected the number he was looking for, and called it.

45

Jackson had kept to himself most of the early morning. The others watched him as he came and went, wondering when he was going to debrief them all on his little field trip. As Maggie finished making breakfast and called everyone to the table, Jackson figured communing over Maggie's eggs and fresh pork sausage was as good a time as any.

"Yesterday, the Andersons told me they very much suspect the Hopewell County Vice Squad planted bricks of heroin on their son, Harper," he said.

Fraggie shook her head as she stabbed at a clump of scrambled eggs.

"Fuckers," she grumbled.

Maggie kneed her underneath the table and mouthed something Jackson couldn't make out.

"If the Vice Squad are the bad actors here," Jackson continued, "my guess is the outside agencies aren't involved. So I made a second stop after the Andersons. I had a face-to-face with Lieutenant Sayre."

At that, everyone stopped chewing and looked up.

"He thinks he's about to be on the outside looking in on the case. Apparently he took a swing at one of the Vice Squad detectives and he was on thin ice even before that. He went back into the Hopewell County Sheriff's Office last night and got some files. Files that, at the very least, call into question what exactly went down the night Bobbie and his friends had their run-in with the police."

"What do you mean?" Bear asked.

Jackson explained to them all what the files said. About the forensics indicating Mason was shot up close, but Franko and Bragg saying he was shot some 30 feet away; the photos and statements indicating Mason had shot at them with his right hand, but that Sayre had discovered Mason was left-handed.

"It's true," Bobbie said. "Mason is—*was*—a lefty. The high school baseball coach called him Southpaw."

"So, what do we do with this? Do we find another lawyer and take this to trial?" Ray asked.

"Shit, better loan him your helmet from your Ranger days, Jackson," Fraggie said.

Maggie kneed her again.

"I don't think so," Jackson said.

"What?" Ray asked. "What do you mean?"

Jackson took a bite of eggs as the group looked at him with varying levels of consternation on their faces. He swallowed.

"If Franko set up the shooting at the courthouse, we're still not safe —especially Bobbie," he said. "Not as long as they're out there."

"So, what do you say we do, then?" Ray asked.

Jackson paused again, taking another bite, knowing his answer would make some of them uneasy.

"We neutralize the threat," he said around a mouthful of eggs.

"Hot damn!" Bear said, slamming his fist down in approval.

"Whoa, whoa, wait, here a minute," Ray said. "You're talking about killing them? Killing *cops*?"

Jackson shook his head.

"Not if we don't have to, no," he said.

"Then what, exactly?" Ray asked.

"Everything's a food chain in this," Jackson said. "These guys want Bobbie. Well, there's someone out there that's going to want a squad full of police officers abusing their power and making bad arrests. We just have to serve them up."

"What about this Sayre guy? You said you think he'll help. And he's state police, not local."

"And may be on his way out. We can't count on him."

"So, who else? I mean, don't police departments have people to investigate this stuff? Internal affairs or whatever?"

"The Hopewell County Sheriff's Office is so small I doubt they have an actual Internal Affairs Division. And, in any case, we couldn't trust that they aren't also a part of this."

"So, who then? The FBI?"

"That's a possibility. I can make some more phone calls."

The table was quiet, everyone eyeing the other. Jackson guessed they were hoping for something more.

"I'll go make those phone calls. See if I can't get you all anything more," Jackson said.

"You'll do no such thing," Maggie said from across the table.

Jackson looked at her, taken aback by her assertiveness. She saw it on his face.

"You're going to finish your breakfast. The same goes for everyone," Maggie said. "We're going to eat, and then we'll all get on with work. That's that."

Jackson smiled and nodded. Maggie was quiet, but she had a matriarchal way about her.

Together, the group finished breakfast and headed out onto the property. Bear and Ray offered to help Fraggie move a round bale of hay into the field for the goats and Bobbie fed the dogs after helping Mia lay down on one of Maggie and Fraggie's sofas. Jackson walked over to his truck and pulled out his phone but turned around when he heard footsteps behind him. It was Maggie.

"Thanks again for breakfast," Jackson said.

"My pleasure," Maggie said. "How are you holding up?"

"I'm good."

"All this craziness with Bobbie, you seem to have taken it head on."

"I guess."

"You have. But you don't have to bare the weight of all this alone, you know. We're all here."

"Thanks, I appreciate it."

Maggie smiled as she crossed her arms and tucked them against herself for warmth.

"I also wanted to say I overheard Ray and Bear talking. About your son," she said."

Jackson didn't say anything.

"I'm sorry, I didn't mean to bring up a sensitive subject," Maggie continued. "It's just—"

"No, no. It's okay," Jackson said. "It's not a state secret or anything."

"I'm sorry you lost him. That's...that's really awful."

"Thanks."

"His name was Evan?"

"Yeah."

"I like that."

"I did, too. So did my wife."

Maggie studied Jackson's face as he looked down into the fields, watching Bear and Ray and Fraggie work.

"You don't talk about him much, do you?" Maggie asked.

"Not really, no," Jackson said.

"You should, you know," Maggie said. "It's important. You loved him. You should keep his memory alive."

Jackson nodded in acknowledgment.

"Have you ever heard of Banksy?" Maggie asked.

"The graffiti artist?" Jackson asked in reply.

Maggie chuckled.

"The artist, yes," she said. "Well, he once said you die twice. Once when you stop breathing and a second time when somebody says your name for the last time."

Jackson, again, didn't say anything.

"Talk about him. Evan," Maggie said. "Keep saying his name. That way, others will, too."

Jackson smiled, but couldn't bring himself to look at Maggie.

"Thanks," he said softly.

Maggie reached out and grabbed his arm, lightly squeezing it. Jackson couldn't bring himself to say it, but he was happy for what she'd said. Maggie stayed there a moment, lingering, before Jackson's phone chimed and buzzed in his pocket. Both of them heard it.

"Well, I'll let you get that," Maggie said.

Jackson pulled the phone out of his pocket and checked the call. It was Sayre. He answered it as Maggie headed back toward the house.

"I'm officially on a leave of absence," Sayre said.

"I'm sorry to hear that," Jackson said. "So are you headed back to Charleston?"

"No, I'm on personal time now. Figured I'd stick around, see what trouble I could get into, assuming I can find a place to stay. You got any ideas?"

Jackson turned and took in the view of Maggie and Fraggie's prepper farm from his truck. Goats and guns and bales and bunkers.

"I might know a place," Jackson said.

46

Together, everyone at the farm watched from the porch as Sayre's police-issue Chevy Impala navigated the rocky dirt drive up to the house. Just two days earlier this man had been tasked with apprehending Bobbie. Now, Sayre was supposedly here in the effort to help keep him out of handcuffs. At least for now.

Sayre pulled up behind Fraggie's tractor. He slid his 6'3" frame out of the sedan and stretched upwards. He reached down for his pistol and slid it into the waistband of his jeans, momentarily revealing a torso contoured in all the right ways.

"Jesus," Fraggie muttered.

"I'm not gay," Bear said, "but he can bunk with me."

Ray snorted. Jackson stepped off the porch and walked over to meet Sayre as the man grabbed a duffel bag from the back seat of his car.

"Hard place to find," Sayre said.

"That's the idea," Jackson said, "Come on, I'll introduce you."

Jackson led Sayre past the cars and back up to the porch. The group hadn't moved or taken their eyes off of their new guest.

"I'm Colton," Sayre said, introducing himself. "Nice place you've got here."

"Isn't that *Lieutenant* Colton? Lieutenant Colton Sayre of the state police?" Ray asked.

"If you want it to be, sure. Though officially I'm on a leave of absence," Sayre said.

"But that badge and gun still work if you decide to use them, right?"

"I'm not here to arrest anyone."

Maggie stepped forward and extended a hand.

"We didn't mean anything by it," she said. "I'm Maggie. That's Ray, Bobbie's uncle. You can understand we're a little protective of Bobbie right now."

"I can imagine," Sayre said.

"That's Fraggie there, and that's Bear in the back," Maggie continued. "You obviously know who Bobbie is. Jackson, too. And that's Mia."

Mia stood behind everyone, draped in a large blanket, her eyes peering out at Sayre through her unkempt hair. They were pale moons in the middle of this otherwise sunny day with dark, heavy bags underneath them. Sayre could tell she was dopesick. Hazards of the job.

He waved at the group. Most of them nodded or smiled respectfully. Bear began to wave back before he realized he was the only one doing so.

"Well," Maggie said, "Fraggie will get you situated."

Maggie turned and walked Mia back inside.

"Is she going to be okay?" Sayre asked. "That looks like some rough withdrawal there."

"She will be. Hopefully," Ray answered.

"She will," Fraggie said. "C'mon, let's take you down."

She led Sayre and the others on an ATV down to the smokehouse. Despite Bear's offer, Sayre took the one remaining unoccupied couch in the living area and plopped down on it. Fraggie opened a door on the far side of the house, revealing a room of shelves filled like a warehouse with dry goods. Preppers, Sayre thought to himself.

Fraggie walked down one aisle of shelves, came back with a blanket, and tossed it to him.

"You need any more pillows besides what's on the couch there?" she asked.

"No, thanks. I'm good," Sayre said.

"Maggie and I have some work to do," Fraggie said, heading for the front door. "Bobbie, you come with me. Let them figure some things out."

Bobbie followed Fraggie out of the smokehouse. Jackson heard an ATV roar to life, then saw it take off down the dirt drive, Fraggie driving with Bobbie wrapped around her midsection.

Jackson grabbed a chair from the dining room table and positioned it opposite Sayre. "I went over those files you gave me. I see what you mean about their statement. You're right, it doesn't add up with the evidence. Bobbie confirmed Mason was left-handed."

"The left and right-handed thing can be explained away," Sayre said. "Right now, the biggest piece of evidence is the forensics of the gunshot wound. But that's not enough on its own."

"I spoke with a couple in Martinsburg. They're convinced the Vice Squad set up their son with two bricks of heroin," Jackson said.

"Would they testify to that?" Sayre asked.

"I'm not sure. They told me, a virtual stranger. So, maybe."

"That might help."

Jackson pulled out his phone, looked up the Anderson's information, and sent it to Sayre.

"The real question is," Jackson said, "who do we go to with this? You said you're off the case now."

"I don't think my office is going to be much help, honestly. Even if I get someone like my partner to buy into it, the second our Captain gets wind of it, he'll kill it," Sayre said.

"And that's all criminal investigations out of state police?" Jackson asked.

"Unfortunately."

"So, what are we left with? The feds?"

"Pretty much."

"Do you know anyone at the FBI in Charleston?"

"Charleston doesn't have a field office. The nearest is Pittsburgh. They cover West Virginia. The FBI has a resident agency – basically a

satellite office – in Charleston. I know a guy or two over there. But this
isn't enough to get them to look into it."

Jackson was quiet, thinking.

"There's another angle to all this," he said, finally. "Have you heard
of VigilOne?"

"They're like a defense contractor, right?" Sayre asked.

"Security services. Officially, anyway," Jackson said. "They're a
private military company. And they supplied and trained the
Hopewell County Sheriff's Vice Squad and SWAT Team. And they've
done the same thing with at least a dozen other rural counties across
the state. Plus, they own and operate the nearest prison and an inpatient rehab program."

"I'm not seeing the smoking gun here."

"There's got to be a reason the Vice Squad is doing all this. You
can't tell me all this is just to get their rocks off. There's got to be a
bigger motive."

"Let me guess: you have a theory."

"From what I've learned, VigilOne's revenue has skyrocketed since
they started focusing their business stateside. They're in the business
of crime, and this New War on Drugs initiative by the governor is the
boom they've been looking for."

"So, you think it comes down to money?"

"You're the investigator. Doesn't it always? I think they've taken
narcotics arrests and turned it into a cottage industry in the corners of
the state where no one bothers to care. And if you've got a cash cow
like that, you'd kill to protect it. We already know Franko set up the
shooting at the courthouse. I think what Bobbie saw that night when
his friends were killed threatens to unravel everything. Like knocking
over the right domino. That's why they want Bobbie quiet. And dead
is as quiet as it gets."

Jackson looked at Bear and then Ray, both of them nodding in
agreement. Sayre was quiet as he parsed out the thoughts in his head.
Trying to kill Bobbie seemed like a strong reaction to a little planted
meth. He thought about Amelia Westfall. Had someone tried to quiet
her as well?

"That's not bad, Jackson," Sayre said. "But the problem is proving it. If money is the motive, then you've got to have the money. The funding for training and supplying police departments is going to all be legitimate. So where is the illegitimate money?"

Ray stepped forward and spoke before Jackson could.

"What if it's with the local departments?" he said. "I mean, Jackson said this Vice Squad brings in more arrests than the rest of the department combined. All these arrests mean money for VigilOne whether the person goes to jail or this NRIP place."

Sayre raised his eyebrows.

"NRIP is the inpatient rehab program VigilOne runs," Jackson explained.

"Exactly," Ray said. "They make money no matter what happens. What if they kick back a portion of that to the guys making the arrests? Like a finder's fee."

"That's some really fucked up finder's fee," Bear said.

"I buy it," Sayre said, nodding. "But like I said, where's the money? We're not going to get financial statements without a warrant, and we're not going to get a warrant with what we've got, even if I was on the case still. Besides, if these guys are smart, it's not going to show up on bank statements."

"So, we find out," Jackson said.

"What do you mean?" Sayre asked.

"Set up on them. We watch them. Watch what they do, who they meet with. There's more than enough of us for a revolving tail on at least one of them. If there's money, it's got to come into play at some point. We just have to be there when it does."

"You do realize you can't do that and hide out here at the same time, right?"

Jackson looked at Ray and then at Bear. Bear met his eyes and gave him a boyish grin. Jackson looked back at Sayre.

"We're done hiding," he said.

47

Wolfe hated waiting on people. It seemed to be the one pet peeve of his where he couldn't buy something or pay someone to get rid of the inconvenience. He stood there, at the river-front park in downtown Charleston, holding an umbrella over his head as a dreary onslaught of cold autumn rain pelted him from above.

From his vantage point, steps away from the frigid Kanawha River, the city buildings towered over him, looking out on the mountains beyond, their facades as gray and lifeless as the skies above them. A trash barge made its way down the river. Wolfe could see the dark figure of a man on the barge's bridge, standing vigilant over the boat's foul cargo.

"You and me both, man," Wolfe said to himself. "Always pushing shit downstream."

The barge flowed past, revealing the far side of the river: a sloping landscape of leafless trees, broken up only by the occasional building. Though much smaller, they were no less drab than the monstrous rectangular monoliths looming behind Wolfe. He turned slowly, still watching the barge fade into the distance, when two men approached him out of the corner of his eye.

The reason he was here. Finally.

"Sir," one of them said, greeting Wolfe.

"King," Wolfe said before looking at the other. "Cobb."

King and Cobb looked every bit the lethal problem solvers that they were. Tall and muscular, they wore matching black coats and watch caps, standard issue for the few clandestine men Wolfe kept on retainer and paid handsomely to do particularly unspeakable things.

"What have we got, sir?" Cobb asked.

"I'm sure you're aware of this matter with the Casto kid up in the panhandle," Wolfe said.

"Yes, sir," King said. "He's a fugitive right? Wanted for the attempted murder of those two detectives."

Wolfe nodded.

"Precisely," he said. "The issue is we're involved. And exposed. This kid may have seen some things that could complicate one of our more profitable business endeavors in the area."

"Copy that," Cobb said. "No local assets nearby?"

"This business of ours up there involves some of the local police—the Sheriff's Office. But so far, they've proved to be incompetent in handling the problem. I want solutions."

"What exactly did you have in mind?"

"We need the Casto kid removed from the equation. Permanently. And quietly. He's evaded us this long because he has help. If that means eliminating those threats too, so be it."

King brought his hands to his mouth and breathed into them before rubbing them together, trying to generate some warmth.

"What's our timeline on this?" he asked.

"Immediately," Wolfe said. "You two are on one of our Blackhawks out of Yeager in twenty minutes. They'll drop you at one of our properties a few klicks outside of Rion. A tactical suite and vehicle will be waiting for you."

"Yes, sir," King said. "You said some of the local law enforcement are assets. Should we make contact when we're in the area?"

Wolfe slid his hands into the pockets of his Tom Ford pea coat. His breath formed a foggy cloud in the cold air as gray as his eyes. "No. Consider your work independent of theirs."

"And if they get in the way?" Cobb asked.

"Nothing gets in your way," Wolfe said.

48

In less than an hour, the group had a game plan. They'd make up two teams: Jackson and Bear would be one, and Sayre and Fraggie would be the other. Their targets were Franko and Starcher, since they were most likely the two shot-callers involved with whatever was going on. Starcher was an obvious candidate as the head of the Vice Squad, and Franko appeared to be something of a lieutenant to him, the senior detective on the squad.

"Are you sure I shouldn't go instead of Sayre?" Ray had asked. "They've been working next to the guy for the last couple days. They'll recognize him if he's seen."

"We need Sayre's skills out there," Jackson had said. "Anyway, we'll all be set up from a distance in order to not be seen."

Jackson and Bear took Fraggie's truck, while Fraggie drove Sayre in Maggie's Jeep. The plan was to watch Franko and Starcher and, whichever of the two did something first, both teams would focus their efforts on that guy.

A call to the Sheriff's Office – using Maggie's pleasant and unremarkable voice – put Starcher at his desk. Franko was simply "not in today". As Fraggie and Sayre headed into town to sit on the headquarters, Sayre called a fellow investigator at his office in Charleston.

"Thomas, BCI," the investigator answered.

"Carter, it's Colton," Sayre said. "How are you?"

Carter Thomas was the baby-faced freshman investigator at the state police's Bureau of Criminal Investigation. Barely old enough to drink, he'd made a name for himself as something of a wunderkind within the department. Most just marveled at the fact that some of the longer-tenured investigators in the office had children older than him.

"Colt, you're top on the boss's shit list today. I think I even heard him utter his first cuss word," Thomas said.

"Tell me something I don't know," Sayre said. "Listen, I was wondering if you could do me a favor."

"You mean do something for you without Captain Smith's knowledge," Thomas said.

"Isn't that a favor? It's not a big deal, I just need the home address of a detective out here. Ronnie Franko. Ronald's probably his legal first name."

"Give me five minutes."

Sayre ended the call.

Fraggie looked over at him.

"So, did you get the info?" she asked.

"He's looking," Sayre said.

Neither of them said anything more until they posted up on the Sheriff's Office. Fraggie pulled into a parking spot half a block away at the community center, a few hundred feet from the Sheriff's Office but with a clear line of sight to the front of the building. With the binoculars Fraggie brought along, they'd be able to identify anyone coming and going.

"What's this Starcher fella look like, anyway?" Fraggie asked.

"Fat and balding with a goatee," Sayre answered. "Basically a bad cliché of a police detective."

Fraggie laughed as she handed the binoculars to Sayre. A plump middle-aged woman studied the two of them with suspicion as she walked down the sidewalk. Sayre grabbed the bill of his ballcap and nodded at the woman. Fraggie met the woman's gaze and offered her one of the five fingers on her right hand. The woman snarled and shook her head as she kept walking.

"The idea is to not draw attention to us," Sayre said.

"Fuck her," Fraggie said. "Nosy broad."

She watched as the lady walked to the end of the street and disappeared around the corner of the community center. Sayre kept his eyes forward on the Sheriff's Office. Two officers – one he recognized as a desk sergeant – were walking in with brown paper bags blotted with grease stains. Probably burgers or cheesesteaks or something else far more likely to kill them long before an armed bad guy ever does, Sayre thought.

"How long you thinkin' he'll be in there?" Fraggie asked.

"When I was there, he held court most days until the end of business."

Sayre turned and looked at Fraggie and saw she wanted a more specific answer.

"Probably around four or five," he said.

Fraggie looked down at the time on the Jeep's dashboard.

"So...we just sit here for a couple hours and wait?" she asked.

"Unless he comes out earlier, yeah."

Fraggie huffed.

"That's the gig," Sayre said.

"Should've teamed up with Bear," Fraggie grumbled. "He ain't much to look at compared to you, but at least he ain't boring."

THE NEXT PARKING LOT OVER, Detective Lucas Staats was leaving the ATM with a fresh wad of cash and heading back toward his truck, the same unmarked black pickup with tinted windows and a hidden light bar that all members of the Hopewell County Vice Squad drove.

Large and beefy—the perfect size to play left tackle just as he had at Division II Fairmont State—Staats didn't have to climb up into his pickup so much as pile in. Backing out of his parking spot, he rounded the corner and had just pulled out onto the nearby street when a small Kia sedan nearly hit what looked to be a rather large woman crossing the street. The woman, now standing in the middle of the street, began yelling at the driver in the Kia. The Kia, in response, wailed on its horn.

"Oh, for fuck's sake," Staats muttered.

Not willing to wait for the squabble to end but equally unwilling to get involved, he nosed the front of his truck around the mess and cut through the parking lot of the adjacent community center. Free of the traffic, he sped up and rounded the building at speed before nearly T-boning an SUV in the process of backing out. Now, the driver of the SUV looked at him expectantly, but he was too far out for Staats to get by.

"Come on, come on," Staats said, fully aware the driver couldn't hear him.

It was just his luck. Work was right fucking there. He could see it. Literally. He could look out and—something caught his eye. There, in a parked car right next to Staats, a man with binoculars appeared to be watching the Sheriff's Office

As the SUV cleared him, Staats drove down to exit the parking lot but doubled back on the street toward the parked car. The man now had the binoculars down and Staats could clearly see his face.

"Son of a bitch," Staats said.

He drove to the end of the block and pulled out his phone.

"Boss," Staats said when Starcher answered, "you're not going to believe this, but I think that cop from Charleston is camped out in front of the office."

49

S tarcher took his plastic cup of coffee and threw it against the wall. The lukewarm joe splattered some papers pinned to a cork board. On the other side of the phone, Detective Staats' face began to turn a feverish red.

"You're telling me that asshole is staking us out or something?" Starcher growled.

"That'd be my guess," Staats said.

Starcher popped out of his chair and stomped over to a window on the front side of the building.

"What's he in?" he asked.

"Jeep Wrangler. Forest Green. And he's not alone."

Splitting a pair of blinds with his doughy fingers, Starcher peered out at the parking lots across the way. He thought he saw the Jeep but couldn't be sure. Either way, he definitely couldn't see inside it.

"Who's he with?" Starcher asked.

"I don't know. Some chick," Staats said. "Skinny. Purple dyed hair."

"Get a tag and then get in here," Starcher said. "Come in the back way, through the courthouse. Just leave your truck back there."

Before Staats could say anything, Starcher had hung up and was calling Franko.

On the third ring, Franko's groggy voice answered the phone.

"What?" he said.

"Where the fuck are you?" Starcher asked.

"What do you mean, where am I? I'm home. It's my fucking day off," Franko said.

"Get into town. That Sayre asshole hasn't left and Staats thinks he's watching us."

"Watching us? For what?"

"Does it matter? I don't have to tell you of all people we need to find out whether or not he knows something."

Franko sighed hard enough that his breath made a staticky grumble into the phone's receiver. Starcher could hear the man struggling to get up.

"Alright, I'll be there in twenty," Franko said. "What do you want me to do?"

"Help us ditch this asshole. Then the whole team is going to meet at the clubhouse and we're going to figure out what the fuck we're going to do about this," Starcher said.

Again, Starcher hung up before his subordinate could answer. He threw the phone on his desk and paced around, thinking. He pictured Sayre, sitting out there, watching. Starcher punched into his open palm. He walked over to the water cooler, grabbed a paper cup and filled it, then tossed in a handful of Alka-Seltzer tablets. As he walked back to his desk, he took a big gulp and swallowed with a grimace.

All the money wasn't worth this stress, he thought. He pulled out his phone and scrolled through his contact list, finally settling on Lane Wolfe. Starcher contemplated calling the man, telling him they still had a problem, but ultimately decided against it. Wolfe was the kind of man you could only go to so many times for help before he decided *you* were the problem that needed fixing. And Wolfe's problems had a good track record of disappearing.

Starcher wasn't trying to disappear. Not just yet, anyway.

He put his phone away and waited for backup to arrive.

50

Jackson and Bear had just gotten to Franko's address – texted to them by Sayre – when Franko came jogging down the front steps. Sliding on a leather jacket that stopped being stylish at the turn of the century, he hopped into his black pickup and took off down the road.

"He's movin'," Bear said, holding a spotting scope up to one of his eyes.

"On it," Jackson said.

He pulled off the curb several hundred yards back and slowly followed Franko. Franko's house, a red brick midcentury with the curb appeal of a trash can fire, was in an unincorporated community north of Rion called Spring Rock. When Franko turned onto the county highway headed south, Jackson pulled out his phone and called Sayre.

"Franko's on the move," he said, "headed toward Rion."

"You think he's coming here?" Sayre asked.

"It's as good a guess as any," Jackson said.

"We're a block and a half away with eyes on the front. If he comes here, we'll see it."

"Got it. I'll let you know."

Jackson hung up.

"He looked in a hurry," Bear said. "Think we spooked him?"

"Doubt it. We weren't there long enough," Jackson said.

As suspected, Franko took the highway all the way into town. When he was at the heart of it, he turned left and headed for the Sheriff's Office. As Jackson saw the courthouse come into view, he reached for his phone to call Sayre back, but Franko drove past the turn for the police station and instead turned two blocks later.

Jackson and Bear followed cautiously. Franko took the road a block or so before it ended at a parking lot, where he pulled over just short of the entrance. Jackson and Bear pulled over quickly into a street parking spot to maintain their distance.

"That parking lot he's in front of, what's it for?" Jackson asked.

"Looks like a church of some kind," Bear said. "Maybe he's tired of all this and lookin' to confess."

"I wouldn't count on it," Jackson said.

He looked to his left. The bell tower of the courthouse peeked out just over the top of a community center. That reminded him of something Sayre said. He called Sayre back.

"Is he coming this way?" Sayre answered.

"No, he blew past the place," Jackson said. "You said you were a block and a half away. Where, exactly, are you?"

"Parking lot of a community center," Sayre said. "Why?"

"Franko just came to a stop a couple blocks away, putting you between him and the headquarters."

"Why'd he do that?"

"Not sure. Could you have been spotted?"

"I don't see how. There's been barely any activity out front."

"Hold on."

Jackson reached into his pocket and grabbed one of his wireless earbuds for his phone. He slid it into his right ear.

"Wait, we've got movement," Sayre said. "Starcher's coming out. He's with two guys. One of them is Bragg, the other I've seen around but don't know his name."

"What are they doing?" Jackson asked.

"Headed to their trucks. Starcher in one, Bragg and the other guy in a second. What's Franko doing?"

"Just sitting short of this parking lot here."

"Well, the three over here are about to move out."

As Sayre said that, Jackson saw the taillights on Franko's truck blink to life. The truck began rolling forward.

"Wait, Franko is moving now, too," Jackson said.

"What do you want to do?" Sayre asked.

"Follow them, assuming they stay together," Jackson said. "If they split, follow Starcher. We'll stay on Franko."

Jackson pulled forward slowly, matching Franko's speed. He was barely doing the speed limit. When Franko took the next left, Jackson hit the gas hard and roared down the block, coming to a stop at the intersection. Franko passed the community center, heading back toward Main Street.

"My guys are headed for Main Street," Sayre said. "Looks like they'll be making a right, moving northwest."

"Franko's headed to Main, too," Jackson said. "Not sure which way he's turning. He could go straight across Main."

A car honked behind Jackson, who winced at the noise, praying it didn't draw Franko's attention.

"Go around, you dumb fuck," Bear grumbled.

A turquoise Ford Fiesta swerved around them, a teenager covered in piercings screaming something at them as it went. It cleared their vision of Franko just in time to see his truck turn right onto Main Street.

"Franko's taking a right on Main," Jackson said. Again, he punched the gas, covering a block's worth of street in just a matter of seconds. The light at the intersection turned yellow, but there was no time. Jackson blew through the yellow, the truck fishtailing as he turned. His pulse quickened as he spotted Franko's truck again.

"Sayre, the black pickup behind you is Franko," he said. "He's right behind you."

"We see him, it's fine," Sayre said. "We've got eyes on the other guys."

But just as Sayre said that, Franko's truck became awash in strobing red and blue lights. A loud *WOOP WOOP* sounded out for good measure.

"Fuck," Sayre said. "He's pulling us over. Someone must've made us. He's going to shake his boys free of our tail."

"He can kiss my ass," Fraggie said, loud enough for Jackson to hear her through Sayre's phone. "We're not stopping."

"No, pull over," Sayre said.

"Fuck that. We're on these guys."

"Listen to me, Fraggie. Pull over. This is what they want. They want a reason to put us in cuffs. Or worse. They want us out of the picture. Pull over."

Jackson heard a slew of four-letter words come from Fraggie.

"Let him take you," Jackson said. "I don't think he knows about us. You guys stop, we'll go on and follow Starcher and the other two."

"Got it," Sayre said. "Sorry, man."

"Nothing to be sorry about."

Jackson and Bear watched as Fraggie and Sayre pulled over in their Jeep. When they were past, Jackson sped up. Main Street became a rural two-lane highway as it headed out of town. Jackson and Bear kept their distance, following Starcher and the others. The road bucked and swayed lazily through a mural of honey and ginger foliage.

The two black pickups continued on for another five miles until they pulled into a gravel lot next to a building just off the road. There was nothing else nearby it; no place for Jackson and Bear to stop without being noticed.

"Keep going," Bear said.

"Yup. We'll double back when we're out of view," Jackson said.

Jackson saw Starcher amble out of one truck as they drove by. Whatever the building was, that was their intended destination. A half mile ahead, the highway turned and wended deeper into the woods. Not long thereafter, it intersected with a one-lane road. Jackson turned onto it and continued on until they came to a clearing in the trees made for the power lines overhead.

"There," Bear said. "I saw this clearing from the highway. This corridor doubles back toward where those guys stopped."

Jackson stopped the car. He and Bear hopped out and armed themselves. Jackson slung the pack he'd brought along over his shoulder, and together, they followed a trail under the power lines through the clearing. A quarter of a mile later, they were back on the highway. They followed the tree line to the building the three vice detectives had stopped at.

The building was a wood-sided commercial structure painted a reddish brown. The adjacent gravel lot seemed far too big for the place, and made it harder to get close without being seen. As they approached, Bear tapped Jackson's arm and motioned across the street. A small creek bed followed the road on that side.

"That'll give us some cover," Bear said, "and a better view."

Jackson agreed. The two backtracked until they were out of view of the building, then crossed the road and followed the creek bed back. Now directly across from the building, they crouched down in the gully.

"What is it?" Jackson asked.

"Hold on, there's a sign above the door," Bear said. He put his spotting scope to his eye. "*The Trail's End.*"

"That's ominous," Jackson said.

"What do you think it is?" Bear asked.

"What it is and what it *was* may be two different things. It looks like it was a restaurant or a bar of some kind. What it is now? God knows."

"Maybe they're kicking off and going to happy hour."

"They had Franko sabotage their tail so they could go get drunk?"

"Shit, I've done less for a beer."

"I don't buy it."

"What do you want to do?"

Jackson picked up a fistful of dirt and ran it through his fingers as he thought. He reached into his bag and pulled out his handheld GPS.

"We'll mark the place on here and come back to it," he said.

"Maybe take a peek inside," Bear suggested.

"Exactly," Jackson said. "But not with them here. We should double back and make sure Fraggie and Sayre are good, anyway."

Jackson punched the location of *The Trail's End* in to his GPS, and then the two of them followed the creek bed back to the trail beneath the power lines.

Twenty minutes flat from when they'd left, they were back in the truck, heading for Rion.

51

Lieutenant Sayre glanced behind at Franko's truck, a dizzying array of blue and red lights commanding them to stop. He flinched as a loud WOOP WOOP bellowed from somewhere underneath the hood.

"Fuck," he said. "He's pulling us over. Someone must've made us. He's going to shake his boys free of our tail."

Fraggie and him began arguing about obliging the Sheriff's detective before Jackson, via Sayre's phone, weighed in.

"Let him take you. I don't think he knows about us. You guys stop, we'll go on and follow Starcher and the other two."

"Got it," Sayre said. "Sorry, man."

"Nothing to be sorry about," Jackson said.

Fraggie flicked on her turn signal and pulled into the parking lot of a 7-Eleven. Franko followed closely, putting the nose of his truck nearly up against their rear bumper.

"Peckerhead," she muttered.

"Play nice," Sayre said. "Play dumb."

Franko got out of the truck and strutted up to Fraggie at her driver's side window with all the swagger he could muster. Fraggie rolled down the window but looked straight ahead into the convenience store.

"Well, hello there, little lady," Franko said. "How are we doing today?"

Fraggie didn't say anything. Franko leaned down and looked into the truck.

"And you, sir," he said. "You are supposed to be headed back to Charleston, I believe."

"I was taken off the case, so I decided to see some friends nearby," Sayre said.

"Were these friends sitting in the community center parking lot, too?" Franko asked.

"Why? Is that a crime?"

"Not yet."

Franko flashed Sayre a fake smile and pulled his radio from his belt. He keyed the mic.

"Victor 30. I'm Code 6 with two in front of the 7-Eleven on Main. Start me another," he said.

"Backup," Sayre translated. "Really, Franko?"

"Just a minute, sir," Frank said. He focused back on Fraggie. "Ma'am, I'm going to need your license and registration."

Sayre could tell Fraggie was about to put up a fight, so he jabbed her subtly and gave her a look, imploring her to go along with it.

"I have to reach into my glove box, officer," Fraggie said in an even tone. "Would that be okay?"

"Just do so slowly, ma'am," Franko said.

Fraggie leaned over and popped open the glove box.

"Like I couldn't get the drop on your dumb ass," she muttered under her breath.

Sayre had to turn away as he chuckled. The two of them heard a buzzing sound come from Franko, who reached into his pocket and checked his phone. He took a moment to read something. The backup patrol car he requested pulled into the parking lot, but now Franko waved him off.

"That'll be it for today, ma'am," Franko said. "I'm going to let you off with a warning about loitering near the police station. Do not do it again. Wait until I leave, and have a good day."

Fraggie did as she was told. She glanced at Sayre; he shrugged. Together, they watched Franko walk back to his truck, back out, and take off down the road.

Neither of them had noticed Franko slip the GPS tracker into the spare wheel on the back of the Jeep.

52

E lijah Hughes was a product of the state he'd lived in his entire
life. Beefy in a muscular way, with a long salt-and-pepper beard
and hair to match, he looked every part the classic mountaineer. He'd
even carved out a decent life for himself working in the mines,
narrowly surviving the Ferrell No. 17 Mine disaster in 1980. In all that
time he'd never made more than $50,000 a year and his only pension
was his horrendous hacking cough. Now, VigilOne Services, Inc. paid
him nearly double that to sit alone in a cabin atop Chaplain's Hill—just
ten miles north of Rion—and maintain a small grass helipad and
observation tower.

He sat there, late in the afternoon, as a large UH-60 Blackhawk
approached for a landing. He walked over to the metal box at the foot
of the tower and flipped the switch for the pad's infrared lights,
markers invisible to all others except the pilots using night-vision
goggles.

The twin-engine helicopter came down, nose tilted up, and settled
easily on the cropped field. One of the two back doors slid open and
two men in gray pants and black jackets trotted out. Before they'd
made it the hundred feet or so to Elijah, the Blackhawk was already
roaring back to life and heading for the cloudy sky above.

As the noise faded, Elijah extended his hand.

"How are ya?," he asked. "Elijah Hu—"

"No names," one of the men cautioned.

Elijah pulled his arm back, embarrassed.

"Is our gear ready for us?" the other man asked.

Elijah pointed to a black Chevy Tahoe parked at the far end of the field.

"A couple of guys dropped it off 'bout an hour ago," he said.

The two men trotted over to the SUV and opened its doors, inspecting everything inside. Elijah assumed the car must be theirs or they must have one just like it, because the two men seemed to know right where everything was. As one of them examined two assault rifles that slid out from storage in the tailgate, the other rooted around through duffel bags on the back seats. Each of them communicated to the other in short, efficient lingo.

"CQBR's are good to go," one said.

"They give us something with 203's?" the other asked.

"Yeah. Got an M4," the first said.

Elijah walked over, marveling at the two going about their inspection. The man at the tailgate eventually stopped what he was doing and looked up at his bearded onlooker.

"Uh, anything I can help you with?" Elijah asked.

"No. We're good," the man said.

"Yeah, actually," the other interrupted, "I'm not seeing any Tac Vests in here. You got any extra?"

Elijah looked at them with a blank stare.

"Kevlar vests with pouches to hold gear," the first elaborated.

"Ah," Elijah said. "Yes, I think they keep some inside."

Jogging as fast as his bad hip would allow him, Elijah ducked into the cabin and came out a minute later with two vests slung around his shoulder. He limped over to the man who had asked for them and handed them over.

"I'm also not seeing any bags either," the man said. "We asked that there be extra."

Elijah chortled and spit out a wad of brown saliva. "I must be dumb or seein' things, 'cause it sure looks like you have a truck full of all kinds of bags."

The man rolled his eyes as he ducked his head back into the Tahoe. Elijah turned to the other man, looking for an explanation.

"Not those kinds of bags," the man said. "Body bags."

53

When Starcher messaged him that they were free and clear, Franko left Sayre and the woman at the 7-Eleven and headed straight for what the Vice Squad called "the clubhouse."

A while back, the reddish-brown building sitting by itself on a lonely stretch of rural highway had been a bar called *The Trail's End*; but when the owners found themselves in a heap of legal trouble—thanks to the help of the Vice Squad and their extracurricular activities—they decided to sell the place for well below market value. Franko and a handful of other squad guys were more than willing to buy it off of them. The idea at one point had been to turn the bar around and run an honest side business, but that all proved to be more trouble than it was worth. Now, the place served as a safe house of sorts—a base of operations for what they simply called "the business."

Franko pulled in next to five identical black pickups parked next to each other like they'd just come off the factory floor. The gang's all here, he thought.

Opening the front door of the clubhouse, Franko was punched in the nose with the odor of stale whiskey and tobacco percolating in the stagnant air. The place no longer had electricity or running water—indulgences the squad wasn't willing to pay for—leaving everything dark and damp and cold. Shades drawn and shutters closed, chairs stacked on top of the tables dotting the open main room, the squad waited in the sparse illumination of construction work lights. Starcher had taken a chair and set up right near the bar, working his way through his third cigarette of the hour.

"You get the tracker on them?" he asked.

"Yes, sir," Franko said.

"Who was the person with him?" Starcher asked.

"Beats me."

"What'd she look like?"

"Maybe five-six, a buck twenty-five. She had purple hair shaved on one side. Looked like she had a scar on the side of her head, too."

Starcher leaned forward and looked around the room for input. The others sat or stood intermittently throughout.

"Could be a fellow state cop from Charleston," Bragg offered.

"Nah, it kind of sounds like this dyke that lives further out, off of Highway 10," Staats said.

Starcher snuffed out his cigarettes and reached over the bar for a bottle of Crown Royal.

"If she's local, ask around," he said. "It shouldn't take much to ID her."

He was addressing Franko, but Franko didn't say anything back. Instead, he was staring down at his phone, transfixed by the screen.

"You said off of 10, Lucas?" Franko asked.

"Yeah, why?" Staats said.

Franko held up his phone to Starcher.

"The tracker is on 10 right now, headed out of Rion," he said.

Now, Starcher stood up, the prospect of a possible lead reinvigorating him.

"Franko, you and Bragg follow the tracker and get eyes on Sayre," he said. "Staats and Reynolds, you go back to the office and see if you can't rundown this woman you think he might be with."

The two pairs nodded and filed out the door.

"What about us?" asked a shorter man leaning against the back wall.

"The rest of us are sitting tight," Starcher said. "No one goes home. I want to know what Sayre knows."

54

By the time Jackson and Bear rendezvoused with Sayre and Fraggie back at the farm, the sun was dipping behind the mountains to the west, bathing the sky in a brilliant tangerine light. Maggie had prepared dinner again for everyone and was fixing plates of chicken and peaches when she heard the shepherds barking out front.

She walked to the door, opened it, and leaned out.

"Come on in, dinner's on," she said.

The group filed in, shedding their jackets and taking turns washing up before sitting down at the dining room table.

"Any luck?" Ray asked.

"Some," Jackson said. "Good and bad."

He grabbed a plate of food and debriefed Maggie, Ray, Bobbie, and Mia on what had happened, starting with how they'd followed Franko into Rion only to learn Franko somehow knew Sayre and Fraggie were watching the police station. Fraggie then stepped in and gave a profanity-laced account of their traffic stop before Jackson picked up the story again and told everyone about the old bar on the side of the highway.

"What do you think is there?" Ray asked.

"Not sure," Jackson said.

"My guess is that's their base of operations for whatever is going on," Sayre said.

Bear nodded.

"That's what we were thinkin', too," he added. "We want to go back and have a look again. When they're not around, of course."

"Is it worth the risk?" Ray asked. "I mean you were in town less than an hour and they figured out you all were up to stuff. Now you want to go poking around where they *really* don't want you to be?"

"You tell me," Sayre said. "Jackson said it himself: you're all done hiding. We need something that'll end this, but it's not just going to fall in our laps out here."

No one responded. Bobbie and Mia played anxiously with the food on their plate. If they were being honest, no one was particularly hungry. Today had supposed to have been about turning the tables. Now, it felt like they were in an even tighter spot than before.

"Anyway," Jackson said, "Bear and I figured we'd double back in a little bit. See if they're gone from the place."

"You want back up?" Sayre asked.

"We'll be fine," Jackson said.

Maggie looked at the two of them.

"No one's going anywhere tonight," she said. "By the sounds of it, it's been a tough day. Everyone needs their rest."

"That's alright," Bear said. "We can sleep when this thing is over."

"It wasn't a suggestion," Maggie said.

Bear raised his hands in surrender. Maggie smiled kindly at him as she got up and headed back into the kitchen. She'd just grabbed a spatula to scoop the last of the chicken off a baking sheet when an alarm rang in the hallway. Jackson leaned over and saw an old school-bell-style alarm mounted high on the wall he hadn't noticed before.

Ray's shoulders were hunched up around his ears.

"What's that?" he asked.

"Perimeter alarm," Fraggie said.

Maggie walked over and switched off the alarm. The shepherds were barking furiously.

"Somethin' has them bothered," Fraggie said.

Jackson and Bear got up when they saw Fraggie grab her pistol from a safe in the kitchen and slide it into its holster. Maggie ducked into a bedroom and came back with a hunting rifle.

"Couldn't it be just some deer or something?" Ray asked.

"The alarm's designed to avoid accidental tripping, like wildlife," Fraggie said. "And the dogs don't alert to 'just some deer.' Maggie, stay here with Bobbie and Mia."

Maggie ushered Bobbie and Mia into the den as Fraggie led Jackson, Bear, and Ray out the kitchen door.

Fraggie looked down toward where the dogs were barking in the far corner of the yard.

"Whatever's got them bothered is to the North," she said, pointing in the direction of the drive leading down to the adjoining dirt road.

"Hardly any light over there," Bear said.

"I've got some night vision stuff in the prep room," Fraggie said.

"I've got thermal with my gear in the smokehouse," Jackson said.

Fraggie motioned for him to go get it.

"Take an ATV," she said. "I'll go get what I've got. Ray, Bear, y'all two keep your eyes peeled in the meantime."

Jackson hopped on an ATV and took it the quarter mile down to the smokehouse. He found his FLIR thermal scope and attached it to the Winchester Model 70 rifle he'd brought with him. In less than a minute he was back out the door and roaring up the drive to rejoin the others.

As he approached the fork in the drive where the entry way split to go to either house, he saw Fraggie and Bear coming toward him. Ray had climbed up on top of the bulldozer by the fork and was looking around with what Jackson assumed were some sort of night-vision binoculars. Jackson stopped the ATV and put the scope of the rifle up to his eye.

Moving the scope from the dirt road down toward the small county highway at the bottom of the property, he surveyed the darkness. Forest creatures dotted the dark blue background like little yellow and orange stars. He saw Bear, a fiery, round silhouette, walking out onto the road near the drive, brandishing his .357. It all appeared as it should be until a strange, amoebous blob lit up his scope. Dropping the scope from his eye, he looked into the night where the blob had been, but saw nothing. He looked back through the scope. It was still there. Whatever it was, it was moving.

Jackson whistled and the three others looked his direction. He pointed to his eyes, signaling he saw something, then pointed in the direction of the unidentified mass. Ray brought the binoculars back to his eyes as Bear began moving down the road in that direction. Fraggie, however, marched straight through the tall brush right toward where Jackson had pointed.

Looking again through his scope, Jackson watched the blob split in two, like cells dividing. He realized now "the blob" was actually two people crouching in the grass. He was about to whistle to the others again when a branch snapped in the distance. Then more branches. Fraggie broke out in a full sprint toward the sounds. She didn't know she was outnumbered.

Jackson hopped on the ATV and drove headlong into the same tall grass. The dry brush whipped at his ankles, as if scolding him for leaving the dirt road.

"There's two of them, Fraggie!" he yelled.

Fraggie drew her pistol. Gunfire rang out from the small copse of trees ahead. Fraggie returned fire. Jackson was trying to catch up to her when he saw a fence barring his path. He veered the ATV left, avoiding the fence, and headed toward the bottom of the hill, looking for a way around. A full-on shootout had broken out to his right.

"C'mon, c'mon," he said.

But the fence went all the way to the highway. Jackson took a dirt mound at the bottom of the hill so fast the ATV went airborne. He slammed back onto the paved road, straightening the quad and pressing down on the accelerator. The ATV bucked backward as it tore down the highway.

Jackson saw Fraggie nearing the trees—she, too, was getting to the end of the farm's property—when two dark figures stepped out onto the open road.

Jackson tried to stop but knew he couldn't. He dove from the ATV as the figures opened fire on him. Jackson's feet hit the dirt next to the road and he rolled to break his fall.

More shots came from his right—Fraggie and Bear returning fire.

Jackson looked up to see three red lights – taillights – glow to life. Two car doors slammed shut and an engine roared in the darkness.

Jackson hurried to his feet, drawing his Beretta as he ran and firing at the retreating vehicle. He kept running and firing until he got to the intersection with the dirt road that led up to the farm's drive. Bear came jogging down just as Fraggie climbed out from the trees in between them.

"You guys good?" Bear asked, panting.

"I'd be better if I hit one of the fuckers," Fraggie said.

Jackson didn't say anything, his eyes still transfixed down the road.

"Jackie boy," Bear said. "You good?"

Jackson looked at him as he answered.

"Tell me that didn't look like a black pickup."

55

Bragg flinched as a pistol round obliterated the passenger-side mirror. Franko had the truck in gear before he was even completely in and now they were speeding down the dark, winding country road. Bragg slid a fresh magazine into his gun and leaned out the door, leveling the pistol at the darkness behind them.

"Are we clear? Is anyone following?" Franko asked.

Bragg lingered out the window a moment longer.

"I don't see anything," he said. "I knocked the one off the ATV. The other two were on foot."

"There could be more with a car."

"There's nothin' behind us."

Franko didn't slow down, though. He took the turns and hills at speed, the truck dipping and swaying like a rollercoaster car. As he came up on a tight, 90-degree turn, he braked and jerked the wheel before punching the gas again. The truck fishtailed, its back wheels nearly coming off the road and slipping down the embankment leading to the farm fields below.

"Did you look at the camera?" Franko asked. "Can we ID anyone?"

Franko and Bragg had been working their way toward the farm-house the GPS tracker led them to when they heard a faint ringing in the distance. Moments later, people filed out of the house, and it wasn't long before Franko and Bragg realized those people were coming for them. Still, in the light just outside the house, Bragg had been able to snap some photos with a telephoto lens.

"I haven't checked yet, hold on," he said.

Bragg pulled out the camera and looked at its LCD display, flipping through the photos. It was a frame-by-frame slide show of four people stepping out from the house.

"There's that broad you were talking about—the one with the purple hair," he said.

"Frances Conway," Franko said. "The property is in her name."

"Yeah, looks like her and a few guys. Don't see Sayre. There's a black fella."

"Casto?"

"No. Older, much older. And two others that—sonofabitch."

"What?"

Bragg held up the LCD screen for Franko. A man's face—sharp jawline covered in a stubbly beard—was half-illuminated in the porch light outside the house.

"That's the guy on the CC video from the courthouse," he said. "The one that was walking with Casto and his lawyer. And come to think of it, that black guy is the one that was with 'em, too."

"How much you want to bet that little half-breed punk is up there with them?" Franko asked.

The two grinned at each other. Franko reached into his pocket and put a celebratory Winston between his lips, lighting it.

"Call it in," he said.

Bragg pulled out his phone and punched in a number, staring at the screen of the camera until Starcher picked up.

"Yeah, boss," he said. "It's me. I think we've got a twenty on the kid."

56

Wolfe sat in the living room of his penthouse condo watching his 85-inch television. Truth be told, he hardly ever used the thing—but TVs were so cheap these days, he thought three grand was a small price to pay to have the best of something.

Tonight, the entertainment du jour was a playoff baseball game. The Yankees were cleaning the clock of the Athletics in a game that was little more than a formality with New York on the verge of sweeping Oakland. Most people probably found the game boring, but Wolfe liked routs. He found amusement in the superior destroying the inferior. Joy, even. And when the Yankees didn't put in their premier $20-million-a-year closer to step on the A's throats, Wolfe booed profusely.

He had just polished off a glass of Pappy Van Winkle when his phone buzzed on the granite countertop behind him.

"Should I get that for you, dear?" his date asked.

"Grab it for me, but don't answer it," Wolfe said.

The leggy blonde rose gracefully from her seat at the dining room table and walked over to grab the phone. She'd been sitting quietly, per Wolfe's demands, waiting for the game to be over and for him to take her into his bedroom. With a gun to his head, Wolfe wouldn't be able to recall her name—Sarah? Nikki? Ashley? It was most likely an alias, anyway. It's how all these $2,000-an-hour girls worked.

The blonde grabbed his phone and walked it over to him, pulling her skimpy dress down as she did. Wolfe answered the call and put the phone to his ear.

"What is it?" he said.

"It's Starcher. Looks like we may have a location on the Casto kid."

"About damn time," Wolfe said. "Where?"

"A farm off of Highway 10, a ways south of Rion."

"Remote?"

"Very."

"Good, take your squad and handle it."

Starcher was hesitant on the other end of the line.

"Is that going to be a problem?" Wolfe asked.

"To be honest, sir," Starcher said, "he's not up there alone. There's at least four others up there and my guys say they're well-armed."

"Yeah, well your team isn't exactly carrying fucking squirt guns now are they?"

Unbelievable, Wolfe thought to himself. This sad excuse for a life form is about to ask me for even more help.

"I just want to end this, same as you," Starcher continued, "But we want this done clean, right? Five shooters that can see anyone approach from a field away? It's going to be messy, just us. I could bring in SWAT, but—"

"No," Wolfe cut Starcher off, "no one else gets read into this. We end it now—quietly—with what we have. I'll send you a team of my mercenary guys. They can be there in a couple hours. Then you handle this."

Wolfe ended the call and stood up. He excused himself from his company and walked into his home office. There, he pressed a board on the wall and opened a concealed compartment. In it, he grabbed a SAT phone. He flipped the antenna up, punched in a number, and waited for one of his guys to pick up.

"The local vice guys have a location on the Casto kid," Wolfe said as the line went active. "I'll get you specifics, but head south of Rion. Highway 10."

"Copy that," King answered. "How do you want us to proceed when we're on target?"

"This Hopewell County Vice Squad is taking one of our teams and hitting the place. Get eyes on. If they fail or fuck up, clean up the mess."

"Yes, sir. What are our operating parameters if we have to go in?"

Wolfe looked out his bedroom window. From it, he could see out across the Kanawha River and the Southside Bridge to the VigilOne facility atop a hill. Large steel and glass buildings were lit up in the Charleston night, forming their own miniature skyline. He'd built a nice little world for himself and done so by eliminating threats to it. This wouldn't be the first time someone was killed to protect it.

"No witnesses," he said.

57

Jackson, Bear, and Fraggie took shifts on watch overnight, meaning none of them got the kind of sleep they needed. Bear and Fraggie had taken their turns sitting in a camping chair in the bed of Fraggie's Tacoma, while Jackson, now on the third shift, walked up and down the drive to the dirt road.

The sky slowly brightened behind the mountaintops to the east, daring to wake the sleeping world below. Twenty yards to Jackson's left, Argos and Maera stalked parallel to him. When they got to the end of their fenced yard, they sniffed furiously, their ears alert. They hadn't dropped their guard all night, either.

Jackson walked to the fork in the drive and then slowly made his way back up to Maggie and Fraggie's house. As he got close, he could see Fraggie and Bear sharing a bench, both of them with a cup of coffee in hand.

"Mornin'," Fraggie said.

"Good morning," Jackson said.

"You can catch some Z's if you want," Fraggie offered. "Bear and I have it from here."

"I'm good, thanks."

"There's hot coffee in the kitchen."

"Maybe in a bit."

Jackson opened the gate to the porch and took a seat next to them, positioning himself in a way he could still look out over the property.

"You still think they're comin'?" Fraggie asked.

"I do," Jackson said. "They were out here for a reason. It won't take much to put two and two together. And then they'll come. More of them."

The three of them went quiet. Jackson had only said what they'd each been thinking all night, but hearing it out loud somehow made it more real.

"Well, we best get ready if we're gonna have company," Bear said. "Probably time you show us what kind of firepower you have 'round here, Fraggie."

"I can do that," she said. "I've been thinking about the county road down there, though. I've got a couple wireless huntin' cameras we can mount on trees thereabouts. It'll give us a heads up if anyone's inbound."

Jackson nodded.

"I like it. Let's do it," he said.

Fraggie handed her coffee off to Jackson and jogged inside. Jackson leaned forward and closed his eyes, letting the rising steam warm his face.

"You sure you don' want some?" Bear asked.

"Yeah. I'm good."

"Goin' to need somethin' in your belly if shit hits the fan."

Jackson didn't reply. He sat there, his eyes focused on the ground ahead.

"How many do you think will come?" Bear asked.

"I don't know," Jackson said. "All of them, probably."

"How many is that?"

"Not sure. Ten? A dozen?"

"We know of four or five for sure?"

"Yeah, but there'll be more. They know we have at least four here, plus Bobbie. They're not going to be interested in a fair fight."

Jackson reached for his Beretta and held it out in front of him, pulling the slide back just enough to double check there was a round in the chamber. There was. He let the slide go and studied the pistol, rubbing his thumb over Evan's initials on the grip.

"You know," Bear said, "I said it when we were in the thick of it on that mountain with that Sara Beth girl and I'll say it here again: You're a good man, Jack."

Jackson snorted and smiled.

"Thanks," he said.

"Your son's somewhere and he knows it, too."

Jackson looked up at him. He nodded, still smiling. He couldn't bring himself to say it, but he loved Bear—he was grateful to have the big guy by his side.

The front door whined as it swung open, breaking up the quiet moment. Fraggie stepped out, dressed head-to-toe in camouflage and carrying a pack with her.

"Got 'em here," she said. "I'll head down and set them up."

Jackson stood up and held out his hand.

"I can do it," he said.

"I don' mind. I'm ready to go," Fraggie said.

"They use cell service, right? You'll need to be here to confirm they're up and running."

"You'll need a radio, then."

Fraggie slid the pack off her shoulder and handed it over to Jackson, then darted back inside the house.

"You sure you don't want back up?" Bear asked.

"I'll be fine," Jackson said.

Fraggie came back out with three radios, handing one each to Bear and Jackson. "It'll connect to our laptop inside. I'll be in there. Bear can keep eyes on you from here."

"Works for me," Bear said.

Fraggie went back inside as Jackson hopped on an ATV and fired it up. He put the pack on the cargo rack in front of him and took off for the dirt road. As he neared the end of the drive, Bear's voice came through the radio, crackling with static.

"You pissed the dogs off," he said. "They're hollerin' again."

But Jackson didn't hear the last part. He felt his body spike with adrenaline as he turned onto the dirt road and looked down it. There, at the end where it met the county highway, two black pickup trucks were parked nose-to-nose, blocking the road. A half dozen men clad in black and armed with rifles stood behind the trucks, watching Jackson.

A third car – a black SUV – pulled up and more heavily-armed men filed out onto the road. Behind them, a hulking armored vehicle slowed to a stop. It looked just like an MRAP from Jackson's Army days, except it was matte black instead of sandy beige.

Jackson keyed the mic to his radio.

"We're too late," he said.

"What do you mean?" Bear asked.

Slowly, the two black pickups backed up, separating. With a roar of its 7.2-liter turbodiesel engine, the armored vehicle lumbered forward.

"They're already here," Jackson said.

PART V

ROMANS

58

Jackson turned the ATV around and throttled the gas as a volley of gunfire from the MRAP punched small craters into the dirt road just inches to Jackson's left. He pushed down harder on the gas and veered right. The machine gun fire continued to nip at the road, snaking after him. Shots clipped the back of his ATV, sinking .50 caliber fangs into the vehicle's carbon fiber body, and Jackson swerved off the road altogether, driving the quad into a gully of tall grass he hoped was out of the MRAP's line of fire. Just as he crossed the gully, though, the ATV hit a rock, sending Jackson headfirst over the front wheels and into the tall grass ahead.

"What in the hell is that?" Bear hollered from the radio.

Jackson groaned through the pain of the fall as he reached for the button on his radio.

"Armored vehicle with a .50 cal on top," he said. "They're sending it up the road."

"The bulldozer near the front," Fraggie's voice chimed in, "can you get to it?"

Jackson sat up. He could see the top of the earthmover. It was maybe fifty feet away through thick brush and felled trees.

"I can try," he said.

"The keys are in it," Fraggie said. "You can block the drive with it like a cork in a bottle. That's what it's there for."

Jackson began crawling up the obstacle-filled embankment. The MRAP was still firing over his right shoulder, clipping branches and strafing the hillside in front of him. But it didn't seem to know where Jackson was. Thank god for that, he thought.

When he cleared the tall grass, Jackson jogged the remaining way to the bulldozer. It took him a moment to figure out the controls, then he turned the key and the engine of the yellow behemoth coughed to life. Jackson pushed down on the throttle and the dozer's large caterpillar tracks crept forward.

The gunner atop the armored vehicle saw the bulldozer moving in to block the drive and redirected his fire. Rounds clinked and clanked off the dozer's metal cab as Jackson shimmied down into his seat. He raised the machine's steel blade to shield himself.

Jackson pushed the dozer forward until its wide body blocked the entire drive, then killed the engine and grabbed the keys. He ducked out the back of the dozer's cab and tumbled onto the ground. He looked up and saw Bear reversing down the drive from the main house in his Suburban. The machine gun shifted left and fired on the SUV as it moved toward Jackson. Bear drove it bumper-first into the bulldozer to cover Jackson, and pushed open the passenger door.

"Thought you could use a lift," Bear said, flashing his boyish grin.

Jackson grabbed Bear's extended hand and pulled himself in as a round from the machine gun shattered Bear's rearview mirror.

"Oh, you assholes better believe we're exchanging insurance cards when this is done," Bear growled.

He put the Suburban in gear and tore back up the drive. Jackson kept his head low until Bear pulled behind the house for cover.

Maggie and Fraggie ran in and out of the basement exit, carrying a pile of weapons and equipment. Jackson jogged over and stepped inside. Shelving made narrow aisles of dry goods and supplies all the way to the far corner where a walk-in chain-link cage housed an impressive array of firepower. Bobbie and Ray were just inside watching Maggie and Fraggie work. Mia sat slumped in the other corner, wrapped in a blanket, her skin pale and glistening with sweat.

The steps leading from the basement to the main floor creaked behind Jackson and he turned. Sayre nodded at him, standing on the steps where he could see into the basement while also keeping an eye on the main house.

Fraggie brushed past Jackson and disappeared into the gun cage. After a moment, she stepped back out of the cage and tossed Jackson a bullet-resistant vest.

"They're coming up the hill spread out in a line, a dozen of them or so," she said.

"I'd bet they've got more using that MRAP to cover their advance from the road," Jackson said.

"What're ya thinkin'?" Fraggie asked.

Jackson looked at all of them: they were waiting on him. Expecting a plan of action. He remembered Fraggie saying Maggie knew her way around a hunting rifle.

"We need some rifles that can do damage from a distance," he said.

Fraggie turned into the gun cage and came out with a pair of Victrix Tormento rifles.

"You mean like this?" she asked.

"Those are some grade-A boomsticks," Bear said.

"That'll work," Jackson said. "Maggie, you and Bear take them and flank out each way, using the woods for cover. You see a threat, put it down."

Jackson turned toward Maggie, making sure she was okay with this. The woman with the soft, kind face now looked at him with hard, determined eyes. This was the other side of that maternal nature he saw in her. The hunter lioness ready to protect what was hers.

Maggie took a rifle and loaded a magazine.

"I'll take south, down to the ridge in front of the smokehouse," she said. "Bear, you can see just about the whole hillside they're coming up next to the cow pen up there to the north."

Bear nodded and took the other rifle.

"Those SCARs there," Jackson said, peering into the gun cage, "we'll need those, too. And a shotgun that packs a punch."

"Here you go." Fraggie handed him the assault rifles, then held up a Benelli 12-gauge.

"That'll work," Jackson said before turning to Ray. "You take it and protect Bobbie and Mia. Fraggie, I need you up on the roof with one of these SCARs. I'll take the other and post up on the front porch."

Ray took the shotgun and began feeding it rounds.

"Where do you want me to take them?" he asked.

"That door over there is to the shelter," Fraggie said, nodding toward the corner of the store room. "Solid concrete and reinforced door."

"No, if they corner them in there, it's all over," Jackson said. "Ray, you all need to be able to move if you have to. I know that's difficult with how Mia's doing, but we have no choice. Stay in the back of the house upstairs and keep low. Watch the back porch to make sure they don't cut us off from behind."

Ray nodded. He went to Mia in the corner and gently lifted her to her feet, then ushered her up the stairs.

Bobbie stayed behind, looking expectantly at Jackson.

"What about me?" he asked.

"Ray will make sure you guys are safe," Jackson said.

"And what if something happens?" Bobbie asked. "I'm not a little kid. I can do what I need to."

Jackson remembered Maggie and Fraggie showing Bobbie how to shoot the other day. He looked at Fraggie; she shrugged.

"Fine," Jackson said. "Get him a pistol."

"Where do you want me?" Sayre asked, taking the last few steps into the basement.

"I need you to contact whoever you've got, anybody that might help us if we get out of here alive," Jackson said.

Sayre looked at Jackson as if it wasn't enough.

"You don't want me out there?" he asked. "I'm probably the best shot besides you."

"Doubt that very fuckin' much," Fraggie said as she loaded one of the pistols.

Jackson leaned in close to Sayre and lowered his voice.

"Crooked or not, that's still your own out there. Fellow officers," Jackson said. "Deputized and everything. You point a gun at them and pull that trigger, that's a line that can't be uncrossed. Especially for someone with a badge."

"You let me worry about which lines I cross," Sayre said.

Jackson looked into his eyes. Sayre was determined. He was probably going out that door whether Jackson asked him to or not.

"Alright," Jackson said. "Fraggie, you got another SCAR?"

"Three's of everythin'," she said.

"Give it to Sayre." He said. "But we still need that help, Sayre. You make those calls, then you meet me on the front porch."

Sayre took the rifle from Fraggie and patted Jackson on the shoulder before stepping outside and opening his phone. The others all looked at Jackson, strapped up in their bullet-resistant vests and gear. Fraggie gave him a reassuring nod.

"I guess that's it, then," Jackson said. "Make sure you've got a radio on you. If anyone gets overrun, fall back *up* the mountain."

"There's an ATV path in the clearin', leads all the way to a livestock gate and stone wall," Fraggie added.

"All right, if you have to move back, that's where we'll rendezvous. Keep your heads down out there."

At that, the group came to life, moving about in varied but deliberate directions like bees in a hive. Fraggie sidestepped Jackson and reached out for Maggie. She pulled her in and embraced her with a hand around her back and neck.

"Try not to get shot," Fraggie said with a nervous smile.

"You do the same," Maggie said. "I love you."

Fraggie pulled her in and sunk her lips into Maggie's. The two of them lingered there, only conscious of each other in that moment.

Bear looked at Jackson.

"Where's mine, bubba?" he asked.

Jackson grinned and held out a fist for Bear to bump. Bear met Jackson's fist with his own.

"You don't get shot, either," Jackson said as they headed upstairs.

Just outside the basement door, Sayre leaned against a shed, scrolling through the contacts in his phone. Anyone he called for help would be a long shot at this point. His boss wasn't about to come to his aid and the rest of the office probably had it on good authority to do just the same. That only left people who weren't in the office. A thought occurred to him. He hit a name on his contacts and waited for them to pick up.

"Sam," he said when his partner answered, "are you still in Morgantown?"

"I am. Where are you?" Hall asked.

"Somewhere outside of Rion," Sayre said.

"Still? I've read the emails on my phone. Sounds like you've stirred up quite the shit storm out there."

"You don't know the half of it."

Detective Hall's laugh crackled with a poor connection.

"Listen, I need a favor," Sayre said.

"Don't you always," Hall said. "What is it this time?"

"I need you to take a little road trip to Pittsburgh. You can be there in an hour if you go fast."

"And what's in Pittsburgh?"

"The FBI."

59

Out on the front porch, Jackson slid a metal cooler and wrought iron bench in front of him to give himself as much cover as possible. He watched as Maggie disappeared down the hill and positioned herself among the trees. To his right, Jackson could see the back half of Bear's large frame sticking out from behind the cow pen.

Jackson keyed the mic on his radio.

"Can everybody hear me?" he asked.

Several variations of *Yes* and *Roger that* crackled at him from the handheld. He rested the barrel of his rifle on the porch's banister and looked down the gun's scope. None of the armed men were advancing toward him yet.

"I don't have eyes," Jackson said. "Can anyone see them?"

"Give me a minute," Maggie radioed back.

"There are a bunch of them in the brush, coming up the hill," Bear said. "They're fanned out in a line. 10 or so. Maybe a dozen."

Jackson looked down his gun's scope again. Nothing.

"I still don't see them, Bear. Can you get an exact count?" he asked.

"Uh, one, two...five...13. Baker's dozen."

"There's another five over on the drive behind that armored car,"

Maggie added. "Plus the gunner on top, and I assume a driver. They look like they're trying to figure out how to move the bulldozer."

At least twenty, Jackson thought. Twenty trained shooters to seven —half of whom were the furthest thing from gunfighters.

"Maggie, do you have a shot at that gunner on the MRAP?" he asked

"Yep," she replied.

"We're going to wait until they come into view up here," Jackson said. "When things start, you take him first. Bear, you take the closest target to you."

"Consider it done," Bear said.

Now, all there was to do was wait. Jackson was calm. He breathed deeply in through his nose and exhaled slowly through his mouth, keeping his heart rate down. His eyes were fixed on the crest of the hill. The autumn foliage swayed back and forth down by the county road; he could hear the leaves rustling on the trees behind the house. Any other day, the setting would be perfect. A crisp breeze blew down the corridor of the porch and out toward the hill, swaying the tall grass back and forth in waves. Then, amidst the dancing vegetation, the first head appeared.

The man was wearing a black tactical helmet, a black mask covering his face, and dark, wraparound sunglasses concealing his eyes. Jackson centered his rifle on the man when another appeared just to the right of the first man. Another appeared to the left. A second later, five more were in view.

"Get ready," Jackson said into his radio.

He waited until all thirteen were visible, but never took his rifle off that first man—he was closest to Jackson. Behind all his gear, the man was anonymous. A black specter with no name. He could be anyone, Jackson thought. It didn't matter. Whoever he was, he'd come here with the worst of intentions. Now, he was going to pay for that with his life.

Jackson keyed his radio again.

"Hit it."

Two shots rang out, one to Jackson's right and one farther down the property to his left. In his peripheral vision, he saw a figure jerk backwards like they'd been kicked by a mule. Jackson squeezed the trigger on his rifle. The lead round exploded out of the barrel of the gun, traveling the fifty yards between Jackson and the man in a hundredth of a second.

Red mist sprayed as the man's head kicked backwards. Through the rifle's scope, Jackson watched his body fall limp, then Jackson was shifting left and firing at his next target. Gunfire erupted all around him. Rounds plinked and planked off the front of the house, shattering glass and punching holes in the siding. None of it fazed Jackson.

His actions were calculated and methodical, a lifetime of drills and training kicking in all at once. Two shots. Target down. Three shots. Another down. Two shots. Winged him. One more. He's down.

Most of the men in the field had been hit when the rest stopped advancing and ducked into the tall grass for cover. Jackson continued suppressive fire in their general direction.

"I can't see them on the hillside anymore," Bear radioed.

"Same," Maggie said.

Jackson emptied a magazine into the field of grass before radioing back.

"Is the gunner on the MRAP down?" he asked over the radio.

"Yes, first one I took down," Maggie said. "They've given up on trying to move the dozer, they're coming around on foot and – oh. Fuck."

But before she could reply Jackson saw it—a double-file line of men coming around the bend in the drive. The two men in front had large ballistic shields.

"They've got shields," Maggie said.

"Maggie's behind them," Bear said. "She should have a shot."

"No, they'll figure it out. It'll give away her position," Jackson said.

He looked down his scope at the approaching men. The shields were just big enough to cover them head-to-toe as they hunched down.

"Fraggie, you're up top. Do you have a shot overhead?" he asked.

"Back, middle of the pack," she said.

"Do it. Bear, if they lift those shields to cover, go for their feet."

Jackson could feel the house shake as Fraggie unleashed a barrage of gunfire from somewhere above him. A couple men fell in the drive as the rest of the others pulled tight together, constricting like an accordion.

"If I'm no good here, I'm moving up," Maggie said.

Jackson saw movement amongst the trees and knew it was Maggie. Then he saw one of the men behind the shields see it, too and fire. The movement in the woods stopped.

"Maggie! Maggie, are you good?" Jackson radioed.

A garbled transmission came back. Jackson didn't wait for a clearer answer.

"Fraggie, Bear, cover me!" he said.

He ran down the porch, jumping over the banister and headlong into danger. Gunfire erupted on both sides. Jackson landed on his feet and took off in a sprint. Bullets slammed into tree trunks as he moved. He could hear Fraggie and Bear's desperate cover fire, but there was only so much they could do with those shields between them and the gunmen.

Jackson leapt over the wire fence corralling the goats. As he got to the drive that led down to the smokehouse, he saw Maggie lying in the middle of the dirt road.

"Maggie, are you okay?" Jackson asked.

"I took one in the leg," she said, wincing.

Jackson slid to a stop and put himself between Maggie and the shooters. He saw the gunshot wound on her left thigh and examined it quickly.

"It looks like it got all meat," he said.

He pulled out his knife, cut off one of the sleeves from his shirt, and tied it tightly around her leg.

"That'll have to do for now," he said. "You think you can move?"

Maggie nodded, still wincing. Jackson helped her to her feet and got up underneath her arm, trying to take as much weight off the leg as he could. With his free hand, he grabbed his radio.

"I've got Maggie. She's hit, but she's okay," he reported. "We're coming up now. Keep covering us."

"Hurry," Fraggie said. "They're moving toward the house."

Together, Maggie and Jackson ran an awkward three-legged race through the woods back toward the house. No one fired in their direction now. In fact, there was no gunfire at all as an eerie calm settled over everything.

"How close are they to the house?" Jackson radioed.

"Fifty feet," Bear said, "but they're using the cars for cover now."

"Ray, get Mia and Bobbie down to the basement. Get ready to go out the back door and fall back," Jackson said.

Maggie groaned with every step her injured leg tried to take. Jackson pulled her in and held her tighter, trying to support her more. The house was coming into view.

"I'm losing them underneath the roof," Fraggie said. "I'm about to be useless up here."

"Just keep covering. We're almost there. Then we'll move."

Jackson got Maggie to the far side of the porch. There, the yard swung low and the deck stood several feet off the ground. Jackson leapt for the banister and pulled himself up, then turned to extend a hand down to Maggie.

"Jack, behind you!" Bear screamed from the radio.

Jackson whipped around to see a man dressed head-to-toe in black standing at the gate on the opposite side of the porch. His gun was leveled squarely at Jackson. Dropping to a knee, Jackson went for the Beretta holstered on his hip. He'd just gotten his hand around the grip when a gunshot broke the peace.

60

Jackson flinched, bracing for the searing pain of the bullet to tear somewhere into his body. When nothing came, he opened his eyes to see the gunman across the porch grasping at his neck. His eyes, the only thing visible on his face, were large white saucers. Jackson was looking into them when two more shots came through the living room window, shattering the glass as they hit the gunman. Jackson drew his pistol as the front door of the house kicked outward. Sayre stepped out between Jackson and the gunman, a rifle leveled against his shoulder. He put a fourth and fifth round squarely into the gunman's head. The man fell off the porch, lifeless. Sayre turned and looked back at Jackson.

"Missed one," he said.

"Thanks," Jackson said.

He turned around and extended a hand to Maggie, pulling her up and over the porch banister. Sayre covered them as Jackson helped Maggie into the house.

"Maggie's safe," Jackson radioed. "Bear, Fraggie: take her out back. Sayre and I will cover from the front of the house."

Sayre stepped up to the shattered living room window and emptied a magazine, dropping two more men. Jackson reached into a pouch on his vest and tossed him another one. Back in the kitchen, Bear came tumbling through the side door, dropping to the floor as bullets chased him inside. Fraggie, who'd just come off the ladder on the back of the house, leaned over looking at him.

"You good there, buddy?" she asked.

"Sons of bitches," Bear grumbled.

A masked man put his gun up and peered through the bullet-riddled kitchen door. Fraggie drew her .460 Magnum and shot the man square through the window. The door groaned in pain as the man's body slumped against it.

"Welp," Bear said, wiping chunks of bad guy off of him, "he don' have a face no more."

He slid to Maggie, and together he and Fraggie helped her get to her feet.

"We're takin' Maggie out now," Fraggie yelled to the front of the house.

"Got it," Jackson yelled back. "Right behind you."

Out of the corner of his eye, Sayre saw a dark figure move toward the front door. Sayre whirled, firing, then quickly ducked behind a couch in the living room. One of the men with a ballistic shield entered through the front door with a pistol poking out from around the shield. The man fired at Sayre, shooting almost without aiming. Jackson came to his feet and fired back, but the man turned his shield in time. Jackson's rounds ricocheted off the large rectangular piece of armor into the walls and ceilings of the living room.

Still, Jackson continued firing as fast as he could squeeze the trigger. The barrage overwhelmed the shielded gunman, and he stepped back through the doorway and out onto the porch. The move bought Sayre enough time to crawl around Jackson and into the kitchen. Jackson retreated back with Sayre, his clip empty.

"This guy's a pain in the ass, huh," Sayre said.

"We're going to have to flank him," Jackson said. "I'll draw him down the hallway. He won't be able to turn easily. Wait here in the kitchen, then drop him from behind."

Sayre nodded.

The gunman moved back into the house. Jackson loaded a fresh magazine and fired at him as he slowly backed down the hall. The man, shield raised, moved quickly after Jackson, cornering his prey. Jackson got to the end of the hall and stepped into a bedroom. The man followed, never seeing Sayre as he passed the kitchen. Sayre came up silently behind the man, put his rifle to the back of the man's neck, and squeezed the trigger.

Jackson came back into the hall and stood over the body, looking at Sayre. Sayre was looking at the man he'd just killed.

"You good?" Jackson asked.

"Yeah," Sayre said quietly

"Come on. I don't hear anything. Let's check on the others."

Sayre nodded and helped Jackson step over the dead body now blocking the hallway. The two filed down the stairs to the basement and out the back door. It was a short hike to the livestock gate they'd agreed to rendezvous at. Jackson was relieved to see everyone else standing there. Bobbie and Mia even had Argos and Maera on their leads.

"I see you took the pooches," Jackson said.

"We couldn't just leave them," Bobbie said.

The group stood together and looked back down over Maggie and Fraggie's land. Bodies dressed in black lay scattered from the house all the way down the drive. Wisps of smoke danced upwards over the macabre setting.

"Is that really all of them?" Bobbie asked.

"Did we really just do that?" Ray asked.

"They did it," Jackson said coldly. "We were just the consequence of their actions."

The quiet lingered on before Argos and Maera pulled at their leads, barking and snarling. Twenty yards down the mountain two more men dressed in black appeared, running as fast as they could away from the group, headed back the way they'd come.

"Two runners," Jackson called out.

Sayre and Fraggie started after them. Bear dropped to one knee and brought the Victrix rifle up to his shoulder. He peered down the scope, stalking the men's movements with the barrel of the rifle, shifting slowly as they ran. Bear squeezed the trigger. A shot rang out. One of the men took an awkward step before falling and disappearing into the tall grass. The second kept running. Bear bolted another round into the chamber and fired again but missed. The second man disappeared into the woods.

Sayre ran to where he'd seen the first man go down. The round had hit the masked man in the abdomen and he was rolling around, writhing in pain. Fraggie continued running in the direction of the man Bear had missed, but Sayre yelled out to her.

"Forget it, Fraggie. They're gone," he said.

He turned back and looked at the man trying in vain to apply pressure to his own gunshot wound.

"Besides, we've got one," he added.

Kneeling down, Sayre reached out and unbuckled the man's helmet. He slid the face mask off a baby-faced man with a military buzz cut. The man glowered at Sayre.

Sayre smiled.

"Detective Bragg," he said, "we meet again."

61

J ackson and Bear jogged over to Sayre and joined him in observing Bragg as he squirmed restlessly on the ground.

"Did you search him?" Jackson asked.

"Not yet," Sayre said.

Bear crouched down and began doing so. Bragg shifted his weight and kicked at Bear like a toddler throwing a tantrum, but Jackson dropped down and knelt on Bragg's wound. He pointed his Beretta at Bragg's face. Bragg howled in agony.

"Don't do that," Jackson said.

"Get the fuck off me," Bragg said.

"I'll go start checking the others," Sayre said behind them, referring to the other fallen gunmen.

Bear methodically worked over Bragg, turning his gear and everything on him inside out. Extra ammunition; a second gun; two knives; tear gas canisters. No identification of any kind.

"I don't see a badge or anything that identifies him as police," Bear said.

"That's because they didn't come here as police," Jackson said.

"Yes, I did," Bragg said, laughing. "Police! You're all under arrest. Get on the ground."

Bragg cackled and continued to squirm. Ray helped Maggie walk over to Jackson and Bear as they huddled over Bragg. Argos and Maera growled as Bobbie and Mia brought them over.

"You came here for him, right?" Jackson asked. "For Bobbie?"

Bragg ignored Jackson's question, propping himself up on one elbow. He gazed up to the peak of the mountain they were on and then down to the county road below. He noted the other mountains in the distance.

"It's nice here," Bragg said, "Pretty. Reminds me of that song."

He started to hum.

"Who sent you for Bobbie? Starcher? Someone higher? The Sheriff?" Jackson said.

Bragg started singing.

"*O beautiful, for spacious skies—*"

"You're going to bleed out here, unless you give one of us a reason to take you to a hospital."

"*For amber waves of grain,*" Bragg crooned, his voice rising.

"Everyone here, who are they? They're not all Vice. Are they County SWAT?"

"*For purple mountain majesties, above the fruited plain—*"

"That's enough."

But now Bragg arched back and screamed more than he sang. "*America! America! God shed His grace on thee—*"

Jackson grabbed Bragg by his vest and pinned him against the ground.

"Stop it," he growled.

"*And crown thy good with brotherhood,*" Bragg chanted in between maniacal laughter, "*from sea to shining sea!*"

Bear drew his .357 and pressed it hard against Bragg's cheek.

"My friend here told you to knock it off," he said.

Sayre came back up the mountainside, wiping his brow. He put his hands on his knees and breathed heavily.

"I checked about ten of them or so," he said. "Half I've never seen before. Not around the Sheriff's Office or anything. None of them have any kind of ID."

Bragg chuckled again.

"You all," he said, "you're so fucking stupid."

"Enlighten us then," Jackson said. "Who are the ones we don't know?"

"Ah man, they're from the company. They're from *corporate*."

Bragg continued chuckling. Jackson, Sayre, and Bear took turns looking at one another. Then Jackson put it together.

"VigilOne," he said.

"Bingo!" Bragg shouted. "And what do we have for our winner?"

Jackson slammed him against the ground again.

"Okay, VigilOne sent you guys help," he said. "To do what?"

"The kid, man," Bragg said, "To kill the kid. To kill all you assholes."

"For what? A bad shoot? That doesn't make any sense."

Bragg laughed again.

"I mean, really, how dumb are y'all?" he said.

"What for, then?" Jackson asked.

"They're a business. You're fucking with business."

"And what about you? Do you get paid something?"

"I am *gainfully employed*."

"Cut the shit. You know what I'm asking."

But Bragg just laughed again.

"You dumb fucks," he mumbled, trailing off.

"Hey, hey," Jackson said, shaking him. "Wake up."

"Give it up. Look at how much blood he's lost," Sayre said.

Jackson pressed down on Bragg's gunshot wound, hoping in vain it would bring Bragg back to the world of the conscious. Bragg's head slipped to the side as blood continued to stream out between Jackson's fingers. Jackson let up, defeated.

"What did he mean? 'Fuckin' with business'?" Bear asked.

"Probably exactly what Jackson thought," Ray said from behind them. "They're all getting kickbacks or whatever for drummin' up bodies for the prison and the rehab program."

"But if we have the full scope of a private military contractor gunning for us," Sayre said, "we're more fucked than we thought."

A QUARTER MILE AWAY, across the county road on an opposite mountainside, King and Cobb lay prone on a flat piece of earth. Draped in camouflage, you could be ten feet from them and not know they were there.

Cobb eyed their targets through a spotting scope as King looked down the scope atop his M40 rifle. He adjusted the turret knobs, dialing in the precise elevation and windage. In between him and Cobb lay the photos of Robert Casto, Jackson Clay, Raymond Byrd, Archibald Beauchamp, Frances Conway, and Magdalena Lynch.

"They're not moving anymore," Cobb said. "Who's the third woman? Younger, skinny."

"Unknown," King said.

"We'll deal with it. Do you have a shot on the black kid? Casto?"

"Negative. There's someone in the way. Raymond Byrd, it looks like."

Cobb backed away from the spotting scope for a moment and looked at the adjacent mountainside with his unaided eyes, using his hand to block the sun. The targets were indecipherable stick figures. He put his eye back to the scope and confirmed what King saw.

"Copy. Boss said to put the others down if necessary," Cobb said. "Fire when ready."

62

The gunshot thundered through the small valley. Jackson and Bear ducked at the sound. A flat thud immediately followed, then Mia was screaming and Ray was flying backwards, propelled by the 51mm round that had punched him square in the chest, exploding his heart and killing him before he hit the ground.

"Sniper! Sniper!" Jackson yelled. "Get down!"

Sayre and Fraggie dove onto the ground next to Jackson and Bear. Maggie grabbed Bobbie and Mia, both paralyzed with fear, and pulled them down with her. Sayre reached out and grabbed the dogs' leads before they could bolt away.

A second shot rumbled, tearing into Bobbie's arm. He screamed in pain.

"That one got Bobbie," Bear said.

"How bad?" Jackson asked.

"In his arm," Fraggie said. "I'm on it."

Jackson rolled to look over at Fraggie tending to Bobbie's arm. He glanced at Ray lying awkwardly on his side, and knew the man was already gone.

"We're caught in the open here," Sayre said.

A third shot crashed into a rock near Fraggie's head.

"Jesus fuckin' Christ," she stammered.

"We need to move," Bear said. "We're sittin' ducks here."

Jackson looked around for an answer. Between him and Bear was the equipment Bear had pulled off of Bragg. He eyed the tear gas canisters turned on their side.

"Everyone make some kind of mask," he said, "and get eye protection if you can. I've got an idea."

Bear glanced at the canisters, then back to Jackson. He grinned. He pulled the goggles off of Bragg's head and handed them along with Bragg's face mask to Mia.

"Here you go, hon. Put these on," he said.

Another round punched into the earth near them.

Mia did as she was told. Maggie took off her sweatshirt and started cutting it into smaller pieces with a knife. Bear pulled a handkerchief out of his pocket and offered it first to Jackson and then to Sayre, but they both declined. He then tried giving it to Bobbie, but Bobbie didn't respond. He lay on the ground, shaking and staring at his dead uncle. He barely flinched as a fourth shot whizzed over his head.

"I'll pop these and use them for cover to get to those bodies over there," Jackson said. "Hopefully they have more gas on them. Then we can make a wall of it and block the shooter's view all the way to cover."

"Alright guys, if you're not shot or helpin' someone shot, put some rounds on that mountainside over there when he goes," Bear said.

Sayre handed the dogs off to Maggie and took Bragg's rifle off of his body.

Bear reloaded his .357 and looked over at Jackson.

"On you, brother," he said.

Jackson popped open the canisters and tossed them into the clearing between him and the next bit of cover. They hissed as yellowish-gray clouds billowed out and blanketed the surrounding mountainside in noxious gas. Jackson took a deep breath in and ran.

Bear and Sayre sat up and unleashed a volley of gunfire. The sniper across the way either didn't see Jackson or ignored him because the return fire came directly at the group. Jackson made it to a jagged rock formation and crouched down. The first body was just feet away from him. He reached out and patted the corpse down, finding another two canisters strapped to the dead gunman's vest. He opened them, tossing one just to his left to give himself more cover and then threw the other in the direction of the rest of the group.

Jackson keyed the mic on his radio.

"Can you guys hear me?" he said.

"I've got you," Maggie radioed back.

"A couple more and you guys should be able to get behind the house for cover."

The gas inflamed Jackson's senses as he crawled forward on his hands and knees. He coughed and his eyes watered to the point he could barely see. He felt around with his hands until he felt another body suited up in polyester and Kevlar. Another dead gunman, supplied with two canisters of gas. Jackson popped them open and tried to fill in the bare spots of the wall of gas that now rose between him and the others.

"Okay, that's the best we're going to do," Jackson yelled into his radio. "Go! Go!"

Huddled down, the group used the smokescreen for cover and ran behind the house. Fraggie, after setting a wounded Bobbie down, ran into the basement. She returned moments later with an armful of proper gas masks and eye wash for Jackson.

"Where's the nearest car?" Mia asked, crying. "We have to get out of here."

"No," Jackson said, "that shooter is set up somewhere across the county highway over there. There's no cover on the drive from the house or the dirt road. They could take out the car easily. Or worse."

Maggie tried to tilt Jackson's head back to administer the eye wash, but he brushed her off.

"Our best bet is to use the woods for cover," Jackson continued. "Either up the mountain and over to the East or down that way to the South."

The group looked up at the foreboding mountain. It had to be another thousand feet or so in elevation and at least triple that in distance.

"I've made that climb before. It's not easy, and Bobbie's shot and Mia's sick," Maggie said.

"Plus we're going to have PMC's on our asses," Fraggie added.

"South then," Jackson said. "But we've got to move now. Time is distance and distance is life right now."

The group pulled to their feet and headed for the trees. Maggie put an arm around Bobbie—still dazed—and ushered him forward.

As they walked, Jackson grabbed Fraggie and pulled her aside. "What's down that way? Where are we going to end up?"

"I don't know, to tell you the truth," Fraggie said. "It's woods like these all the way to the end of our land. I haven't had a reason to go beyond that."

"Well, now we do."

Jackson reached into his pocket and grabbed his handheld GPS, holding it up for Fraggie to see.

"I assume you've worked one of these before?" he asked.

"Of course," she said.

"Take it and figure out what's up ahead. You take point for the group."

"What are you going to do?"

"Hang back and watch our six."

"Don't hang back too far."

Jackson nodded and slowed his pace, allowing the others to gain distance. If anyone questioned what he was doing, no one said so. He trailed the group fifty feet back, his rifle in hand. When he wasn't looking behind for their pursuers, he was scouting the earth around him, searching.

A half-mile into the woods, he found what he was looking for. A large sycamore maple had toppled over, its root system taking the surrounding ground with it, and dammed up a small creek. The wadded clump of roots sat in a now-dry creek bed, covering a body-sized ditch. It was the perfect spot.

Jackson stopped and watched the group continue on. Bear looked back, opened his mouth to speak, but Jackson shook his head. He put a finger over his mouth and pointed to his radio before holding up three fingers. Bear took his radio and switched to Channel Three.

"Be right there," Jackson said. "You all need to go on like normal."

"What are you doing?" Bear radioed back.

"Ending this."

Bear lingered for a moment, unsure. His instincts told him to help his friend, but he trusted Jackson. Reluctantly, he continued to walk ahead.

"Good luck, brother," he said quietly into the radio.

JACKSON SLID into the ditch and dug with his hands, making it a bit deeper, then laid down and covered himself with the dirt and leaves and pine needles he'd dug up. He left his face exposed but smeared it with mud and wedged it under the mop of dirt hanging from the tree's roots.

He had a narrow line of sight each way, both the way they had come and the way they were headed. More importantly though, with the forest quiet all around him, he could hear everything.

He closed his eyes and forced his heart rate down again. His mind kept returning to Ray's death and Bobbie being shot – how he had let that happen on his watch – but he forced those thoughts away, pushed them down deep. Jackson took a deep breath in through his nose and exhaled slowly through his mouth. He imagined Evan lying next to him, the two of them out hunting together. Posted up and waiting for the moment to strike. Evan never lived past a few years old, but Jackson could picture him perfectly as a teenager now. Scrawny with disheveled brown hair and a bulging Adam's apple just as Jackson had had when he was a teen. Evan looks at him and smiles before turning his gaze down range again. A branch snaps in the distance and together they look.

"Is that them?" Evan asks.

Is that them? Is that? Jackson came back to reality. He hadn't imagined the branch snapping—it had really happened. He turned and looked in the direction the sound had come from. Something moved in the distance. Flat, dull thuds thumped on forest floor, crunching leaves. Another branch snapped. The movement was human. No forest creature moved so clumsily through their own environment. He could hear the movement shift. From his right, to directly behind him, and eventually over to his left—the same way the group had gone.

"Here," a voice said. "More matted leaves, continuing east."

Two pursuers, Jackson realized. At least. As the sounds slowly moved away from him, he shifted his weight to get a better view. From under the clump of roots he could see two pairs of feet walking in the direction Bear and the others had continued on.

Slowly and quietly, Jackson pushed himself away from the fallen tree. Rising to one knee, he now saw the rest of both men. They were wearing tactical camouflage, not the Mossy Oak kind you picked up at Bass Pro Shops but the kind military or paramilitary wore. Each of them had on wide-brimmed boonie hats, concealing their faces in the shadow.

Jackson raised his rifle and put its sights on the man closest to him. If he had to, he felt confident he could engage the man as he moved, but a real hunter waited for his best shot. Jackson put his feet underneath him and stood up. He placed a foot outside the ditch and in one graceful motion stepped out quietly. Never taking his eyes off his target, he moved with the man, keeping his clean shot. And when the man stopped to sidestep a rocky ledge, Jackson took it.

He squeezed the trigger and hit the man squarely between the shoulder blades. The man hadn't even fallen before Jackson had the second man in his sights, but the second man was faster. Jumping to his right, the man ducked behind a tree as Jackson's shot went wide. Jackson fired twice more, hoping to catch the man stepping out on the other side of the tree, but the man played it smart, peering out just enough to see where he was shooting and returning fire.

Rounds kicked up the leaves at Jackson's feet and he ran forward, grabbing cover behind the thick trunk of an empress tree. He tilted his head just enough to see where the man had fired from. Jackson watched the man move from tree to tree, trying to swing around Jackson's position like a hand on a clock. In turn, Jackson moved with him, keeping the man downhill of himself. When he caught the man in an opening, he brought his rifle to his shoulder and fired again. The man threw himself to the ground and rolled off the rocky ledge behind him. The move saved the man but gave Jackson the advantage.

Jackson moved toward the ledge, gun raised. There, he leaned forward and pointed the barrel down. The man was gone. He must be tucked up underneath, hoping to catch me run past, Jackson thought. Slowly, he got down and placed his rifle on the ground. He unholstered his Beretta and crawled to the lip of the rock. He took a deep breath in, then out, and did it.

Dropping to his belly, he reached his arm over the ledge and pointed the gun at the earth underneath. But there was nothing but dirt and leaves. And when leaves crunched behind him, Jackson knew he'd made a grave mistake.

"Hands out," a voice behind him said.

Jackson did as he was ordered, stretching his arms out, holding his Beretta in his right hand.

"Now, drop the—"

A gunshot cracked through the air. Jackson flinched. He rolled over just in time to catch what remained of the man's head collapse and hit the rocks at Jackson's feet. Bear walked over, holstered his .357, and grinned at Jackson.

"Bear," Jackson said, confused.

"C'mon," Bear said. "You didn't think I was going to let you have all the fun, did ya?"

63

Bear was helping Jackson wipe off what dirt and forest muck he could when the rest of the group came running back.

"We heard gunshots," Maggie said. "Are you okay?"

"Yeah, fine, thanks to Bear here," Jackson said.

"What happened?"

"I hung back to get a drop on our pursuers."

"Without telling us?"

"I needed you to continue on like I hadn't stopped to make sure."

Maggie shook her head.

"That was dumb," she said. "Reckless and dumb."

"Call it what you want," Bear said, "but it worked. We got two more dead bad guys to prove it."

"You think that's all of them?" Fraggie asked.

Jackson kicked over the mostly headless body at his feet and checked the dead man's pockets.

"Hard to say. At the very least, I don't think there's any more with these guys," he said.

"Maybe we could turn around, then?" Mia said. "Go back to the farm."

"Too risky. For all we know, there's more back there trying to figure out where we're headed," Jackson said.

"Well, where *are* we headed?"

"That's a good question."

Jackson stood up and brushed himself off some more before turning to Fraggie.

"You figure out what's ahead yet?" he asked.

"There's a road about a mile away," Fraggie said. "It leads into the town of Kaybee. I've been there. Not much of a town, really."

Jackson extended his hand, asking for the GPS. Fraggie handed it over. He switched the map over to a satellite overlay.

"Looks like there's a building on that road with a parking lot," he said. "Gray roof. A white tower of some kind, maybe."

"It must be that church over there," Maggie said. "What's it called? Kaybee Assembly of God?"

"Do you know the pastor there?" Jackson asked.

"Not personally, no."

"So, you don't know what they'd do with a bunch of armed strangers escorting a wanted fugitive?"

Jackson took the group's collective silence as a no. He sighed and looked down at the screen.

"Do we have much of a choice right now?" Sayre asked.

"My thoughts exactly," Bear said.

"There's got to be a better option then going to someone who's first call will be the police," Jackson said.

But nothing came to him. He handed the GPS back to Fraggie and looked at the group. They were tired and scared. Bobbie was shot. If he was going to put faith blindly into something, Jackson thought, he could do worse than a church.

"Let's go," Jackson said.

It took them a little more than twenty minutes to cover the mile through the woods. At the end of it, they stepped out onto a small, paved road that ended at the tree line. Halfway between them and the intersection down the road sat the church Jackson had seen on the GPS.

Kaybee Assembly of God was an unassuming red brick T-shaped

building with shallow roofs rising up to a steeple that felt too small for the chapel it grew from. A pair of glass doors at the front led to a parking lot that hugged the building like a horseshoe.

"If anyone's got a better idea, now's the time to speak up," Jackson said.

No one said anything.

"Alright, then. Leave the guns here," he said.

"I'm not going in there unarmed," Fraggie said.

"Fine. One pistol each. Concealed," Jackson said. "But, Bobbie and Mia, you guys drop everything. And someone has to stay here with the dogs. At least for now."

He looked at Mia, holding the dogs' leads. The hike had exacerbated the symptoms of withdrawal. Her olive skin was pale now. Jackson half expected her to keel over any moment.

"I'll stay here," she said. "Church isn't really my thing, anyway."

"Just until we check it out," Jackson said. "Then we'll come back for you."

Jackson and the rest of the group formed a pile of firearms hidden at the tree line before heading for the church. They found the front doors open and Jackson led them inside. The chapel was dimly lit, with ten-foot pews running a couple dozen rows deep on either side of a central aisle leading toward the altar. Burgundy carpeting ran from one beige wall to the other.

"Hello?" Bear called out.

Fraggie jabbed him in the ribs. A man in a black shirt and coat with a white clerical collar stepped out from a door and gave the group a warm smile. He was young and handsome, clean-shaven with short, cropped hickory-brown hair.

"Hello, there," he said. "Please, come in."

He ushered them forth, still smiling. The group, with Jackson in the lead, approached hesitantly.

"You just missed noon mass I'm afraid," the pastor said. "Not that it has much fanfare on a weekday."

"I'm sorry to say we're not here for mass, father," Jackson said.

"Oh, please, Reverend Asher is fine," the pastor said, "Or Asher. Or even Ash, if you'd like. Please, then, what brings you here?"

Just as he'd finished asking, the Reverend spotted Bobbie, bleeding from his arm.

"My goodness, son, are you okay?" he asked.

"He's been shot," Jackson said.

"He needs a doctor," the Reverend said.

"He does. Truth be told, we could all use some help. A safe place. We were hoping this might be it. There's one more of us outside, too, with two dogs."

The Reverend stood there, taking in the group. The six of them were dirty, disarranged, and tired looking. He extended his arms outward, his palms open.

"John 3:17," he said. "'But if anyone has the world's goods and sees his brother in need, yet closes his heart against him, how does God's love abide him?'"

The group looked at one another, unsure of how to answer.

Reverend Asher chuckled again, and gave them yet another warm smile as he explained himself.

"What I'm trying to say is, you are safe here."

64

Starcher paced on his back deck waiting to hear back from his men. He'd told them, along with the men Wolfe sent him, to go back to where Franko and Bragg had seen Sayre and the others and end this nightmare once and for all. But when Franko finally called him, the news wasn't good.

"Boss! Boss!" Franko yelled breathlessly as Starcher answered his call, "It's bad."

"Is the problem handled?" Starcher asked.

"No. Fuck no," Franko said in between gulps of air. "It was a fucking massacre."

Starcher felt a burning sensation in his chest. He stopped pacing and leaned against the banister overlooking his backyard.

"What do you mean? Tell me what happened," he said.

"The thing was a fuck up from the start," Franko said. "We couldn't get the MRAP up to the property. They started picking us off one by one. They had serious fucking firepower."

"I sent two dozen of you! You said there were no more than four or five of them."

"Boss, I'm telling you. These were trained fucking shooters. Not just Sayre. A half dozen of them."

"And you had four times that many."

"Yeah. Had."

Starcher gripped the banister, feeling as if his legs might collapse underneath him.

"Had," Starcher repeated. "How many of our guys are down?"

"I don't know," Franko said. "All of them. Almost all of them. I said it was a fucking massacre."

Starcher moved for the closest chair and flopped into it. He was sweating now as if it were the dog days of summer, not a cool autumn afternoon. "The cover for this was that you guys were on a training exercise. What kind of training exercise gets the whole fucking team killed?"

"I know. I mean, I don't know. I think you need to call the higher-ups again. We need help."

"No. Uh-uh. You do not understand how fucking close our balls are to the band saw on this. You want me to tell them we just lost all their men *and* Casto is still out there? Forget it."

Starcher rubbed his eyes and thought. He needed a way out. But to get that, he needed time. And if there was a field full of dead bodies somewhere, he didn't have a lot of it.

"You," he said. "You and I. We're going to go back there and we're going to make this look like something we can control."

"How do we do that?" Franko asked.

"The mercs. There's no way to trace them back to VigilOne. They'd make sure of that. We fix this. Our boys were on a training exercise and the property wasn't secured. They came across unknown gunmen, things went south. The Sheriff will want a pound of flesh and we'll be the guys to get it for him. *We* control the narrative."

"I don't know, boss. This is a fucking mess. We can't just cover this up."

"Listen to me. We are out of fucking time on this one. The moment they discover that place as it is, the jig is up. You understand? We're talking jail time. Real fucking jail time. No. No, we are going to fix this. And then we're going to figure out how to end all of this."

Franko sounded hesitant as he answered Starcher.

"Alright," he said. "You're the boss."

"I *am* the fucking boss," Starcher said. "Meet me at the place."

"What if they're still there?"

Starcher snorted.

"We should be so fucking lucky," he said.

65

Jackson was trying to clean himself up as best he could in the men's restroom when Sayre stepped in. He looked Sayre over from head to toe, then handed him a stack of paper towels. Sayre chuckled and began cleaning himself off.

"Thanks," he said.

Jackson finished up with his face and arms and worked down his lower legs. A wad of soiled towels amassed on the counter next to the sink.

"It's nice of the reverend. All this," Sayre said. "But you know we can't stay here."

"I know," Jackson said.

"Even if he really is interested in keeping us safe, anyone can walk in here. And we're still in Hopewell County."

"I know, Sayre."

"Then what?"

"We need help. Real help. Did you find anyone with your phone calls before everything went down?"

"My partner promised to drive up from Morgantown to the Pittsburgh FBI Field Office. I have no idea what happened with that."

"Can you call him back? Or make some other calls? I'm about to do the same here in a minute now that we've got service again."

Sayre nodded and finished up wiping off his arms and hands and stepped back out. Jackson placed his hands on the counter and turned on the faucet. He closed his eyes and let the water run. The sound was calming. It helped him recenter himself. Refocus. We're not done, he thought. We've still got to fight.

He pulled out his phone and called Special Agent Bailey. She answered in a hushed tone.

"Jackson," she said.

"Yeah, it's me," Jackson said.

The line went quiet for a moment and he could hear various sounds in the background. He assumed Bailey was getting to a private place where she could talk.

"What's going on?" she asked. "I haven't heard from you."

"I know," Jackson said. "I'm still out here. Working this problem."

"How's it going? Last I heard, the authorities were still looking for the kid. Well, for you too, I guess."

"That's still the case. But it's worse."

"Worse? How so?"

"It's...complicated."

"Oh. It's bad, huh?"

"Yeah. Listen, you know I wouldn't ask if it wasn't absolutely necessary, but we're out here without a lifeline. I could really use some backup."

The line went quiet. Jackson thought maybe he couldn't hear her for some reason and shut off the faucet, but it was indeed quiet. And when Special Agent Bailey spoke again, her voice was soft and regretful.

"Jackson, you know I want to help," she said. "If there was anything I could do, I would. But, no matter what the story is, you're still harboring a fugitive. You know I can't be connected to that. And I couldn't ask anyone else like me to do that, either."

Jackson took a deep breath in and sighed.

"It kills me that I can't help," Bailey added. "You know that, right?"

"I know," Jackson said. "Don't sweat it. Really. It's more than I could ask for."

"If the situation changes, you let me know."

Jackson ended the call. He looked at himself in the mirror. He thought about everything that had happened. How he'd ended up here, in a church bathroom in a small town in West Virginia. He'd never been the kind to believe in prayer, but he was open to it at this moment.

He cleaned up his mess and walked back into the chapel. The others were sitting in the first few pews, drinking water and eating peanut butter and jelly sandwiches Maggie had prepared with what Reverend Asher showed her in the church's pantry. Jackson raised an eyebrow when he saw Mia was now back with them.

"We grabbed her and the dogs," Fraggie said, catching his expression. "Turns out they have a fenced-in playground here. It'll work as a dog run in the meantime."

She tore her sandwich in half and offered an end to Jackson. He shook his head, but Maggie got another sandwich on a second plate and handed it his way with a look that said declining was not an option. Jackson nodded in thanks and took a big bite, acknowledging a hunger he'd suppressed until now.

"I heard you on the phone," Bear said. "Any good news?"

Jackson shook his head.

"No, afraid not," he said. "Sayre apparently sent his partner to the FBI before everything at the farm. Hopefully, he's got something for us."

"I do," Sayre shouted from across the chapel.

He jogged down the aisle in between the pews and joined the group at the front.

"My partner pitched the FBI our theory and they bit," he said. "I told him about the shootout and how they have a good dozen dead bad guys and ID-less cops for evidence. They're sending us a couple cars and a team is hitting the farm. They'll get us and then we'll join them there."

"We don't know if the farm is secure," Jackson said.

"It sounds like it's about to be secure as shit," Bear said.

Sayre pointed at Bear, underscoring his point.

"There's just one thing," he added.

"What's that?" Jackson asked.

"Bobbie," Sayre answered. "He's got to go in."

Jackson stood up and stepped in front of Bobbie as if Sayre was going to arrest Bobbie himself.

"Uh-uh. No deal," he said. "What's the one thing we know? They'll kill him to keep him quiet."

"Hold on, hold on," Sayre said, his hands out in front of him, "he won't be going with Hopewell County, he'd be going with the FBI. I told them he was shot, so he needs medical attention anyways. They agreed Hopewell Memorial not having a trauma center is enough reason for him to go elsewhere. He'll be in Winchester, in *Virginia*, with a uniformed *FBI* police officer outside his room. They said Mia could go, too."

"What about the charges? What he's wanted for in Hopewell County?"

"Hopefully by the time he's healed up, we've blown this thing apart and it's a non-issue."

"That's a hell of a gamble."

Sayre turned his palms upward in a giving motion.

"You wanted a way to take these guys down," he said. "This is what I have."

66

Three hours later, Jackson watched a small convoy pull in and fill up a good portion of the church's parking lot. Two black Chevy Tahoes escorted a 12-seater van emblazoned with *FBI Police* on the side and an ambulance. The four-car posse came in from the far end of the road and circled back, pulling up driver's side to the front of the church.

Two men in FBI windbreakers stepped out of the first SUV. The driver extended a hand toward Jackson.

"Hello, sir," the man said. "Agent Grayson Meadows. This is my partner, Agent Brant Fields."

"Meadows. And Fields," Jackson said skeptically, shaking his hand.

"Yeah, we know," Fields said.

Both Meadows and Fields had short brown hair and were within an inch of each other, somewhere around six feet, but Meadows was of average build and had his hair parted just so, looking almost scholarly. Fields, on the other hand, was thicker, with straight, bristly hair that matched his mustache perfectly.

Bear and Sayre led the others out as a third man climbed out of the back of the Tahoe dressed in golf clothes. He nodded at Sayre, who nodded back. Jackson took him to be Sayre's partner.

Bobbie peered out from behind the group and looked at the idling ambulance.

"Is that for Bobbie?" Jackson asked, pointing at the ambulance.

"Yes, sir," Meadows said. "Medical transport directly from Winchester. Nothing local to Hopewell County. I talked to them briefly. They've never even been out here before."

Jackson turned and faced the group.

"Guys, these are Agents Meadows and Fields," he said.

Fraggie snorted.

"Who's your boss, Agent Pasture?" she quipped.

Agent Fields grimaced and seemed to growl at her.

Meadows laughed politely and extended her his hand.

"Like we said, we've heard them all before," he said.

Fraggie took his hand and shook it reluctantly. He then moved to Bobbie and Mia.

"Agent Meadows," he greeted. "You must be Bobbie and Mia."

"I am," Mia said.

Bobbie didn't say anything. He looked for Jackson. When their eyes met, Bobbie's welled up.

"I can't go," he said. "I can't. I didn't do anything wrong."

Jackson put a hand on his shoulder.

"You're going to be fine," he said. "No one here is getting in trouble. Not if I can help it. They're going to take you and keep you safe. And then I'm going figure everything out and make sure everyone knows what really happened."

Bobbie looked at the ambulance then down at his feet, still unsure.

"Hey," Jackson said. "You want this to be over, right? This is how we end this."

Bobbie nodded slowly without making eye contact. Jackson turned and motioned to Meadows that they were good.

"Okay, Bobbie and Mia to the medical transport," Meadows said. "You'll be going to Winchester. Like Mr. Clay here said, you'll be safe there. Everyone else, we've procured this fine van for you. It'll take you back to what I understand is Ms. Lynch and Ms. Conway's property."

"Hold up," Agent Fields said. "By my headcount, we're one short."

The group shared confused glances. When Bear realized where the confusion lay, he sighed. His shoulders drooped.

"Ray," he muttered under his breath.

"Raymond Byrd," Jackson said to the agents. "He was killed by the gunmen that stormed the farm."

"Well," Agent Meadows said in a quiet, sympathetic tone, "we have men hitting the property as we speak. Hopefully, we can get you some justice. Why don't we head over there if you're all ready."

Everyone moved like herded livestock for the van. Jackson stood with the two agents, watching the others climb in. He saw Mia step through a side door on the ambulance as the two paramedics helped Bobbie onto a stretcher. They were just about all loaded up when Reverend Asher stepped out from the chapel.

Jackson walked over to him and extended an open hand.

"Thank you for everything, reverend," he said. "I think I speak for all of us when I say it was very much appreciated."

"Think nothing of it," Reverend Asher said. "Are you going to take your guns over there in the woods?"

Jackson looked at him, surprised that the Reverend knew. But Reverend Asher just smiled and chuckled.

"Yeah, I'm sorry about that," Jackson said. "I didn't want to bring them into, you know, your place of worship."

"And you were thoughtful to consider that," Reverend Asher said, "but I think you're forgetting where you are. This would not be the first time I've had guns in my Assembly of God."

"I guess that must be true. The FBI probably doesn't want us bringing those along. They already had us hand over what we had on us. Do you think you might just forget those are there for a while?"

"I can't in good conscience let someone just come across them, but I'll tell you what. Why don't I say I found them, not knowing who they belonged to, and decided to hold onto them for safe keeping. You know, until their owner comes for them."

"That would be incredibly kind of you. But I feel like I have to tell you – maybe you know since you seem to know more than you let on – that's not exactly hunting equipment. Lives were taken with those guns. Isn't that against your good book?"

The reverend stepped toward Jackson and put a hand on each of his shoulders.

"You're right—'Thou shall not murder' is one of the Ten Commandments," he said. "But taking a life is not always murder. I know this and the Bible knows this. There are times to be peaceful, but there are also times when it is necessary to fight."

"I've never been much of a Bible reader," Jackson admitted.

The reverend smiled warmly.

"That's okay," he said. "It's never too late to start. And when you do, I'd suggest Romans 13:4. It reminds me of you."

Jackson began to say something when Agent Fields leaned out the open window of his Tahoe.

"It's time to go. Now," he barked.

Jackson tried again to say something, but Reverend Asher simply squeezed Jackson lightly with his hands and smiled.

"Go with God," he said warmly.

Jackson went to the second Tahoe where Sayre was holding the door open for him and climbed in. A moment later, the quartet of vehicles rolled forward and left the church parking lot. Reverend Asher stood there, waving and smiling as they left.

In his seat in the back of the second SUV, Jackson pulled out his phone, Googled Romans 13:4, and read:

For he is God's servant for your good. But if you do wrong, be afraid, for he does not bear the sword in vain. For he is the servant of God, an avenger who carries out God's wrath on the wrongdoer.

67

The drive back to the farm took less than fifteen minutes. Halfway through, the ambulance split off from the others and headed for Winchester. Jackson was uneasy about letting Bobbie go, but he knew this was the best thing for him. For all of them, really.

He sat quietly as the three cars made their way through the woods down the country roads. The sun, low in the late afternoon sky, flickered through the bare trees. As they approached the clearing where the farm sat, Jackson expected to see the area swarming with FBI vehicles. Instead, the drive was jammed full of black-and-gold sedans emblazoned with *Hopewell County Sheriff* on the side. His heart sank.

The FBI agent in the passenger seat answered his phone as it rang.

"Yeah?" he said.

Someone said something on the other end of the line.

"Okay, got it," the agent said, and hung up.

He turned to the man driving.

"We're going to pull up here just ahead," he said. "There's a fuck-up or something."

"What do you mean?" Jackson asked from the back.

"Don't know," the agent said. "We'll figure it out here in a minute."

Jackson suddenly felt incredibly naked without a gun. The three cars pulled onto the dirt road that led up to the farm's drive and stopped with the van bringing up the rear and blocking everyone else in.

As everyone climbed out, a side-by-side Utility Terrain Vehicle – it looked like a golf cart on steroids – headed toward them down the road. In it were two men in Hopewell County Sheriff uniforms.

"What's going on here?" Agent Meadows said. "My team up ahead says you blocked them from entering that property. We have a warrant to execute."

The man in the passenger seat of the UTV slid out and walked with a slight limp toward Meadows. He was older, with salt-and-pepper hair cut into a 70s-era buzz cut, and skin that looked tough and weathered like rawhide.

"Well, I don't know about your warrant," he said, "but I'm guessing my crime scene trumps it. Somebody – or somebodies, rather – gunned down nine of our boys out there while they were on a trainin' exercise."

Jackson felt both rage and fear building inside him. What bullshit exercise? Those men had come to kill him and the others.

"Now I've got twice as many bodies to work my way through," the Hopewell County man said. "And I don't have much time for any federal types steppin' on my toes."

"And you're the Sheriff, I presume?" Agent Meadows asked.

"I am. Sheriff William Davis. So, I don't know what all this is about, but it's just going to have to wait."

Sheriff Davis looked over Agent Meadows' shoulder at the rest of the group.

"I do see someone I have been looking for, though," he said. "Hello, there, Mr. Clay. I have a warrant for your arrest."

Jackson felt his pulse thumping angrily in his neck.

"Warrant?" he said. "For what?"

"Aiding and abetting one Robert 'Bobbie' Casto," the Sheriff said. "Something, as a matter of fact, I believe the lot of you are wanted for questioning in connection with."

"Hold on," Agent Meadows said. "These men and women are all

witnesses for a series of potential federal criminal investigations, which some in your own department are now the subject of."

Davis sneered at Agent Meadows and stepped toward him. Another UTV with two more sheriff's deputies came down the road.

"That's all well and good," he said. "You do your investigatin'. But you're not gettin' on my crime scene. And I already have the warrant in hand for Clay. I have him on CCTV leading Casto away from the courthouse where he was supposed to turn himself in."

"That's bullshit," Jackson said. "There was a fucking gunman. I was getting him to safety."

"Safety!" Sheriff Davis said, amused. "Why didn't you just go to a deputy? We *are* the safety 'round these parts."

"You and I both know very well why I didn't go to anyone with a badge in this ass-backward place."

"If you have a complaint about our department, you're welcome to file it. You'll be down at our headquarters, anyway."

Agent Meadows raised a hand, beckoning for the two of them to stop.

"You know this little charade won't hold up," he said.

"That may be," the Sheriff said, crossing his arms, "but unless you got somethin' better up your sleeve, it's gonna carry the day for now. And I'm takin' *that one* into custody."

Two of the deputies stepped around Agents Meadows and Fields and headed for Jackson. Maggie, Fraggie, Bear, and Sayre collectively stepped in front of Jackson, blocking their path.

"You'll have to go through us," Fraggie said.

"Ask your boys how that went," Bear added. "It didn't work out so well for them."

"Guys, stand down. This is not the way to do this," Agent Meadows said.

A Hopewell County Sheriff's car came down the highway and pulled around the budding standoff at the intersection to the dirt road.

"Hold on, wait," Jackson said. "This is all about the Vice Squad. They're the ones that did this."

"They're just about all dead halfway up that mountain," Davis said,

"I already know you abetted an attempted cop killer. Now, I'm going to find out if you're a cop killer yourself."

The door of the Sheriff's car opened.

"No, wait," Jackson said, backing up, "Listen. Meadows, Fields, this is what we're talking about. Their Vice Squad. They're trying to cover all this up."

"We'll figure this all out," Agent Meadows said. "But I can't stop their arrest. You've got to go with them for now."

Jackson knew that wasn't an option. If he let himself get taken by this sheriff's outfit, he'd be charged with who knows what. Or worse, they'd just take him out into the woods somewhere and kill him. No, he didn't know what to do, but he knew if he went with them it was all over.

He turned and looked at the man climbing out of the cruiser. Jackson recognized the man as the silver-haired deputy he'd run into the night he helped Sayre take the files out of the Sheriff's Office headquarters. The man looked at him, puzzled for a moment, but then seemed to recognize him, too.

The deputy stepped toward Jackson and offered his hand, seemingly oblivious to the drama going on.

"Public works, right?," he said. "Deputy Hill. Good to see you again."

"I'm sorry about this," Jackson said.

He took the deputy's arm and in one swift motion bent it backwards. The man howled. In a split second Jackson was behind the man, unclipping the pistol from the deputy's holster.

PART VI

THE TRAIL'S END

68

The deputies fanned out in a semicircle around Jackson, their weapons drawn. Sheriff Davis unholstered his own pistol, holding it by his leg. His trigger finger twitched. He started toward Jackson, but Agent Meadows stepped in front of him.

"Clay, what are you doing?" Meadows asked.

"What I have to," Jackson said. "Everyone, guns down. Now."

"You don't want to do something here you can't undo," Meadows cautioned.

Jackson grabbed Deputy Hill's arm and bent it further backwards. The officer hollered in pain again. Jackson put the officer's gun behind him, making it look as though he had it pointed squarely at the officers back. In truth, it was pointed at the ground.

"I'm not going to tell you all again," Jackson said. "Everyone drop your guns."

The deputies looked at the sheriff for guidance. Davis stood there, glaring at Jackson, trying to read the man. His eyes shifted to Meadows, who nodded. Slowly, Davis bent over and laid his gun on the ground. The deputies quickly did the same. Meadows, in turn, put a hand on the grip of his own holstered pistol.

"Don't do that, Meadows," Jackson said.

"Don't do something to force me to."

Jackson stepped back toward Deputy Hill's patrol car and its open door, bringing Hill with him. Jackson took the officer's handcuffs and placed them on Hill's wrists. He then reached around to the front of the man, grabbing the extra magazines for his pistol and Hill's radio and tossed those into the car.

"Do you have some hearing protection?" Jackson asked the deputy.

"What? No," Hill said.

"Then I'm sorry about this in advance."

Jackson raised the officer's gun, pointed it over the man's shoulder, and fired a round into each of the two exposed tires on the FBI Police van. He then leveled the pistol at the van's engine block and unloaded the rest of the magazine.

Meadows crouched down, ducking, as Sheriff Davis and his deputies ran for cover.

Inside the patrol car, the radio came alive. *113, shots fired! Shots fired!*

Still crouching, Meadows met Jackson's eyes.

"Don't do this, Clay," he said.

But it was done. Jackson slid into the patrol car, put it in gear, and took off, leaving a dazed Officer Hill behind. The disabled FBI van blocked in the other vehicles and prevented anyone from pursuing. Still, as Jackson drove, he heard deputies radioing for back up.

Dispatch, advise all units suspect fleeing in a Hopewell County cruiser. Car number 6-4-1. Last seen headed north on Highway 10.

107 responding. I'm on 10 headed south.

Jackson was running headlong into more sheriff's deputies. He took the next turn that came. As that road emptied, he took another turn, doing his best to work his way away from the county highway. The radio chatter continued.

107, where did you say he was again?

Headed north. Highway 10.

Copy, I'm almost to you, still no visual.

Alright, we need to set up a perimeter.

Jackson drove harder. He needed to get past their dragnet before it ensnared him. The road he'd taken slithered through the West Virginia wilderness, trees and brush encroaching on the road and scraping at the patrol car as he flew by. When the road emptied onto the largest thoroughfare he'd seen for miles, Jackson pulled to a stop. The road signage indicated it ran north to south.

He turned and headed north. Before long, he started to recognize where he was, and when the road intersected with the main highway into Rion, he turned and headed for town.

The radio chatter died down as the deputies struggled to locate Jackson and their missing car. Still, marked police cars were meant to be spotted, and Jackson knew it was only a matter of time before he was seen by the wrong person.

A quarter mile outside of Rion, he pulled off onto a gravel turnout and nestled the cruiser up into the woods beyond. Jackson reloaded the officer's pistol, tucked it and the radio into the waistband of his jeans, and slid the spare magazines into his pocket. Ditching the police car, he headed on foot toward Rion, his hoodie up and ballcap low.

He walked into town a few minutes later, just another fellow Rionian out for a stroll on a cool fall evening.

AGENT MEADOWS TURNED and faced Bear, Fraggie, and Maggie as a couple deputies tried in vain to chase after Jackson.

"Where the hell is he going?" Meadows asked.

"I think he left the oven on," Bear said.

Meadows stepped up to Bear.

"Do you think this is funny?" he asked.

"You guys didn't give him much of a choice," Sayre interjected.

Now Meadows turned and got in Sayre's face.

"It's *us* that have limited choices here," he said. "We come out here on some story your partner tells us. So far, I haven't seen a single damn thing indicating anything here is like you say it is. Give me one good reason why I shouldn't just cut bait and go home?"

"Because nothing's changed," Sayre said.

"Oh, nothing's changed? What about the part where one of the supposed victims in all this just stole a deputy's car at gunpoint?"

"We told you about the shootout at the farm, right? Look up there, we weren't lying. Nothing about that has changed. But every minute you're not up there getting control over the situation is another minute you let them cover this thing up."

"I need a reason to override their authority, and for a reason I need evidence."

"Well, that's a real fucking Catch-22 because the proof is up there. Starting with the body of Raymond Byrd. Assuming they haven't made him disappear yet."

"Well, if I can't get to that evidence, then tell me where I can find something else."

One of the men in an FBI polo stepped in and leaned in toward Meadows. He spoke quietly, but everyone could hear him.

"Local police have run the highway between here and Rion," the man said. "No sign of Clay. They're starting to set up a perimeter now."

Bear snorted and shook his head.

"Good fuckin' luck findin' him," he said.

"What was that?" Meadows asked.

"I said good luck findin' him. The man lives in woods just like these. This all might as well be his backyard. He's in his element, now."

"And I have an entire Sheriff's Office at my disposal."

"You're in the eastern panhandle of West Virginia, slick. That's some 3,500 square miles of country roads, mountains, and woods. Trust me. The only way you're going to find him is if he wants you to."

Meadows glanced at the others. Their faces told him Bear knew what he was talking about.

"Alright, then," Meadows said. "What do *you* suggest we do?"

"You've forced his hand," Bear said shrugging. "For now, it'd probably just be best to stay out of his way."

"And why's that?"

Bear nodded up toward the farm, now dotted with patrol cars and wrapped in yellow police tape.

"Those bodies up on the mountain?" he said. "Those were the last guys to get in his way."

69

S tarcher sat in his unmarked black pickup in the parking lot outside the Sheriff's Office headquarters. He and Franko had spent the better part of two hours doing the best they could to make what had happened out on the mountainside look like anything but the truth. Still, though, the truth would come. But Starcher wasn't planning to stick around to pay its price.

He'd sent Franko home to nurse his wounds. If he had to guess, the man was probably halfway through a fifth of Jim Beam, watching wrestling or some western on TV. When he was asked how he was the only one to survive the gunfight, Franko had been vague and deflective. Starcher assumed the truth involved some details the man wasn't particularly proud of.

A pair of deputies looked at Starcher sympathetically from the front doors. News had gotten around. To them, he was a superior officer in mourning. And the fact of the matter was there *was* a little truth there —he had really lost nine of his ten men. But everything else was lies. There were no mysterious gunmen. Those gunmen and his men had gone up that mountain together to kill. Maybe his dead men got off easy, he thought. They didn't have to carry the burden of their sins any longer.

He was staring ahead, looking at nothing, thinking about every-thing, when his phone buzzed in his breast pocket. Without looking at the caller ID, he answered the call and put the phone to his ear.

"I'm guessing the fact that I have not heard from you or the others means that things were not handled," Lane Wolfe said.

"Yes," Starcher said, "but I can—"

"No, I'm afraid there's no need to explain. You had a job to do; you didn't do it. Quite honestly, it's been your modus operandi through this whole shitstorm."

"You're right, the job's still not done. But, sir, Franko and I handled the mess. We can fix this. I can fix this still."

"That's okay, Mr. Starcher."

Starcher stopped talking. He couldn't say he knew Wolfe very well —they'd only met in person a couple of times—but he talked with him enough to know how the man operated. And if you thought him berating you with four-letter words was scary, wait until he started being overly polite. Like a guard escorting a prisoner to the electric chair.

"Tell me, Mr. Starcher," Wolfe said, "do you know how they make the decision to amputate someone's limb?"

Starcher didn't dare answer. A cold sweat beaded on his forehead.

"It's all a simple calculation," Wolfe continued. "It seems crude to put it in such terms, but it's the truth. A doctor – or whoever has the saw, really – has to look at the appendage in question and assess the damage."

Starcher tried to gulp, but suddenly found it hard to swallow. He searched around for something to drink. All he could come up with were a couple mini bottles of Smirnoff he had stashed in his center console. It would suffice in more ways than one.

"Usually, you don't get to this point unless the appendage is in really rough shape. Extensive nerve and tissue damage, stuff of that nature. That sort of damage, left unchecked, can prove to be fatal to someone. Or something, should this be an analogy."

Starcher finally worked up the courage to interject.

"Sir—"

"It's not easy, the decision to amputate a limb," Wolfe continued. "I mean the patient, quite literally, is attached to it."

Wolfe's sick giggle crackled through the static-filled connection.

"But the calculation has to be made," he said. "Do you take a limb in order to save the body? Do you take in order to save?"

I'm guessing no one ever asks the arm's opinion, Starcher thought.

"So, what are you saying? You're burning this bridge?" he asked.

"A different analogy – yours, not mine," Wolfe said. "But in so many words, yes."

"Mr. Wolfe—*Lane*—I'm telling you that is not how this needs to go."

"Let me ask you another question, Mr. Starcher. When you say you handled the mess, what did you do? May I guess? You made my men some band of *nefarious* criminals that ambushed and killed your men. Is that about right?"

"Sir—"

"Did you stop and think what kind of position that puts me in? The sheer amount of shit-shoveling I'll have to do to ensure that all that does not get back to me? No, you didn't. You were out to save your own ass. Well, Mr. Starcher, *I'm* saving *my* own ass. And unfortunately for you, I'm better at it than you are."

Starcher felt anger welling up inside of him. He grabbed the steering wheel with his free hand and squeezed it until his knuckles were white.

"I have documents, Wolfe," he stammered. "Ledgers. Papers. *Money*. Enough damning shit to bury you and—"

"And I have a fucking army!" Wolfe hissed. "You say you have money. Good. I suggest you take it. Take it and run. Disappear. Before something bad happens. Because that's all that's left for you in this. Do you hear me? Bad fucking things."

The line went quiet. Starcher heard Wolfe clear his throat and imagined the man recomposing himself.

"That'll conclude our business today and in the future," Wolfe said, his voice calm and professional again. "I suggest you kindly lose this number. Goodnight."

The line went dead. Starcher held the phone down by his side, seething. He was angry. And he was scared. He clenched the phone and threw it at his dashboard, then grabbed the steering wheel with both hands and shook it furiously, as if he were trying to tear it off its assembly.

Starcher ran out of energy more than he calmed down. Sweating and panting, he sat back in the driver seat and unbuttoned the top button of his shirt. He looked down at the watchful deputies. They probably thought the grief of losing nine men to a senseless act of violence had gotten to him.

In some ways they were right.

In others, they couldn't have been more wrong.

70

J ackson walked the main thoroughfare of Rion until he got to the courthouse. There, he turned right at the town's only intersection with a traffic light, and headed up Peak Road, the town's other major artery. The walk made for a fitting reflection of his time there. There was obviously the courthouse and the day Jimmy Green, coerced by Ronnie Franko, drew a pistol and tried to kill Bobbie Casto. Then there was the street itself, where Bear came roaring through a downed barricade in his Suburban to take Jackson, Bobbie, and Ray to safety. Across the lawn behind the courthouse was the Sheriff's Office headquarters, where Lieutenant Sayre handed him the critical evidence that proved something wasn't right about the night Bobbie's two friends were shot and killed. Now, he was headed to one other place he'd been before.

Peak Road took him north and east, headed out of town. Commercial and municipal buildings gave way to quaint city residences. Yards got bigger and the distance between addresses grew until eventually city homes were replaced by farms and rural ranches outside of town.

Twenty minutes up the road, he returned to Spring Rock, an unremarkable cluster of houses and shops—one of which was the home of Detective Ronnie Franko. Jackson turned onto Franko's street, walking past the house once to check it out. One of the Vice Squad pickups was parked curbside and the electric-blue glow of a television emanated from the front window. Ronnie Franko was home.

Jackson walked the next block over, then cut through a neighboring yard and hopped the fence into Franko's backyard. There, he drew the Glock 19 he'd taken off Deputy Hill and approached Franko's house.

The back door opened onto a small wooden porch that was slowly rotting. Jackson checked the door and found it locked, but the window next to the door was half-open. Confirming no one could see him, Jackson reached in, unlocked the door, and let himself in.

The stench of stale cigarettes hung heavy in the air of the kitchen. From somewhere deeper in the house, Jackson heard muffled gunshots pop from a TV. He leveled the Glock out in front of him and moved slowly toward the sound. Ahead of him, a hallway bent at a right angle. Beyond it, Jackson saw the flickering light of the television.

"Well, it must be one of you assholes from the mountain," Franko said as Jackson stepped into the room.

The detective's words were slurred, his voice thick with alcohol.

"All the assholes I know use the front door," he added.

Jackson assumed a gun was nearby, but Franko, faced away from him, didn't move.

"Hands," Jackson ordered.

"Go fuck yourself," Franko said.

Jackson sidestepped around the room in a circular pattern, keeping his distance from Franko until he came face to face with the man. Franko sat still, a cigarette burning slowly in his hand. His left leg was bandaged and propped up with a raggedy sofa pillow. His foot hung off a coffee table otherwise covered with beer and liquor bottles.

"Well, it is you," he said. "The one and only Jackson Clay. That is, based on the description put out on the radio."

Franko patted the police radio lying on one of his armrests.

"That wouldn't be the Glock you pulled off of ole' Ben, would it?" he asked.

"I'm borrowing it," Jackson said.

"That old fuck should've retired years ago." Franko nodded as he took a drag from the cigarette.

"It's over, Franko. Even if you covered up what happened at the farm, Bobbie and Mia are in federal custody. Protected. And they'll testify to what they saw."

Franko chuckled.

"Mia...That dumb bitch came to you?" he asked before shaking his head. "Should've known. Fuckin' junkie whore."

"We kept her safe," Jackson said. "And she can name you, specifically, entrapping her into trying to kill Bobbie."

"If it's all over, then where's the FBI? Why are you here and not them?"

Franko shook his head again and took another drag from his cigarette. He grinned.

"No, I don't think anything is over," he said.

"It is," Jackson said. "But I'm here to make you one last offer. Give me hard evidence that ties VigilOne to everything you've got going on here. Do that, and maybe I forget I found you here."

Franko cackled a smoker's laugh that turned into a brief-but-substantial coughing fit.

"You really are desperate, aren't you?" he said. "You're the one intruding. You've broken into a cop's house. You took a patrol car at gunpoint, came here, and are now pointing that same gun at another cop. You'd be lucky if you made it to your trial alive."

"That seems to be a thing around here," Jackson said. "So maybe I call the FBI, tell them where to find me. Let's see what else they find here. Or do you guys keep everything at *The Trail's End?*"

The grin disappeared from Franko's face.

"I guess you didn't know we knew," Jackson said. "There's a lot you don't know. Like those VigilOne goons you stormed the farm with? There's two more dead deeper in the woods. I'm guessing they won't fit into whatever story you all spun for Sheriff Davis."

Franko still didn't say anything, just snarled at Jackson from his recliner.

"So, last chance," Jackson said. "Give me VigilOne, and I'll walk away."

"If you know everything, then you know this is all run by *him*,"

Franko said. "Lane fucking Wolfe. You think you can do something to me he can't?"

"Turn state's witness and you'll be protected."

"I'd rather eat a bullet."

"Your choice. Last chance."

"Like I said. Go fuck yourself."

Franko reached for a pistol stashed under the pillow propping up his leg. Jackson put two rounds in Franko's chest. Franko's arms flopped to his sides. Jackson came up and stood over him. Franko looked up at Jackson with bloodshot eyes, jaw agape.

Jackson slid the barrel of the Glock into Franko's open mouth and leaned down.

"This is for Ray," he whispered.

Outside, one last gunshot disturbed the otherwise peaceful night.

A moment later, Jackson opened the front door and jogged down the steps to Franko's black pickup. With Franko's keys and phone in hand, he opened the truck and got in. As he fired up the engine, the phone buzzed. The name Red Starcher flashed across the screen.

He took the call.

"Franko? Franko, you there?" Starcher asked.

"Franko's dead," Jackson said. "Now, I'm coming for you."

71

I t took almost two hours for the FBI to send another van to replace the one Jackson had shot into early retirement. By then, Meadows' calm, librarian-like demeanor had degraded to the point where he was grouchier than Agent Fields.

He'd watched helplessly as the Sheriff's Office combed over the mountainside, doing Lord-knows-what with any evidence that might be damning to one of their own. The sheriff himself had tried numerous times to take custody of Sayre, Maggie, Fraggie, and Bear, calling them "persons of interest in an ongoing investigation," but Meadows refused. The Sheriff's Office had the crime scene, but the FBI had the witnesses. The two were at a legal and jurisdictional impasse.

When the new van arrived, it pulled around the first—which had been towed out of the way—and attempted to pull onto the dirt road before a pair of sheriff's deputies sternly waved it away. No one was getting blocked in again.

"Everyone get in the van," Meadows said. "We're going."

"Goin' where?" Fraggie asked.

"Martinsburg," Meadows said. "At least until we figure out what to do with you all. Or Mr. Clay materializes."

Fraggie frowned. She wanted to object, but figured their chances were better with the FBI than the Hopewell Sheriff's Office. In any event, it was clear sleeping in their own bed tonight wasn't an option.

"What about our dogs?" Maggie asked.

"We'll have to put everyone up in a motel," Meadows answered. "We'll make sure it's pet friendly. Now come on, we've got over an hour's drive ahead of us."

Bear, Sayre, Maggie, Fraggie, Argos, and Maera filed into the van followed by Meadows, who apparently was giving up his seat in his SUV to keep an eye and ear on the group.

"Let's go," he said to the driver.

But as the driver put the van into gear, the scene behind the sheriff's police line became frantic with activity. A short, younger deputy jogged to a tree and started ripping down the yellow tape cordoning off the road. Just as he got it clear, a pair of patrol cars tore down the road and turned onto the county highway, speeding off into the distance with their lights and sirens blaring.

"What the hell is going on?" Meadows grumbled.

"Maybe Krispy Kreme's on fire," Bear said.

Meadows shot him a look before climbing out of the van, leaving the door ajar. He was yelling at the squat deputy, demanding information when Agent Fields climbed out of his SUV and jogged over to him.

"Shots fired. North of Rion," he told Meadows. "A neighbor called it in. The tenth Vice guy, the one that wasn't killed here. Ronald Franko. It's his address."

"Christ," Meadows said. "That has to be Clay, right?"

"You bet your ass it is," Bear said under his breath.

Fraggie heard him and grinned.

Fields answered Meadows with a shrug. Two more patrol cars came down from Maggie and Fraggie's farm and took off down the highway.

"What do you want to do, boss?" Fields asked.

"I don't know. Give me a minute," Meadows said.

Bear was watching Meadows pace around on the side of the road when the sudden vibration of his phone underneath him caused him to jump and bang his head on the van's ceiling. Fields and Meadows looked over at the commotion, but Bear waved in apology.

He didn't recognize the number, but answered anyway.

"Hello?" Bear said.

"It's me," Jackson answered.

Instinctively, Bear shirked down in the van and turned his back to Meadows and Fields.

"Hey, uh, now's not really a good time, buddy," Bear said. "We're still stuck here in the principal's office, if you know what I mean."

"I figured. Put Meadows on."

"I don't know if that's a good idea. Did you shoot Franko? They just found out about that."

"Just put them on."

"You're the boss."

Bear sat upright again and leaned out the open van door.

"Hey, uh, Agent Meadows, phone's for you," Bear said.

Meadows looked at Bear skeptically, but when Bear raised the phone, Meadows took it and walked to the back of the van with Agent Fields. He put the call on speaker.

"Is that you, Clay?" he asked.

"It is," Jackson said.

"You've made things worse on yourself, Clay, doing what you did."

"I think I know how we can both get what we want."

"Oh, yeah? And how's that?"

"Simple. Come to me."

72

S tarcher swerved into the parking lot of *The Trail's End* then yanked the wheel right, nearly hitting the row of parked Vice Squad pick-ups. His headlights pointed directly at the sign by the road, and he now jerked the wheel to the left and slammed on the brakes, causing the truck to fishtail and slide to a stop.

A brutal mixture of fear and hard liquor had him heavily intoxicated. He stumbled out of the truck and, for a moment, studied his parking job. His pickup was angled awkwardly compared to the others. Fuck it, Starcher thought. It didn't much matter. Not anymore.

He slipped and tripped his way to the back door of the bar and let himself in. Of course, the interior was pitch black. He felt his way along, banging every pot and pan as he made it through the kitchen and into the small office adjacent to it.

The office safe was open and most of its contents gone. Shit, Starcher thought to himself, had Franko come here? Had he taken the stuff before this Clay guy found him? Starcher needed a drink. *Another* drink. A gun that couldn't be traced back to him *and* another drink— both of which were behind the bar.

Working his way through the darkness again, Starcher stepped into the main room and felt for the bar, then followed it to the flip-top door on the far side and stepped through. He crouched down and felt around beneath the bar. Finding a bottle of booze proved to be about as easy as expected in a bar, but that pesky revolver eluded him.

"If you're looking for the .38 Special you had there, it's with me," Jackson said from across the room.

He clicked on a flashlight and shined it in Starcher's direction. Starcher shot upright, raising a hand to shield himself from the bright light.

"I left you the booze, though," Jackson said. "I'm not unreasonable."

Keeping his hand up, Starcher felt his way back around the bar, stepped out, and began walking toward Jackson.

"That's far enough," Jackson said. "Why don't you have a seat there. The one to your left, right there."

Starcher did as he was told, still trying to process everything that was happening. Jackson lowered the light and pointed it at a stack of files on a table in front of him.

"I was betting if you had anything proving what you all were doing, it'd be here," he said. "But this? This is more than I could've hoped for. Ledgers, receipts, names and locations of meets. I hit the jackpot."

Starcher opened up the bottle of Crown Royal he'd grabbed from under the bar and took a heavy swig before coming up for air.

"By the way, the next time you have a safe, make the code something a little more creative than your badge number."

Jackson lifted a separate stack of documents.

"Got these from the case files Lieutenant Sayre took from the Sheriff's Office and gave me," he said. "I'm guessing you didn't know about these."

"The sher—the sheriff," Starcher struggled to say. "The...sheriff's on his way here. You—you'll be arrested. And all that will g-go away."

"I doubt that. But if he is, I guess it's a good thing I snapped photos of most of this stuff while waiting for you and sent it to all the friends I've made out here. How much you want to bet your police buddies can stop them all before one of them shows the feds?"

Starcher wiped the sweat off his brow and put the bottle down on the table. "Stop. Just stop," he begged.

His speech was suddenly more lucid, like his fear was having a sobering effect.

"We can work this out. All this can go away just as quick as you found it. And you and everyone else could be paid for your troubles."

"I don't know," Jackson said. "That's a lot of mouths to feed."

"We've – *I've* got the money," Starcher said. "There's plenty. You've killed everyone else. Most of the guys have money just lining their walls. We can get it. We can get it all. We can fix this."

"What about Bobbie and his family? And Mia? And Maggie and Fraggie? Those are the women whose farm you ransacked today, by the way. They still have to live here with you goons policing the area."

"I'm telling you, it's a shit-ton of money. Like six figures a head. They could go anywhere and start a new life."

"Maybe they want to live here. Why should they have to leave and you get to stay?"

Starcher leaned forward and put his hand to his chest.

"Are you kidding me? I'm *gone*," he said. "I'm fucking gone after all this. Then there won't be anyone left from the business."

"So, the Vice Squad was the only part of the department in on it?"

"Yes. I mean, Sheriff Davis isn't stupid—he knew something was going on. But he'll shut up. He's a fucking politician. He'll do whatever he needs to save his own ass."

"That's what I'm worried about. Retribution against any of us. Especially Bobbie."

"Look, we can call him right now, work something out. He knows about the money—I'm sure he'd like a chunk of it, too. Everyone gets paid, no one gets dead. We can make this work."

"And what about VigilOne?"

Starcher went quiet.

"I told you," Jackson said. "I know everything. It's the CEO calling the shots, right? Lane Wolfe?"

"Yes," Starcher mumbled.

"You guys get kickbacks for putting people in his company's private prison and rehab center."

"C'mon, you said you know all this."

"I'm just making sure. Does he know your busts are bullshit?"

"They're not all bad busts."

"But most are."

"Whatever. Yes, he knows about that."

"And those were his goons at the farm this morning. Not *against* your Vice Squad but *with* them. Trying to kill us, to silence people who'd witnessed what you all were doing."

Starcher slammed his fist on the table.

"Jesus, what do you want me to say?" he said. "Yes, yes to all of it! It was a bunch of mercenaries Lane Wolfe sent to help my boys take you out. I told you, we can get past this. There's enough money to go around."

"And then you and Franko went back there today and set everything up to look like those mercenaries were gunning for your guys. To cover up what really went down."

"Yes. God Almighty, why won't you get past it?"

"I have a hard time getting over people trying to kill me."

"Then what's your price to get over it? Everyone has a price."

Jackson was quiet. Starcher shifted his weight in his chair, leaning forward in anticipation of an answer.

"Fifty percent," Jackson said. "How much would you guess that is?"

"I don't know. All the boys have their own cash. It depends how much they all spent," Starcher said.

"You're a smart guy. Guess."

"Two million, maybe."

"Two million dollars, and I'll walk away. Maggie, Fraggie, Bear, Sayre, Bobbie, and Mia split 35 percent. Ray Byrd's next of kin gets 10 percent – which you will make look like an insurance payment after you file a police report of his accidental death – and you get five."

"What? No, to hell with that. I'm not getting no measly five. And two mil is only a guess."

"This isn't a negotiation. I get two mil. You get five percent. Everyone else gets what I said. Everyone stays silent."

Starcher leaned back in his chair, uncapping the bottle of Crown

Royal again and taking another large swig. His one hand lowered the bottle between his legs while the other wiped off his mouth and mustache.

"Fine," Starcher said. "If everyone makes this go away, they'll get paid."

"Good. We can add that to the other charges then," Jackson said.

"What? What the hell are you talking about?"

"You really ought to put some lights in this place. You never know who – or what – is around you."

Jackson tilted his flashlight over to the table next to Starcher, pointing it at a phone sitting there.

"I hear the audio quality on these new iPhones is just amazing," he said.

"You goddamn sonofabitch!" Starcher yelled.

He stood up, grabbed the phone, and threw it as hard as he could against the wall. He then stumbled over to the pieces, threw them into the sink behind the bar, and turned on the faucet.

"Good thinking," Jackson said, "except it was on a phone call. To the FBI agents who'd been alerted this morning to everything going on. I'm sure they were recording, though. They've been down the road waiting to say hello."

Jackson and Starcher heard vehicles rumble into the gravel parking lot outside and skid to a stop. Doors open and shut. Red and blue lights flashed through spaces in the boarded-up windows.

"I told you I was coming for you, Starcher," Jackson said. "This is me coming for you."

The front doors kicked open and flashlights illuminated the dark interior. FBI personnel moved swiftly into the room, fanning out, covering every corner.

"FBI! Hands up!" someone ordered. "Show me your hands!"

Starcher raised his hands but started retreating for the back of the bar. He was almost to the office door when Agent Fields came up from behind, grabbed one of Starcher's arms, and slammed his upper body against the bar top.

"Red Starcher," Fields said, "you are under arrest. You have the right to remain silent. Anything you say can and will be used against you..."

Fields' Mirandizing drifted off as he escorted Starcher out the back of the bar. Jackson stood up and walked to the front door. Men in navy blue polos and windbreakers flowed around him like water around a boulder. Before he could leave, though, Agent Meadows entered and blocked Jackson's path.

"Mr. Clay," he said. "Good work. Nice touch with the bribery bit, too. That's at least a couple more charges, potentially."

Jackson handed Agent Meadows the .38 special he'd confiscated before Starcher had arrived.

"He was looking for this," Jackson said. "Is it too much to hope you can tack on attempted murder, too?"

Agent Meadows smiled and chuckled for the first time all day.

"Probably," he said. "Don't worry, though—he's beyond fucked."

"That's the idea."

"And that stuff about VigilOne, we're not stopping here. We'll go after them. You have my word on that."

Jackson extended a hand. Meadows looked down at it, offered his in return, and shook.

"I'm going to hold you to that," Jackson said.

"I wouldn't expect anything less," Meadows said. "Your friends are inbound, by the way. Give them my best."

Jackson nodded and walked off into the parking lot. Meadows stood there, watching him leave, when Agent Fields approached.

"Starcher is cuffed up," Fields said. "The guys back at the office are working on getting a court order to get the sheriff's office off that crime scene on the mountain."

Meadows didn't say anything, still watching Jackson walk away.

"I guess if we believe that guy's story," Fields continued, "he and his buddies held off twenty-something armed mercenaries and dirty local cops, killing most of them, only to turn around and pin a slew of felonies on the remaining."

"I guess so," Meadows said.

Fields snorted and headed back into the bar.

"Remind me not to piss that guy off," he said.

73

The next morning, the sky was awash in cornflower-blue as the sun, still tucked below the horizon, pushed the coming dawn into wakefulness. It had been hours since the FBI arrested Starcher and had begun itemizing evidence in the shuttered bar, but the gravel lot was still full of emergency vehicles.

Maggie lay in the back of an ambulance with two paramedics tending to her gunshot wound as Fraggie and Bear stood by.

Sayre walked up behind them and shook his head.

"You know," he said, "this all started for me at the back of an ambulance just like this, taking statements from Franko and Bragg."

"What a swell couple of guys they turned out to be," Bear said. "The beginnin' of all this feels like a lifetime ago."

"Many lifetimes ago," Sayre said. "To think of everyone that's been killed over this..."

"I'll miss Ray and the innocent ones. Always. The others can go to hell."

"Here's to hoping they did."

Sayre raised a disposable cup of instant coffee then drank from it.

"Is it true Franko's dead?" Fraggie asked.

"They found Franko shot and killed in his home," he said. "A loaded pistol was in his hand."

"Guess someone was faster on the draw."

"Guess so."

"That's a shame. I wonder if Jackson knows."

The two smiled along with Bear.

"Where is Clay, anyways?" Sayre asked.

"Feds took him to Winchester Medical Center," Bear said. "He wanted to tell Bobbie personally it was all over."

"I guess as over as it can be, anyway," Sayre said.

"What do you mean?"

"VigilOne. Lane Wolfe. They just get a pass in all this?"

"They'll get theirs one day, hopefully."

Fraggie shook her head and fired a wad of spit in disgust. Maggie gave her a look of admonishment from the back of the ambulance.

"Haven't been as lucky so far," Fraggie said.

"I don't know about that," Sayre said. "We could all very easily be dead a couple of times over. I'd say we *were* pretty lucky, everything considered."

Bear shook his head.

"That wasn't luck," he said. "*That* was Jacky boy."

SOME 40 MILES AWAY, Jackson stepped off an elevator in the hospital and walked down a cream-colored corridor lined with thick wood railings. He was about to ask someone at the nurse's station for Bobbie Casto's room number when he saw a uniformed police officer at the end of the hall sitting on a folding chair.

Jackson walked to the end of the hall and flashed a courteous smile when the officer looked up.

"Family friend. I'm here to see Bobbie," Jackson said.

"I'm sorry, but no one goes in without prior approval," the officer said. "You're welcome to—"

The officer was cut off by the sound of the door opening. Jackson was surprised to see Mia standing there, cleaned up and wearing a fresh pair of scrubs no doubt loaned to her by the hospital. She looked better than at any point since he'd known her.

"Hello," Jackson said. "It's good to see you again."

Mia smiled shyly and looked down at her feet.

"It's good to see you, too," she said quietly.

"I like the new outfit," Jackson said.

"Thanks. Actually, one of the nice nurses gave these to—"

"I know. I'm kidding. I just meant you look like you're doing much better."

"Oh. I am. They gave me a counselor to talk to. She told me about free programs for people who want to get clean. She said she'd do what she could to try and get me into one."

"That's terrific. I'm really proud of you for doing that."

"Thanks."

"Is Bobbie awake?"

"Yeah, I was just saying hello. You can talk to him."

Mia stepped back and opened the door wider for Jackson. Jackson looked at the officer; the man waved him in. After he stepped through, Mia walked out, but stopped before closing the door and turned back to Jackson.

"Jackson," she said.

"Yeah?"

Their eyes met and Jackson watched her as she struggled to say whatever it is she wanted to say. Eventually, she gave up and lunged into him, her arms open to embrace him. Jackson caught her.

"Thank you," Mia said, beginning to cry. "For everything."

"Don't mention it," Jackson said.

"You saved my life."

"Don't sell yourself short. You were there, too. You're a fighter. In more ways than one."

"No, I'm not talking about stopping me on the road or when they came for us at the farm. Before. I hated my life. I hated myself. I hated where I was. I don't hate where I am anymore."

Jackson held the hug until Mia let go.

"If you need anything, you let me know," Jackson said.

Mia nodded as she wiped at her eyes, working for a moment to compose herself, then smiled once more and left, closing the door behind her. The thud and metal click muted all the noises of the hospital until there was only quiet. Jackson turned to see Bobbie looking up at him from his hospital bed.

He smiled as he walked over. Bobbie raised an arm covered in wires and medical tape and waved.

"How are you doing?" Jackson asked, pulling a chair up to Bobbie's bed.

"I'm okay," Bobbie said. "How's everyone else?"

"Everyone's just fine."

"So, it's over?"

"It's over. You may have to testify to what you saw, but no one's coming after you anymore. Not even the authorities."

"We had beer and weed, though. That part was us."

Jackson grinned.

"I think, all things considered, the county attorney's going to let you off with a warning on that," he said.

Bobbie felt a sharp pain at that word. *You.* As if the word had stabbed him. When everything happened, there were three of them, him with his two closest friends. Now it was just him. *You.* The only one left.

Jackson saw the consternation on his face.

"Hey. What's up?" he asked.

"Nothing," Bobbie said. "It just made me think of Mason and Emma. I don't think I've thought about them since we were at that lawyer's house. It feels like forever ago. But they're still gone."

"They are. And I'm sorry that you have to deal with that."

"And Uncle Ray. I mean, he died trying to help me."

"He *wanted* to help."

"But how do I deal with that? Knowing he'd be alive if it wasn't for me."

Jackson sat upright and scooted his chair closer.

"Hey, look at me," he said.

Bobbie looked up at met his eyes.

"This isn't your fault," Jackson said. "You hear me? Those officers and whoever was doing this with that company, they did this *to all of you*. You were all victims."

"But I'm alive and they're not."

"That's true. And you're going to have to live with that. It'll hurt, and I know you think it isn't fair – hell, it isn't – but that's no excuse. You're alive. So you have to live."

"Like you with your son?"

Jackson sat back in his chair, the question hitting him like a jab to the gut. Truth be told, he couldn't remember if he even knew Bobbie knew about Evan.

"I'm sorry," Bobbie said quickly, "I didn't mean – It's just, I heard Ray and Bear talking about it once."

"What happened to Evan was...different," Jackson said. "I could've stopped that."

"Or maybe you just feel that way. Like I do about Uncle Ray."

Jackson nodded and smiled. He couldn't deny the kid had a point.

"I just don't know what to do when my mom and her husband get here," Bobbie said. "I feel like they're going to have a million questions."

"You only have to talk about what you're ready to talk about."

"How do I tell them about Uncle Ray?"

Jackson smiled again and reached out to put a hand on Bobbie's shoulder.

"You tell them the truth," he said. "You tell them he was there because he loved you."

Bobbie nodded. A tear formed in the corner of his eye but he was quick to brush it away.

Jackson patted him on the shoulder and stood up.

"I'm going to make sure everything works out with the county attorney," he said. "In the meantime, if you need anything, here's my phone number."

He pulled out a piece of paper and handed it to Bobbie.

"Your address, too," Bobbie noted.

"Bear's actually," Jackson said. "He asked me to give it to you. Said if you're ever near your uncle's old place to stop on by. You're always welcome."

Bobbie stared at the piece of paper quietly.

"Your uncle might be gone, but you've still got all of us. Don't forget that," Jackson said.

He started for the door but stopped and waved one last time before stepping out.

"I'll be seeing you," he said.

Bobbie watched as the man who Bear had called for help, who'd shown up at his uncle's door, walked out, disappearing just as fast he'd come into Bobbie's life a few days prior.

A nurse came in, knocking on the door.

"Do you need anything, hon?" she asked.

"Do you know where my wallet is?" Bobbie said.

The nurse opened a cabinet and fetched a plastic bag with all of Bobbie's belongings.

"Here you go, hon. Anything else?"

Bobbie shook his head and thanked her. When she left, he dug into the bag and grabbed his wallet. He opened up the bill fold and pulled out a photo he had in it of his Uncle Ray. Bobbie studied it for a minute, smiling, then slid the piece of paper Jackson gave him behind it and tucked both away.

All his extended family in one place.

74

Hollywood Cemetery sat in the heart of Richmond, Virginia, nestled on the north bank of the James River. 130 acres spread out over rolling hills with sweeping views of the southern end of the city. Two sitting presidents and countless congressman, justices, and generals – both Union and Confederate – found their final resting place within Hollywood's stone walls.

Jackson, Bear, Bobbie, Mia, and Lieutenant Sayre came to the cemetery a few weeks after everything had ended to say one final goodbye to Ray. It was an unusually cold Saturday in early December, and a thin coat of snow blanketed everything as a small group of mourners gathered at plot 25-84 to see Ray Byrd laid to rest next to his brother in their family's section. As the casket was lowered, attendees got in line to toss flowers on top before filing out. Jackson, wrapped in a black bomber jacket and ballcap with dark sunglasses, stood underneath a naked gum tree and watched the crowd thin. Bear was a good head and a few belt sizes over everyone else. He knelt down at the foot of the casket, whispered something, and stood. As he turned, he saw Jackson in the distance and nodded as he walked up to him.

"I'm glad you came," Bear said.

"I was happy to," Jackson said. "I'm surprised Maggie and Fraggie couldn't make it out."

"They wanted to. They got a hold of me a couple days ago and said they wouldn't be able to come. Something about finishing up stuff with the farm."

"Well, it was a nice service."

"It was. Tough to plan, but it came together once the coroner released his body. Still makes me angry what those assholes did. Trying to get rid of him in a shallow grave on the farm like that."

"Well, the ones who aren't already dead are facing hard time."

"Have you heard anything about VigilOne or Lane Wolfe yet?"

"No, not yet."

"Still can't believe the governor resigned."

"He had to after the news he'd been steering contracts to VigilOne. State's Attorney General is pursuing charges against him."

"I saw that. You know he hired Landon Rhodes as his lawyer? Liam Harper's partner. Wonder how much money it takes to forget your partner's death."

"I guess it's like Starcher said: everyone has their price."

The two of them watched as Bobbie took his turn at the front. Instead of one flower, he held a whole bouquet. He dropped them in, then turned and buried his face in his mother's arm. Mia came around from behind them to console Bobbie.

"I hope he'll be okay," Bear said.

"Me, too," Jackson said. "Anything I can do?"

"For him? Nah."

"What about for you?"

"Actually, I was going to talk to you about something. I didn't plan on here, but since you mentioned it."

"Shoot."

"Well, with Ray being gone and all, I have no business partner for the store."

"Not sure I know anyone that'd be a good fit."

"I was thinking you."

Jackson crossed his arms and sighed.

"I know what you were thinking," he said.

"Well?" Bear asked.

"You know I want to help," Jackson said. "But I'm not the business type."

"Be a silent partner, then."

Jackson didn't say anything.

"See, you've got the hang of it already," Bear said.

The two men laughed quietly.

Jackson took off his sunglasses, met Bear's eyes, and extended his hand.

"Whatever you need," he said.

A boyish grin stretched across Bear's face and he moved inside Jackson's hand, opting instead to grab the man and wrap him tightly in his beefy arms. Bear's nickname fit him very well.

Jackson stepped away as he was released and moved back.

"Where are you parked?" Bear asked. "Do you need a ride?"

"No, I think I'm going to walk," Jackson said.

"Alright then, brother. I'll be seein' ya."

Jackson waved before turning and heading down the hill. He followed the road as it swooped down and toward the James River. In the center of the overlook was a large stone structure. Palmer Chapel was a mausoleum on the far south end of the cemetery. At the heart of it was an open-air corridor leading to the resting places of a select few. Jackson walked down the passage, wind blowing the powdery snow around his feet, until he came to the name he was looking for.

Evan Randolph Clay

Taking off a glove, he put his hand to the engraved lettering, slowly running his fingers across it. Thirteen years and a thousand things had changed, but not this. His son was still here. Here and gone. In the years since, he'd tried desperately to make meaning of his loss. It had driven him into this, his new life. One where he fought to save others where he couldn't save his own. Now, that journey brought him back here, having saved Bobbie Casto—but at the cost of his loving uncle.

Jackson had closed his eyes when footsteps echoed from the far entryway. He turned to see a petite woman in a black beanie and wool coat. She stood just outside the mausoleum with her hands over her mouth.

"I am so sorry," she said. "I didn't mean to startle you."

"That's okay," Jackson said.

She stepped into the corridor and took off her beanie, revealing a full head of blonde hair, shaking the snow off of it. "It's crazy. It never snows here."

Jackson smiled, agreeing. He turned back and looked at Evan's name. The woman walked over, read Evan's name and the years below it – just a few numbers separating birth and death – and put it together.

"I was just out for a walk," she said again. "I didn't mean to interrupt you if—"

"No. No, you're fine," Jackson assured her.

The woman watched Jackson as he stared at the entombment.

"Was he your son?" she asked.

"He was," Jackson said.

"I'm sorry. If I'm prying, I don't—"

The woman trailed off, seeing Jackson smile. A thought came to him. The woman's words reminded him of what Maggie told him at the farm, about keeping Evan's memory alive and talking about him. He wanted to do that.

"No, I'm glad you asked," Jackson said. "His name was Evan. Evan Randolph Clay. And he was the greatest kid."

The woman stepped up to Jackson and joined him in front of Evan, listening and smiling as the man she'd only just met told her about his son.

75

W olfe sat in the back of his chauffeured Mercedes, phone to his ear, listening as his lawyer berated him, listing how much trouble VigilOne and Wolfe, specifically, was in.

"I've met with the rest of our in-house counsel, sir," the lawyer said, "and we all agree we should hear what the other side has to say in terms of a plea deal."

"Giving up? That's what you're talking about," Wolfe said. "Surrendering. Losing. I don't know if you've looked outside whatever corner office I put you in, but that's not the business we're in."

"Sir, with all due respect—"

"Oh, cut the shit, Carl. I've seen you do blow off the ass of a girl half your age. Fuck respect—this is about who survives."

"That's exactly right, Wolfe. This *is* about survival. You talk about VigilOne like it's some sort of entity still. Well, it's not. The Titanic has hit the iceberg and it's everyone for themselves. And, news flash, Lane, there aren't lifeboats for everyone."

"What are you saying?"

"I'm saying not everyone has your resolve. People are going to flip. And more specifically, they're going to turn on you."

Wolfe sneered before punching the passenger seat in front of him.

Outside, the city was embellished with Christmas decorations. String lights accented building edges, and wreaths and trees adorned the glass-enclosed lobbies he drove by. The festive atmosphere disgusted him.

"Look," Carl said. "Just hear what they have to say. If they offer something without jail time, I really would consider taking it."

"I'm about to pull up to my place, Carl. When we meet tomorrow, I want a better plan than get down on our fucking knees for the feds."

Wolfe ended the call and had his door open before the car had fully stopped. He hopped out, ignoring his driver wishing him well, and trotted into the lobby. There, the man at the front desk said something, but Wolfe ignored him, too. He didn't have time to ingratiate himself to the peons. Not with the shit day he'd had. He needed a release. He needed what was waiting in his penthouse for him.

Wolfe took the private elevator up to his penthouse apartment. When he stepped off, he saw the woman waiting for him by his bar.

"Good evening," he said. "You must be my ten o'clock."

The woman smiled. "I guess so, handsome."

A form-fitting indigo dress did little to conceal her impressive physique. She had on black heels and evening gloves that reminded Wolfe of Audrey Hepburn. She approached him and slid off his coat.

"Let's get you out of some of these stuffy clothes," she said

Wolfe grinned.

"I like that accent. And that hair," he said.

The woman smiled coyly, twisting and winding her black locks around her fingers. Wolfe didn't seem to notice it was a wig.

"Do you really?" she asked.

"I do. What's your name?"

The woman leaned in warmly like she was going to kiss him, but pulled up just short and lingered before pulling back.

"Frances," she said softly.

"Frances," Wolfe scoffed. "That's a stupid name."

Wolfe didn't see her roll her eyes as she turned her back to him. She stood up, walked over to the bar, and began fixing a drink.

"I'm sorry, handsome," she said. "What would you like to call me then?"

"I don't know. Aren't you supposed to have some sort of sexy name?"

"Hmm...How about Magdalena?"

Wolfe beamed brightly.

"*Magdalena*," he repeated, "I *like* that."

The woman calling herself Magdalena smiled back at him.

"I like it, too," she said. "It's my girlfriend's name."

"Your girlfriend? Don't tease me and tell me you play for both sides, now."

"I don't. Normally, I'm a real ladykiller. But for you, I'll make an exception."

Wolfe chortled with pleasure as he sipped the scotch from his glass. The woman climbed onto his lap and undid his tie before rubbing his shoulders.

"Oh, you," he said. "I like you. What's your story?"

"I don't know," the woman said. "What do you want it to be?"

"Mmm, something good."

"Well, how about I'm just a West Virginia gal, from right here in the mountains."

"Local girl. Okay, I can dig that."

"And I've got a farm with goats and sheep and cows."

"Okay, like a farmer's daughter sort of deal. I like it."

"No. My father's dead. It's me, I run the farm now."

"Okay, okay. So, you're in charge."

"I am. I look out for my farm and my family."

"Oh yeah?"

"Yeah, I protect them. From anyone. Anyone that tries to hurt them."

Wolfe looked at her, confused. She eased up on rubbing his shoulders and sat back, putting space between the two of them.

"Okay, that's not *as* hot," he said.

She noticed his glass was empty and took it, climbing off his lap and walking back over to his bar.

"I'm sorry," she said. "I'm just telling you my story. It's the truth."

"Yeah, well, I'm not paying you for the truth. I'm paying you for fun."

"Actually, you're not paying me at all."

"What?"

"You paid another woman to come here tonight. And then I paid her to take the night off."

Wolfe watched as the woman calling herself Magdalena turned around, a silenced pistol in her hand. He felt himself getting enraged, but as soon as the anger came it dissipated. He was getting drowsy. His limbs felt like cement. Wolfe looked up at the woman, confused.

"The Rohypnol is starting to take effect," she said. "I'm guessing you didn't taste it in your drink a few minutes ago."

"What...the fuck," Wolfe said, straining for the words.

"Like I said, I protect my family and my farm. From all threats."

"You...bitch."

"Threats like you. You sent your men to my farm to kill us. The only problem is you failed, and pissed me off in the process. And the name *is* Frances. My friends call me Fraggie. So, you can call me Frances."

She walked over to him. Wolfe tried to say something but couldn't.

Fraggie pointed the gun at his head.

"Just in case you were wondering who it was that killed you," she said.

She squeezed the trigger twice, firing two hollow point rounds into his forehead. Wolfe's head whipped backwards and leaned awkwardly over the back of the sofa, blood, bone, and brain matter splattering the floor.

Fraggie turned and put the oversized sunglasses she'd been wearing back on. She grabbed her thick faux-fur coat, the one that concealed her slender figure, and took the elevator down to the lobby. The man at the front desk waved as she walked by.

"That was fast," he said with a perverted smile.

"He didn't last long," she said.

Stepping out into the frigid West Virginia night, Fraggie walked around the block and slipped into a black pickup truck, that, if anyone ever traced it, would come back as being owned by the Hopewell County Sheriff's Office Vice Squad unit.

After she closed the door, locking out the blustery winter weather,

Fraggie began to shed. First the sunglasses and coat, then the wig and hair net that prevented any of her brilliant violet hair from being left at the scene of Lane Wolfe's murder. Finally, she slid off the gloves that concealed her fingerprints.

"Are you okay?" Maggie asked from the driver's seat.

"I'm good," Fraggie said. "Let's go."

Maggie put the car in gear and headed for the interstate. Five minutes later, they were out of Charleston and driving headlong into the night. But as they approached an exit, Fraggie sat up.

"Get off here," she said.

"What for?" Maggie asked.

Fraggie smiled and held Maggie's hand as she answered her.

"Take the country roads home."

ACKNOWLEDGMENTS

I cannot emphasize how grateful I am to the team of family and friends around me that continue to make my writing possible. First, I would like to thank Austin Shirey, who both beta read and edited this novel. Your tireless and patient support elevated this novel to a level I simply could not on my own. You are a saint for putting up with my rants and ravings. You are more than a friend, you are a brother. Second, I want to thank my other beta readers, Elizabeth Ellis and Emily Trautwein. Your thoughtful input helped shape this book and make it a better story to share with everyone. I also would like to thank my parents, Debbie Bleviss and Bill Lienesch, who continue to be in my corner through everything. But most importantly, I want to thank my wife, Meg. I am, each and every day, marveled by your unconditional love and relentless enthusiasm for my work. You believed in me before I believed in myself, and words cannot express what that has meant to me.

ABOUT THE AUTHOR

B. C. Lienesch is an emerging author of crime thrillers. He is a former freelance writer and featured columnist and editor for GuysNation.com, but has done everything from owning a bakery to selling fireworks out of a pair of shipping containers. Born in Washington, D.C. and raised in Northern Virginia, he now lives in the same area with his wife Meg, their two dogs, Kaia and Aria, and two cats, Luna and Hitchcock. COUNTRY ROADS is his second novel. He previously wrote THE WOODSMAN.

Visit www.bclnovels.com or follow @bclienesch on social media for more.

ALSO BY B. C. LIENESCH

The Woodsman

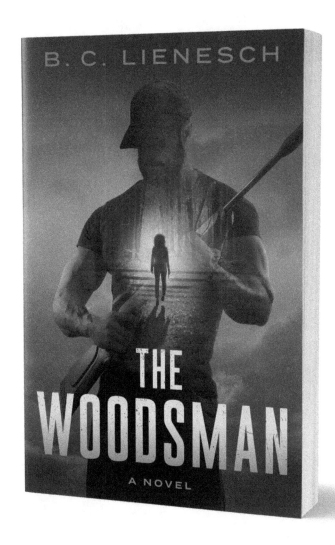

CPSIA information can be obtained
at www.ICGtesting.com
Printed in the USA
LVHW041314020622
720142LV00004B/95